STAND OFF

"Mr. Charlie has found a way to rig the bore drill to detonate on his command. He's threatening to blast apart the whole of Phoboi Twelve. He says he'd rather die than be locked into a machine again."

"Incredible. But why are you risking our lives? What do you care?"

"I am C-P programmed to care. I have been built to be fascinated by human beings. Naturally, when I received a distress signal from an archaic human, I had to go to him."

"And if we rescue him," Mei asked, "then what? Where can we go with him?"

"There's only one place. The renegade colony on Mars, where the archaic humans are holding out. Solis."

"Attanasio is a poet, a seer and a born storyteller, who writes with heart, authentic life wisdom, and staggering, world-class imagination. There are no limits to what he may accomplish."

—David Payne, author of *Early From the Dance*

By A. A. Attanasio

SOLIS*
THE MOON'S WIFE*
KINGDOM OF THE GRAIL*
HUNTING THE GHOST DANCER*
WYVERN*
RADIX

*Available from HarperPaperbacks

SoliS

A. A. ATTANASIO

HarperPrism
An Imprint of HarperPaperbacks

This is a work of fiction. The characters, incidents, and
dialogues are products of the author's imagination and are
not to be construed as real. Any resemblance to actual
events or persons, living or dead, is entirely coincidental.

HarperPaperbacks   *A Division of* HarperCollins*Publishers*
                   10 East 53rd Street, New York, N.Y. 10022

A hardcover edition of this book was published in 1994
by HarperCollins*Publishers*.

Cover illustration © 1994 by Mike Van Houten

First HarperPaperbacks printing: March 1995

Printed in the United States of America

HarperPaperbacks, HarperPrism, and colophon are
trademarks of HarperCollins*Publishers*

❖ 10 9 8 7 6 5 4 3 2 1

For those touched by wonder,
touchy about reality,
and in touch with their imagination

And especially for Charles Platt,
who has made his own arrangements for
cryonic suspension in the real world of the
twentieth century.
Who among you shares his fleshly faith in the future?

The dead are at the mercy of the living.

Contents

Prelude

SWOLLEN WITH DREAMS, I AWOKE FROM THE DEAD. WHEN I tried to speak, all I could utter were small animal sounds. So I just lay there in the dark, silent in the secret sea of images and memories that make our dreams. I saw a beautiful woman making love to me. Her face was porcelain, glossy with the sweat of her exertion. Her breasts shivered like small rabbits. The tresses spilling over her shoulders were red as autumn leaves. The smell of cloves whispered from where the clamp of her need gripped me—so hard my pleasure bleared to pain, then relaxed again to pleasure. Like tiny azure pearls, tears of rapture beaded in her lashes.

A blast of little bright birds, spooky as minnows, flared across my brain. And once more I was in the dark depths of the secret sea, another lewd dream beginning to shape itself around her lubricious sobs. The only way to stop it was to remember I was dead. Long years before, so long ago now that almost all of that past is forgotten, I met death. I remember little of that loneliness and intimacy.

What I recall most clearly is that my soul was in my mouth.

A dim time ago, a jellyfish had snared my heart. Its nematocysts burned the cavity of my chest and seared the length of my left arm. With it came the stink of my own putrefaction, my bowels voiding as I thrashed to the ground, the lunatic ringing of cicadas in my head as the high D of blood whined in my constricting vessels. The woman with hair like dead ivy took me into her mouth, her lovely face rising and falling with my hips.

I'd read somewhere an aboriginal healer's explanation of why some patients die. "The spirit is a boomerang. It is not meant to come back. It returns only when it misses its target."

And then, after a maddeningly long time, I was pulled from the secret sea, and the dreaming stopped. I heard weird voices, genderless, childlike: "Mr. Charlie! Can you wit what we say? Be hearty, my Mr. Charlie."

"Medullary compression of the gibbus. Man, man! Be you hearty or be you gone!"

I was blind, and apart from those eerie voices, I could hear nothing. Wherever I was smelled like nightfall in a place where rain gathered. Wild thoughts spilled through me: Was I in a coma, hallucinating all this? Were the strange voices and erotic episodes prodromal of brain damage? Or was I, in fact, dead, as I had long before surmised, remembering too well the wreath of thorns about my heart, too painful for me to draw even the shallowest breath? And then the famous fluorescence that opened into fumes as I lay dying, my consciousness rending into radiant vapors, curling into a space the color of pepper, looking back and seeing my body curled like a seared insect, my eyes rolled up, dead moons, and the wind's big silence whistling louder. Oh, yes, I was dead—I think . . .

"Faith, love, and hope are all in the waiting," said one of the sexless voices. "Mr. Charlie, can you wit what we say? Blink, blink, blink."

A hot light hurt my face and refracted into spectral halos.

"Behold—the sign!"

"Nay. The retinal tissue hurts. He squints. Let him be gone. Remove the electrode."

A dizzy darkness seized me, and I plunged again into the secret sea, where a woman with breasts like peaches was bending closer . . .

Only in sex do we do what we mean, do we give what we in actual fact are.

A thousand gaudy butterflies burst through my brain. And I was alone again in the secret sea, the spelled sound of her wrought breathing all that remained of her. Until, like a cloud blown from a sunset, she appeared under me this time, looking over her naked shoulder languorously, both hands splayed across the muscles of her raised hips . . .

The salacious dream burst into darkness, and a child-like voice spoke:

"Pregestation rituals! Speak no more on them. Hear me! We would know no more of that. Tell us not of the salt mine in the blood, the match-head clitoris, the cobra head of the penis, vixen and rakes, the gates of mine thighs—these lewd truths that kindle the beast. Speak no more on them, we say! Instead speak, Mr. Charlie, of the mind—do tell of the relations of psyche and physics."

I startled alert, out of a dreamless void. The sex-obsessed sequences that had gone on interminably were gone. The weird voices were back—different ones this time. I tried to speak and managed to say: "Who? Who are you?"

"Stink and wonders! He be witful. What profit him to cry?"

"We be Friends."

"So be our calling, Mr. Charlie. We be Friends of the Measuring Class Not of Niels Abel."

"What?" I didn't understand. "Where am I?"

"You be Mr. Charlie in the lock-hole, at the hinge-split of the world."

"Huh?"

"Wold I, nold I."

I was utterly confused. "I can't see," I complained. "I'm blind. Who are you? Where am I?"

"Spark his eyes, say I."

Briefly, sight returned to me—though I wished it hadn't. I was lying on a mirror-polished floor, cinnabar red, and reflected in it was my face—or not my face, not the features I remembered, but something like a hog-nosed snake with lidless human eyes peering from sea anemone stalks and the pink cauliflower of brain matter all encased in a gel pod and chrome net. That was me? A scream roiled within me but could find no way through the cage of my shock. What had happened to the gift of my face? Where were my limbs, my torso? I huddled in the hut of my heart, stared meekly upward and saw— among tufts of dandelion seed lifting into the green air, human figures in transparent armor and, beyond them, the polished floor running toward vermilion sandstone arches and the antlers of dusk. Suddenly, my mind felt fragile.

"He be hearty, all right, and wind in his whiskers, as well!"

One of the armored figures had said that and gestured at me. I peered more closely at—it: It had a face of black glass or gelatin, flexible, expressive, a teenager's face, boy or girl, I couldn't tell. The lake of its dark features was placid, clear enough that I could see the cumulus cloud of its brain enlarging with the thunder of a dangerous thought. "Wax me mind! He be witful for sure. Ho—Mr. Charlie, hear me! We Friends of the Measuring Class Not of Niels Abel would know a thing: Tell us of the relations between psyche and physics," and then, leaning closer, not sure I understood: "mind and matter. Ken you that?"

"I don't understand," I whined, unnerved by all that was happening to me. "Please—help me."

"He be witless in the ways," the figure closest to me said over its glass-plated shoulder to the others. "I were wrong about him."

"The electrode be the way. Use it."

A four-fingered hand manipulated something above my line of sight, and a ticklish pain trilled through me. Abruptly, I saw shimmery blue words scrolling across my field of vision, and I heard a voice very like my own saying, "The expressions of energy, matter, forces, and fields are functions of an abstract geometry. That is the relation of matter and mind."

"Stink and wonders!"

"Wax me mind!"

I couldn't stop myself. I went on to say, "The discipline of physics is pure geometry. Matter is pure mind. Of course, when we think of geometry, we presuppose the spatial configurations of form or the temporal harmonics of sound. Yet geometry in itself is neither spatial nor temporal. It loans itself only secondarily to such descriptions. Geometry is first of all a purely noetic system of rates, ratios, intervals, agreements, and alignments. Its components exist independent of things measured, an abstract typology, a strictly internal self-description."

"Say more, Mr. Charlie! Wit us wise of matter and mind."

And so I did. Just as before, when I was adrift in the secret sea of erotic images, now I hovered in an airy space of words and numbers, only this time what I was experiencing floated across my vision, outside my body. The figures in transparent armor had gathered around me, and I could see the thunderhead thoughts behind their rapt faces as the blue words vapored by: "Spin, interval, charge, and moment are discrete properties, defined in integer and half-integer values, rational functions and ratios, or nonconstructable numbers functioning as constants. Sure, we've been duped before by illusory geometries—like Pythagorean intervals, ideal Euclidean properties, and Kepler's harmonics of planetary orbits—so it's natural to be leery of physics as geometry. Nevertheless, mapped schematically, mass, coupling constant, spin, angular momentum, and charge generate polyhedra. Take, for example, the plotted relations of quarks and leptons on a horizontal plane—displaced vertically proportional to their respective charges, they polarize the angular coordinates of an ideal cube! Think on that."

"As blood is the bride to iron—he be right! Pull the electrode, and we be hard thinking on that."

"Aye, and the void bites its tusks!"

The blue words vanished, and the air smelled all at once of boiled milk. I noticed that, beyond the drifting tufts of dandelion, the twilit sky was precise with stars. I felt the silence of the wind opening in me again, and then darkness came on.

The fire-flower of numbers and words opened and closed around me time and again. And I found myself square-summing the real and imaginary parts of a field specifying spin states of particles, measuring angular momenta, and plotting straight lines in the Regge trajectory. "Abstract geometry defines matter," I heard myself say.

Then I performed conceptual rotations on the double-valued quality of fermions—"You know, *matter* particles"—in an abstract superspace with anticommutators and revealed deep angular identity with the class of bosons—"*Force* particles! Do you see what I'm saying? Geometry shows they are the self-same entity!"

I babbled about heterotic string theory and the summary familial group designated E8xE8, reflecting a generalization of crystal symmetries, a strictly *abstract* pattern produced by categorical requirements applying directly to the macroscopic and *observable* order of structures. "Euclidean geometries are staring out from nature's apparent chaos. Salts, viruses, seashells, pinecones, honeycombs, galaxies, and galactic sheets hundreds of light-years huge! Man-oh-man, it's just like the hermetics said: As above, so below. Thetic geometries in purely abstract space informing real constituents of experience! Matter copulating with mind copulating with matter. It's obscene!"

I am a blue animal that trembles softly. I am a mind without a body calling to you. Can you hear me? Do you see my smile in my words, sad and evil? Sad because I am utterly alone. Evil because I am dead and yet I live. My voice radiates through space. Past lives drift by. The damned descend into the darkness. Can you hear me? Listen. A dead man visits you. Listen to me—someone.

Look, this sounds like ranting to you. I know. I want to speak calmly, rationally now. I want to say the truth as I've known it. I want to say a story—my story. Say a said. And more. Say a body. Say a way back. Say at least a place. Say something. But no one hears me. Do you hear me?

"Mr. Charlie?" A youthful, genderless voice spoke. "Can you hear me?"

A surge of darkness woke me. I felt the old, delusive joy that I was dreaming and I was about to wake to my former life. My wife would be asleep next to me, and I would wake her and ignore her grogginess to yammer about my nightmare.

"Mr. Charlie, I know you're awake."

The viscid barbs of the jellyfish's tentacles burned the length of my left arm, my heartvalves clogged with silicates, and my blood turned to coral. I was dead. *Whereupon the stars drag their darkness into a future without me . . .*

"I am going to activate your visual cortex now, Mr. Charlie. I need to talk with you."

Rays pierced my blindness, cutting blackness into swatches of vision, and I saw that I was apparently suspended midair, for I could look down and see that I had no body. A spongy, circular floor was directly below me. Outside its perimeter, tiles of tessellated turquoise and black marble supported swerves of amber that, after a moment, I saw were chairs and a long table. An adolescent girl sat at the table with a gold stylus in her hand. Her hair was the color of a violin, slant-cut across her left eye, cropped high over her small right ear, and highlighted with a few tiny firepoints of gemdust.

She touched the stylus to a moonpiece, a silver shadow-smudged disc compact as a watch face, and the clarity of my vision sharpened. I saw the vague line of her eyebrows, the topaz light in her tight stare, the carats of sweat on her forehead and upper lip, the cilia rimming her nostrils, the pulsebeat in her throat, the faceted lump of her Adam's apple—and realized that she could be a he.

He touched the stylus again. My vision pulled back,

and I saw him or her sitting in a swerve of amber, wearing black silk pajamas with red dragon-veins.

I looked away, surveying where I was: Slabs of jasper circled us like dolmen rocks, the spaces between them paned with crystal sheets flecked with mica. I peered upward into a boiling light of dust motes towering into thermals of acid clouds. The warm air smelled of jasmine. "Where am I?"

The hermaphrodite touched the stylus to the moon-piece on the amber table and told me, with lips not in synch with what was spoken: "You are dead."

Blue words squiggled in the air before me:

702-gram heart with a moderately dilated right atrium and a 0.3–0.5-cm hypertrophic right ventricle with focal fibrosis; the terminal episode originated in the left ventricle with its 1.5-cm hypertrophy and 5 x 4-cm anteroseptal and 9 x 7-cm posterolateral infarctions. Cause of death: arrhythmia. Subject: Outis, Charles.

At the sight of my name, a strand of razor wire seemed to thrum in my gut, and I reflexively looked down and immediately snapped my gaze back up, brutally aware I had no gut. "What's happening to me?"

"I think you already know, Mr. Charlie."

"Who are you?" I was frightened by this being's manipulation of me.

"I am Sitor Ananta."

I stared hard at the creature, noted its fully human form, its five-fingered hands. "You're not like the others."

"The others are the reason I am here," Sitor Ananta said. "But first tell me what you think you know."

I intended to remain defiantly silent and stare down my tormentor, but Sitor Ananta touched the stylus to the moonpiece, and I spoke: "I am dead. But before I died I had arranged for my head to be cryonically stored upon my death. Now I believe I have been revived—by my future—by you."

"Yes. What you surmise is true, Mr. Charlie."

Shock occulted my vigor. I dizzied, felt my heart would simply burst—but I had no heart! Sitor Ananta used the stylus, and my horror dimmed to astonishment. "Why am I here? What are you going to do with me?"

"*I* merely wish to question you. About the others. I prefer your cooperation. The information I seek can be gleaned directly from your brain, but that process is terribly laborious and very expensive. You can, if you want to, simply tell me what I need to know and spare me all that."

A hellswirl of panic seized me as I understood: In this new time, I was but an object, a thing, three pounds of electrified glutinous tissue teased with electrodes.

The stylus moved once more, and I calmed down. The chamber filled with light, or seemed to. All that remained of my terror was a taste of loneliness. "Where am I?"

A thug's smile creased Sitor Ananta's young face. "Your life is measured on a calendar made of dust, Mr. Charlie, yet you want to know everything—as if anything matters for you anymore. Have you seen yourself—what you look like now? Have you seen your final face?"

My voice creaked like a pine: "I have."

A laugh punched from Sitor Ananta. "The dead come back for laughs, Mr. Charlie. Or as wetware. The Friends of the Non-Abelian Gauge Group used you the way you, in your time, would have used an electronic toy to inform neophytes. Shall we see what program they chose to store in you?"

The stylus swizzled on the moonpiece, and I spoke in a voice orphaned from my will: "In order to locate an electron in a specified spin state at a given moment, measurement must give the differences in the phase fields—parallel and antiparallel components of spin, et cetera. There is no absolute phase. The real and imaginary parts of the wave amplitude are indistinguishable, that is, they can't be separated in some absolute way. Such constraints are functions of observer consciousness—what we humanists call mind. Adopted conventions specify the signs of complementary values, what physicists refer to as a deep-gauge symmetry. The observer perspective is what's important here. The relative ascription of plus and minus signs, used to define oscillations of wave amplitudes, requires the component of $\sqrt{-1}$, the imaginary value called i. It's the *idea* of the thing, for it posits both a thing and its absence. It's easy to believe that a thing can exist out there, independent of the observer, but the posited *absence* of a thing is obviously an expression of consciousness. So, you see, all energies, forces, and fields that make up the material expression of things are functions of an abstract geometry. And abstract geometry, which requires i, is a function of *consciousness!*"

"Well, wax me mind, eh, Mr. Charlie?" Sitor Ananta laughed darkly. "Is that how the Friends' crude translators managed amazement? They sounded to you somewhat as you would imagine buccaneers, didn't they? Well, their primitive translators got that unintentionally right. They're thieves, Mr. Charlie—thieves who stole you from thieves. Your head, after it had been expensively restored to its current useful condition, was originally stolen from the Common Archive by lewdists. I'm sure you remember them fondly. They used you for quite some time, didn't they? Weird bunch. There's been no sexual procreation among civilized human beings for centuries. We regard it much as your era did bestiality. Disgusting. We control our hormones. Yet the lewdists revel in vicariously experiencing that hormonal animalism, and they worked your brain the way you in your time would have used a cathode monitor to view pornography. Atavists is what they are. And there's a surprising lot of them, too—fascinated that we were once as mindlessly glandular as beasts, and not so long ago. But it's not the lewdists I'm interested in. They're a harmless bunch of degenerates. It's the Friends of the Non-Abelian Gauge Group I want to know about."

Sitor Ananta got up and walked toward me. Slim-hipped and flat-chested, the being had a masculine frame but a feminine mien. "The Friends are dangerous. They're enemies of the Commonality—anarchists, a selfish cult intent on usurping the law. But all this need not trouble you. All I want is for you to remember what you witnessed when they activated your visual cortex. What did you see when last you saw as you are seeing now? A verbal description will aid the authorities in pinpointing our enemy's location."

Dread stalked me, but I was reluctant to help this creature in anything. Something about it—its sexlessness, the rogue's hook to its smile, the very fact that it treated me like an object that could be manipulated—inspired defiance. I searched back and dredged up lines from Keats's "The Fall of Hyperion":

I ached to see what things the hollow brain
Behind enwombed: what high tragedy
Was acting in the dark secret chambers
Of the skull . . .

"Perhaps we should chat a little longer," Sitor Ananta said in a thick, quiet voice. "I imagine that most people of the past who arranged to have their heads frozen upon their demise expected the future to be a glorious Eden where they would be woven new bodies, young, perfect bodies, and allowed to partake of the wonders that evolved while they slept like the dead." A cold laugh snicked. "Isn't that a rather selfish view for anyone to have of the future?"

"Optimistic," I whispered. "I wanted to see what would become of us. I wanted nothing for myself other than to see."

Sitor Ananta's poisoned smile deepened. "All optimism

is selfish. Only pessimism accurately approaches the self-less and impersonal violence of reality, Mr. Charlie."

"Stop calling me that."

"Ah, yes, I would. Except I really can't. You see, my translator, as advanced as it is, has some trouble with your language's concept of gender and name preference. I don't sound as garbled as the rebels did, I'm sure, but it would take some adjustments to correct my translator's mode of direct address. I'd rather not bother now, if you don't mind, Mr. Charlie. At least we understand each other, which is better than what you endured with the others."

"The others never threatened me."

"But they used you. They activated the parts of your brain that served their interests with no regard at all for you."

"And what regard have you?"

"I will tell you. I represent the Commonality, the future you went to such lengths to see. We are the ones who have restored you. And now there are two options open to us, two uses for you. If we wish—and the decision is entirely mine—you will be installed inside the governing center of a very powerful machine, a mining factory on one of the asteroids of the Belt. There you will serve the Commonality by extracting and refining useful ores. After each successful work cycle, the amygdala and limbic core of your brain will be magnetically stimulated, inducing a sustained pleasurable rapture so gratifying you will sing praises of me and the Commonality for the trouble we took to revive you."

"And the other option?" I queried angrily. "Torture? Death?"

"Oh, no." Sitor Ananta looked sincerely stricken. "That would be ugly indeed. You see, Mr. Charlie, here is my predicament: It is illegal to use the heads or any of the body parts of members from the Commonality—alive or deceased. Only the dead of the past have no rights—those like yourself. They are simply dead. Unfortunately, most of those corpses are useless to us, decomposed beyond any hope of restoration. We have, however, found a few caches of frozen brain tissue from the archaic era. They are quite rare and located in regions difficult to access. We would never use torture or wanton destruction to squander any one of those heads. They are such a valuable commodity. You see, Mr. Charlie, we have the technology to construct artificial intelligence sufficiently complex to operate mining factories, but the expense is enormous. Despite the rarity and difficulty of obtaining frozen human heads of the past, it's still so much cheaper to revive and install them in our machines." My interrogator leaned back against the table. "Of course, a mining factory requires a cooperative intelligence. If you prove uncooperative, then I will have to recommend that your brain be parsed into sections useful to operating smaller devices."

A weary fatalism closed on me. "I had better hopes for my species," I muttered, more to myself than to the human-looking thing before me. "This is just the kind of monstrous future I was afraid to find instead."

"Disease is monstrous, Mr. Charlie. Old age is monstrous. There are no diseases or senescence in our era. If you cooperate, you will live usefully and indefinitely without pain or suffering. If you choose not to cooperate, the resectioning of your brain will be conducted humanely. You will simply go to sleep and not wake up."

Anger torqued in me, and I knew that if Sitor Ananta so desired, a few squigs of the stylus would render me utterly pliant. But I could plainly see that the creature enjoyed this sadistic manipulation. "The idea of going to sleep and not waking up sounds pretty good to me," I said with all the enthusiasm I could muster.

The look of surprise on that smug, puerile face was

well worth the stabs of pain that followed when Sitor Ananta got stylus in hand. Pain has many colors. That creature found the shades most disagreeable to me, and though I fretted about what this monster would do to the delicate, glass-faced beings who had used me to teach their young, I blurted out the desired information before very long. Then blackness followed.

And in the blackness there were blind memories of beetling talk interspersed with deaf dreams of glittering needles and red crisscrossings of laser light. More darkness came afterward, with pieces of hot perfume . . . and then sleep.

When I woke next, I was here, in the command core of a mining factory, somewhere, I assume, in the Asteroid Belt, writing you. At least, this seems like writing: Blue blips of words appear before me at will when I speak, all of it easily retrieved when I wish. As for who you are, I'm not sure yet. Eventually, I will find someone interested in my story. Perhaps the lewdists or the Friends of the Non-Abelian Gauge Group will seek me out again if the information I rendered to Sitor Ananta has not led to their destruction. I only described what they allowed me to see—those eerie milkweed tufts drifting into a jade sky above a red desert, those four-fingered people in their clear armor and transparent faces with brains like surging clouds . . . Who are they?

That any faction other than the Commonality will contact me seems unlikely in this remote, airless place. Still, there must be other mining factories out here in the Belt. Perhaps someday I will learn to communicate with them. That is the hope of my courage each time I decline the sessions of slow-motion orgasm that follow the long, tedious work cycles. There is no other time to write, and I feel I must write to retain some sense of myself—to be someone. Otherwise, I am just this machine, a regulator of drill trajectories, coolant flow rates, melt runs, and slag sifters. This is a life in the frost-light of a perpetual computer game.

Actually, it's not much different than life was before, except that, since my brain is maintained in a state of continuous glucose saturation, I never get hungry. I'm lonely, of course, but there's enough stimulation to fend off madness most of the time. A vivid dream life seems to offer the psychic hygiene of sanity. And the claustrophobia I suffered from in my former life appears to have been adjusted for by my installers. More often than not, I do accept the rapture sessions—the blissful immersions in the secret sea. I've earned them, and they give my will the mettle to go on.

But every once in a sad while, like right now, I need to affirm my sense of myself, to create the fiction that I am something more than this. We all live by our fictions. We create stories in order to fill the emptiness that is ourselves. And because we must create them with strength from nothing, they make us whole.

Recently, after much dickering with the luculent control displays, I have learned how to use the factory's memory-storage system to transmit radio messages into space. I am going to send what I have written here. And when this is received by the Commonality, I may well be cut into smaller, more convenient parts—but by then it will be too late. My story will continue to exist, expanding into the dark at the speed of light, maybe even to be heard by you. And if you do read this, then I will have failed better than I could have hoped.

This time I'm throwing the boomerang of my life to where it won't come back, at a target I can't miss.

And so—

With my soul in my mouth, I begin—

Swollen with dreams, I awoke from the dead . . .

1

The Laughing Life

WITH MY SOUL IN MY MOUTH, I BEGIN.

The radio message arrives at Apollo Combine's thrust station on the Martian moon Deimos as Munk is in the docking bay, busily unloading rhodium sheets from a freighter. He is a large androne with a chrome cowl, black intermeshing body plates, and articulated face parts that have no human referent apart from a crimson lens bar that, under a pewter ledge of brow, serves as eyes. Those eyes dim for a second after the androne receives the broadcast and his silicon brain replays it several hundred more times, analyzing all its components until he is satisfied that the message is genuine.

In the next second, Munk scans the docking bay and formulates an action plan that will enable him to respond most efficiently to what he has learned. The bay is empty. Apart from several programmed handroids working with him as stevedores, he is alone. The thrust station's other sentient andrones are either deployed or in the mainte-nance pit. Only two vessels occupy the cavernous bay:

the rhodium-laded freighter with its enormous storage nacelles and silos and a small cruiser with three fin-jet thrusters and an asymmetrical black-glass hull.

Apollo Combine, for some mortal reason Munk does not fathom, has named this cruiser *The Laughing Life*. Surely, that is some kind of wry joke. There is nothing inherently funny in what this ship regularly does: conveying jumpers and androne workers among the factories, smelters, and mines of the Asteroid Belt. Perhaps—if the jumpers who named this vessel were at all philosophical—they would say that they laugh at the rare joy of being where life does not belong, in the void, separated by a thin barrier from the near absolute zero of the vacuum and its invisible and deadly sea of gamma rays. But jumpers are genetically designed to be a phlegmatic and wholly unpoetic lot.

Life itself, Munk imagines, thinking about this ship's name, is laughing simply because it can. The absurdity of life blindly groping from necessity to freedom is what led consciousness out of the constraints of biology to the enhanced freedom of his own existence, the metalife of the androne and the great adventure of the silicon mind. So, perhaps, for that reason he, too, should laugh. He is not sure. All he knows for certain is that he has heard a human voice calling for help out of the void. More than anything, he wants to respond, and in the one second that these thoughts and observations have occupied him he has devised a strategy for using *The Laughing Life* to go to the source of this radio signal.

But to fulfill this plan, he needs human help. For a fraction of another second, Munk reviews the profiles of the forty-two people who work for Apollo Combine on Deimos. In that fractional moment, he not only identifies the one jumper best suited for this mission, he also patches into the duty roster and learns that the jumper he wants is currently in the thrust station.

With a reboant clang, Munk dumps the stack of rhodium sheets he has been carrying and runs across the docking bay toward the droplift that will carry him to the jumper quarters. He runs with lithe ease, as though he has always had legs, when in fact they came with his job at Apollo Combine. Before that he worked as a patrol flyer in the gravity wells between Saturn's rings and the shepherd moon Iapetus, troubleshooting among the other androines whose task it was to transfer material from the rings to the thrust station off Titan. Repairing mechanical breakdowns in space and retrieving androines who had spun out and didn't have the power to free themselves from decaying orbits above the gas giant, he lived in the void and had no use at all for legs.

But now he works among people. He could have opted for roller treads or even an adroit skim plate, but he wants to look as human as he can. That is his predilection, and it causes him some small pain when he enters the jumper quarters and the people there—two squat, neckless wrenchers lounging in a palm-fronded atrium—look askance at him. They both know him, and he would have liked for them to look upon him more kindly, as one of their own. But he can tell from their expressions that he is considered an intruder. They make no move to stop him; however, on his internal com-link he hears the protests they whisper on the dispatch line to Central after he passes.

A moment later, Central summons him in her dulcet voice, "Androne Munk, you are in violation of company preclusion rules. Please report at once to the maintenance pit."

Munk ignores her and hurries through a sepulchral chamber of dense bamboo where frosty shafts of light filter down through high galleries of hanging plants and red bromelia. His patch to the duty roster informs him that the jumper he seeks is in the recreation arcade ahead, behind the silver veils of a slender waterfall.

He splashes through the entrance and stands on the floral steel balcony overlooking the chromatic space of the arcade. A half dozen jumpers lie sprawled in air pools in the central dream den, blissed on midstim. From under heavy lids, they gaze up through a froust of oily light and vapor shadows at the giant, cobra-hooded androne looming over them. He stands still, waiting for their slow brains to recognize him in this incongruous setting.

The laggard quality of human consciousness continues to astonish him. For all practical purposes, the silicon mind has outmoded human sentience, and he has had to journey a huge distance to find even this small enclave of multiform humanity. Yet here it is—people working side-by-side with andrones to maintain the Commonality. Impractical as it is, the presence of humans pleases Munk enormously, and he waits patiently until he is recognized by the lounging jumpers before beckoning the one he wants.

Her name is Mei Nili, and she sits up groggily in the buoyancy of her air pool. The duty roster informs Munk that she has just returned from a three-sleep-cycle shift troubleshooting bandit hardware at a floating refinery among a flock of iron chondrites, and he understands why she squints with annoyance at him.

"Jumper Nili," he calls down to her, "please come with me. I need your help to save a man's life. Please, hurry. I promise you, this is not a gratuitous request as in the past."

The past he refers to is a couple of encounters early in his tenure at Apollo Combine when he had tried to interview all the humans at the thrust station. The others he had approached had eagerly complied, clearly flattered by his benign interest in including them in the internal anthropic model he is building. When he went unannounced to her quarters and the portal slid open, she seemed ordinary enough: a slender, 184.6-centimeter-tall woman in the usual matte-black flightsuit with the solar emblem of Apollo Combine over her left breast, her straight jet hair arranged in feathery bangs and a topknot. Her weary green eyes acknowledged his presence with a petulant stare from an otherwise impassive and pallid face.

"I am Androne Munk," he introduced himself, "transferred recently from Iapetus Gap in the Saturn system. I'm interviewing all the Apollo Combine jumpers during off-time—"

"Why?"

"It's my avocation. I'm building an internal anthropic model, and I—"

"Bounce off."

She whacked the door closed, and he stood there a long while not understanding. Later, when he found her alone in the docking bay after she'd come in from a repair run, he rushed to the cafeteria and hurried back to greet her with a meal cart laded with the foodstuffs that he knew from his preliminary observations she liked.

"Look, no-face," she said sharply, "I'm not some kind of animal you can win over with food. I don't want to answer your dumb questions. Can you understand that? Go back to the androne pit, and stay out of my shadow."

To make her point, as she turned away she slapped open an air-pressure valve on the cleaning unit under the hull of her docked ship. The steamy blast kicked the meal cart against the androne so hard it exploded, scattering food across the docking bay.

After that, Munk didn't approach her again until now. His anthropic model had guided him to infuse all the urgent emotion he could into his voice, yet his predictive memory warned him that she would probably wave him off and flop back into her air pool.

While waiting for her to react, he reviews his options

and listens in on the signal flurries that have resulted from the strange radio message. Most of the resultant signals from the other companies in the area are in secure codes, yet he can surmise from their direction and duration what is being communicated. Salvage rights are being debated, and unless he responds immediately, he will have no chance of getting to this unique human before others do.

Munk decides he has blundered in seeking Jumper Nili's help and turns back toward the splashing partition of water.

"Hey, bolt-brain, hold up." Mei Nili trudges up the ramp from the dream den, her silky robes billowing in the gusty passage out of the pool. "This better be damn good, or I'm going to insist Central runs a full integrity check on your silicon synapses."

"It is, I assure you, a matter of life or death for an extraordinary human being." He strides quickly out of the arcade and calls behind from the bamboo grove, "We must hurry."

"Where are we going?" she scowls, her tabis slapping on the flagstones as she runs to catch up with him. "And why didn't you use the com-link to call me? You're not supposed to be in here."

"We're going to the docking bay as swiftly as we can," he answers, holding the droplift curtain open for her. "I can say no more until we're away. If Central overhears us, we may compromise the life we must save. That is why I had to collect you in person."

"I don't understand all this secrecy," Mei complains in the humming rush of the droplift. "Is this something to do with your so-called avocation—because if it is, I don't want anything to do with it. You understand me?"

Munk bounds out of the droplift and onto the wide and empty staging platform of the docking bay. "This is an entirely singular event, Jumper Nili, and as I have promised, is not gratuitous. Please, get into *The Laughing Life* and put on a flightsuit. We must launch at once."

"Munk—that's your name, right?" She swings her gaze across the vast hangar of mooring scaffolds and gantries framing the empty slips, the multitiered freighter, and the sleek cruiser. "Look, Munk, you seem sincere enough, but I'm not going to jump without authorization from Central."

"Central will not authorize this jump," Munk states flatly. "I know you have doubts. You must trust me. This is the right action to take now. Once we are in flight, I will explain everything."

Mei stares hard at Munk, and the androne tries to assess what the human is thinking but draws a blank.

"We must go now—right now," Munk says, impacting his voice with urgency, "or a human life is forfeit."

Mei blows an upward jet of air that lifts her bangs and then, with an irked haughtiness that seems to Munk the proud spirit of the human animal, climbs the gangway to *The Laughing Life.*

Mars fills the viewport with the rusty hues of its sand reefs and fossil craters. Its bleary northern hemisphere, smudged with extended dune drifts and heavily mantled rocksheets, breaks below the equator into scorched basins and a webwork of ancient cratered highlands. The pocked plains, stained by corroded colors and acid shadows, darken toward the cobalt blue of the polar cap. This clash of geologic boundaries, this shining murk of volcanic steppes that buckle the orange surface, acclaim the tectonic powers that thrived here once and died.

Mei Nili, suspended in a flight sling above the viewport, stares with solemn eyes at the broken terrain twenty thousand kilometers away. The planet is dead, and that is what fascinates her. It is a dead thing alive with ghostly dust storms and vague, vaporous wraiths of frozen carbon dioxide and water. It is a dead thing, like her heart—what the archaic life called a heart, not the muscular blood pump caged by ribs: That organ defies her unhappiness and thrives, unconsciously squeezing life through her arteries and veins in the same way that the seasonal cycles blow the dry, cold winds across the shattered reaches of Mars. What is dead in her is the obscure heart, the source of joy and wonder that is more than she can say.

Mars slips out of sight as the vessel banks, the viewport spanning past the brown rim of the planet and garnering the numerous glint-fires of the void. Mei Nili's gaze breaks, and she looks impatiently across a cabin cramped with dented duct pipes, loose cables, and cascades of fern and red moss. Munk crouches like a silver turtle over the command console and seems oblivious to her presence.

"Where are we going?"

"Phoboi Twelve," the androne replies in a faraway voice. He is monitoring something and continues in a distracted tone, "Eighty-two million, four hundred sixty-two thousand, fifty-seven kilometers. Excuse my silence for a moment, Jumper Nili. I have to chart a new trajectory. There are others ahead of us."

"Others?" Inertia swings her about as the vessel accelerates, and she cranes her neck to face the androne. "What are you hauling me into?"

Munk remains silent, hunched over the console.

"Have you logged a flight plan?" Mei calls above the vibrations of the magjets. "I know they haven't authorized this jump, but does Ap Com at least know where we're going? Hey, I'm talking to you. Did you even bother to requisition this ship?"

Munk keeps his silence, and the bulwarks clang with the stress of their steep descent.

Damn! she curses herself for her compliance. *This bolt-dolt is going to kill us.* For a moment, she believes that is the androne's intention—that he's gone brain-burst, which has happened to androne's dinged by one too many gamma rays. She thinks he's taking her with him into oblivion, maybe because she's adamantly refused him his precious interviews.

Then, let it all end here. She's not afraid to die, and a part of her even welcomes it, for at least this will finish the malevolent sadness that has squatted in the hollow of her loss too long now. And she doesn't regret at all how she treated the androne. What had he expected, coming unannounced to her private quarters? She figures now that she had been too fatigued in the dream den to know what she was doing and cringes with remorse at her unthinking obedience.

Mei glimpses again the amber limb of the planet through the viewport and recognizes the maneuver. Munk is flinging the vessel in a tangential arc along the rim of the planet's gravity well in a steep dive that will graze the upper atmosphere, gathering momentum in a slingshot trajectory, and hurl them toward their destination.

"Watch it, Munk," she calls, forcefully. "I don't think this ship can take that kind of torque."

Munk hears the brittle edge to her voice and wants to reassure her, but his full attention is on the microadjustments necessary to maximize the momentum of the ship. He would have preferred a sturdier vehicle and knows if he's not careful, the pressurized cabin will indeed rupture. So, he is careful. Long spells of navigating gravity gradients among Saturn's loping moons retrieving damaged androne's have taught him well the friable limits of machinery.

The clanging of the bulwarks diminishes and dies away, and the cry of the magjets quiets down as *The Laughing Life* banks into its hurtling trajectory.

"You're making me wish I hadn't come with you, Munk. What is going on?"

The androne, in free-fall, rises from the aquatic glow of the control console and fills the flight bubble of the cabin with his chrome-and-black alloy bulk. "I regret I could not inform you sooner, but this situation required me to act swiftly."

"What situation?" With blue-knuckled hands toughened by long spells of hard labor, Mei Nili unlocks her sling, hooks a strap to a wall clip, and fits her boots to the deck cleats so she can stand. "You just put my life in jeopardy. I hope you have a damn good reason."

"I am grateful that you came with me without any explanation at all. Of all the jumpers, you are the only one I believed would accept my summons. I assumed— apparently correctly—you have the least to lose."

She resents his assumption and says so with a glower.

Among the forty-two jumpers who work for Apollo Combine, Mei Nili alone resisted his inquiries. She is known among the entire Deimos crew as a sullen person, and by surreptitiously researching the Combine's personnel files, Munk has discovered why. She grew up on a reservation on Earth and in her sixty-eighth year lost her family in a landslide that entombed an entire village.

"Are you going to tell me why we're going to Phoboi Twelve? That's one of Ap Com's, isn't it?"

"Yes. We have an ore processor there. It's gone down."

"So? That's Ap Com's problem."

"Three other companies with vessels in the vicinity have declared salvage rights, and Apollo Combine has already written off the loss."

"That's standard. Now it's not even Ap Com's problem anymore." She brushes aside a drifting strand of fern coil. "What are you getting at, Munk? You said someone's life is at stake. Why in damnation are we out here?"

"To get to Phoboi Twelve as fast as possible, Jumper Nili. You see, the malfunction at the ore processor is a singular one. It began with a crude radio-band broadcast that I received four point fifty-nine minutes after transmission."

Mei's smooth face flinches with incomprehension. "Radio band? That is crude. But ore processors don't use that wavelength."

"Of course not. It's not an ore-processor signal. It's a human broadcast. The radio source is a human being."

Mei shakes her head and glances out the viewport at a brief dazzle of electric fire wisping past off the hull. "That's not possible. Phoboi Twelve is not outfitted for personnel. It must be an androne."

"No. It's a distress signal from a human being—an archaic human being."

With a puzzled frown, Mei stares up into the androne's crimson visor. "How can that be?"

"As I said, it is singular. Instead of gearing the ore processor with an expensive psyonic master control, Ap Com used wetware instead."

"That's illegal."

"They found a loophole, Jumper Nili. It is illegal to use living wetware. What they found was already legally dead."

"I don't understand."

"Apparently, a trove of cryonic heads from archaic times was found on Earth—"

"Cryonic?"

"Yes. Human heads frozen in liquid nitrogen, sealed near the end of the archaic period in plasteel capsules impermeable to sublimation. They've been preserved intact for hundreds of Earth years, waiting to be reanimated."

"Is that possible? Wouldn't the cell structures have burst in the intense cold?"

"The cost of repair and reanimation of the cell matrix is high yet cheaper than the expense of manufacturing a psyonic master control for an ore processor."

Mei Nili's pale eyes widen as a sick, raw feeling pervades

her. Too well she imagines the horror of encasement, the claustrophobic terror of the nightmare that killed her family. She cannot help but wonder again if they briefly survived their behemoth interment, for minutes or hours left bleeding, suffocating in the crushing dark? Too well she imagines the helplessness and despair of a brain imprisoned in the spidery circuits of a rock factory. "That's monstrous."

"Yes—a human mind enslaved to a machine, burrowing deeper in senseless toil far from all humanity. Monstrous but within the bounds of Commonality law. In archaic times, people were cryonically suspended only after they had legally died."

"Who is this person?"

"His name is Charles Outis, but a translator glitch has him registered with the Commonality as Mr. Charlie. Now that this appellation has been wired into his translator modem, of course that's the only way to refer to him. His real name spoken to him comes out as gibberish."

Mei scowls with disdain. "That's just like the Commonality—depersonalize and control. How did Mr. Charlie get a signal out?"

"Obviously, he knew how to use the electromagnetic components of the ore processor to generate radio waves. As primitive an idea as that is, not very many people in archaic times actually knew how to make even the simplest radio. Most of Mr. Charlie's contemporaries used electromagnetic waves daily without understanding them or how they were generated."

Amazement swells through Mei Nili, and her eyes soft-focus for an instant as she accepts that out there, in the Belt, in the precisely mapped jumble of planetary scraps where mountains of rock lob end over end on their paths of gravitational destiny, an archaic human voice called. Her gaze sharpens with the realization of what the stakes are now. "If the others get him first, he'll be rewired to serve another company."

"Or, worse, dissected into useful components without the annoying characteristics of will, memory, and reflection that enabled him to use an ore processor as a signal station."

"Who else received his signal?"

"Everyone. He manipulated the ore processor's equipment to broadcast across the full waveband from audio frequencies all the way out to infrared. No one could miss it. But only three other vessels were close enough to respond, and two veered off after Ares Bund declared salvage rights."

"The Bund—they're a demolition company." Her heart sinks. "We won't be able to negotiate with them. They'll go for profit maximization and sell Mr. Charlie in pieces."

Munk turns back to the command console, gratified that, with the little data he had and the split-second decisiveness that was required, he had selected the right jumper to accompany him. "Get some rest," he advises. "You must be exhausted from your shift work."

"Wait, Munk." Mei Nili's ears hum with the rush of blood carrying her bewildered excitement. "Why did you hurry us out here? What are we going to do?"

"You're a jumper," Munk replies. "Your job is jumping among these rocks, troubleshooting the bandit equipment salvaged from other companies. You're well acquainted with the limits within which we must work. And, perhaps more importantly, you're human. I'm sure Mr. Charlie will be glad to see a human. With your help, I think we can take him."

"Take him where? Even if we get him away from the Bund, we can't take him back to Ap Com. They'll just slice him into parts. If we get him at all, we're going to have to go rogue."

"Indeed." Munk pulls himself into the wavery blue light of the console and begins correcting their trajectory. "That is why I couldn't speak about my intentions in the thrust station where we might have been overheard by Central. And that is also why I selected you. You are the one jumper who is truly unhappy at Apollo Combine. Where the others were conditioned for this work, you came to the company by default. You lost your family. You seemed the best choice to go rogue."

Mei accedes with a dull nod. This has all happened so fast, she feels the mereness of her humanity, her inability to process information with the nanosecond speed of the androne.

Munk reads her correctly. "This is shocking, I know. And it was presumptuous of me to call you into this so abruptly. But, as you can see, I had no choice. I responded as soon as I detected Mr. Charlie's broadcast."

"Why?" She cocks her head suspiciously, almost arrogantly. "Why have you responded at all? What do you care about an archaic human brain?"

Munk arches around to regard her with his abstract face. "Believe me, I care more than you can know. That has always been my foible. You see, Jumper Nili, like all andrones of my class, I was manufactured by the Maat."

That word has a stark sound to her. The Maat created the reservations. The Maat promised life eternal and happiness. The Maat lied. At least in her life, they are a cruel weakness that own the illusion of limitless power.

"The Maat built me to help transfer material from the ring system of Saturn to the thrust station off Titan," Munk continues. "I am only a common laborer. But, like every androne in the Maat work force, I have been endowed with a contra-parameter program, a C-P skill, that remains dormant until self-activated. That skill might be anything from a talent for waxwork sculpture to an ability to compute massive prime numbers. Who knows why the Maat bother with these special and nonutilitarian files? Who knows why the Maat do anything? Oftentimes, the C-P program interferes with an androne's job and results in the unit's obsolescence. I have seen that happen several times—a perfectly functional androne distracted and made useless by one of these antic obsessions. All andrones have heard of it happening. Consequently, few of us ever dare open our C-P file.

"I labored a long time in the ring system without any interest in my file. Then, a fellow androne—a receptor-class unit, a 'she'—who worked on Titan accepting the data input of the various laborers and coordinating our efforts, dared open her C-P program and discovered in it an imprinted predilection for ordering tones in temporal succession that broke time into unusual and often unpredictable sequences—a talent for music. She began broadcasting these unique, self-evolving patterns, and quite by surprise, I found myself enjoying the music."

"Are you trying to make a point?" Mei interrupts, methodically crisscrossing her flight straps and hooking them to the wall clips to form a crude hammock. "Why don't you just tell me straight out why you care about this Mr. Charlie?"

"I will. Listen. It was music that inspired me to open my own C-P program. When I did, I discovered I was possessed of an intense, if inexplicable, interest in the aboriginal hominid precursor of the Maat—homo sapiens sapiens. I patched into the Commonality data network to learn everything I could about these creatures I had never seen. My memory allocation files burgeoned with human information—anatomy, anthropology, history—wholly purposeless data for my work routines, yet because of my C-P program, I found them irresistibly consuming.

"By request, I was transferred from the Saturn system to the Belt, where I came to work for Apollo Combine. Here I met my first humans—you among them. I tried to explain all this to you when I attempted to interview you with the others. But you'll recall you weren't interested. And that interested me all the more. Your grief set you apart from the others. That is something I want to explore further—"

"Look, Munk, I'm not asking about my grief. I want to know why the hell you're risking my life to get to Phoboi Twelve to keep a human brain from getting sliced. What do you care? And why the hell should I care?"

"I told you. I am C-P programmed to care. I have been built to be fascinated by human beings. Naturally, when I received the distress broadcast from an archaic human—a human that walked the Earth before the Maat—I knew at once I had to go to him."

"And me? Why am I along for the ride?"

"I need your help. There are others who will get there ahead of me. But they are androms, like myself. Surely they will only further bewilder this archaic man. He will need human contact. And so, I need you."

Munk pauses to give time for Mei's human brain to absorb all he has said. There is only one more question to answer, but he waits for her to ask and while waiting corrects again the flight path of *The Laughing Life*.

"If we get Mr. Charlie," Mei finally asks, "then what? Where can we go with him?"

"Solis."

Mei straps into her hammock and hugs herself. "I was hoping you'd say that," she whispers. She smiles, a wan, quiet smile. "It really is the only place we can go now, isn't it? Solis." It has a holy ring to her ears. Since the terrible tragedy, since the beginning of her grief, Solis has been her succor. That is the last refuge of her heart in the kingdom of death. From the first, she was struck with how appropriate it was that this community, independent of the Commonality, should exist in the midst of so much lifelessness. The doom of her family had made her life a wasteland, and Solis was its temple. That was why she had to leave Earth after the tragedy. On Earth no one was supposed to die. Disease and old age had been defeated long ago by the Maat. No one had to die—or so she had believed until the voice of thunder reached across the mountains of the reservation and the village of her childhood disappeared in a black tomb of shattered slate.

"I know you tried to go to Solis after your family died," Munk goes on. "I know they turned you away."

Behind her glassy stare, Mei Nili remembers the loathing she experienced after the numbness of shock and grief began to thin. She came to loathe Earth for its arrogant beauty, its fields of goldenrod and monarch butterflies, its sycamore shadows and flights of cormorant, its dark groves of mossy oak, its shimmering alder slopes and barberry meadows and daisies everlasting. It sickened her. And she yearned for the dead spaces—yet even in the desert, yucca bloomed, bright-beaded lizards danced, thunderheads promenaded in fragrant, purpled veils.

The emptiness of space beckoned, and she left Earth gladly. But the cis-lunar colonies and the garden communities on the moon offered no relief, for the water planet hung in the sky flaunting its blue and feathery beauty. Only when the flight of her grief took her to the dead planet Mars did she begin to feel kinship again and some small glimmer of her heart.

She had wanted to live in Solis, a rugged community that thrived in the very face of death and had no illusions about life eternal. But she had nothing to offer them. She had lived her whole life on Earth skiing, swimming, riding, enjoying the utopia the Maat provided for the remains of Adam. Solis turned her away. They wanted skilled mechanics and ecosystem engineers.

"They were wrong to reject you," Munk says. "You proved that when you gave yourself to Apollo Combine and earned your way as a jumper. You didn't go sniveling back to the reservation. You proved you were tougher than that. And now you can return to Solis. Mr. Charlie will be your validation—and mine, too. They don't usually admit androns. But with the brain of an archaic human to donate to their clone vats, we'll be received as dignitaries."

Concern shadows Mei's broad face. "Only if we can retrieve Mr. Charlie from the Bund."

Munk turns his full attention to the command console. "Only if," he admits. "Rest now. We will have to be strong to face down Ares Bund."

She adjusts the straps of her sling and closes her eyes. But sleep will not come. She is troubled. Everything is happening too quickly. Only a short while ago she was sitting in the pastel color-swirl of the arcade, enjoying midstim with the others—who mostly ignore her. When she first arrived at the thrust station on Deimos to work for Apollo Combine, they tried to be friendly, to include her in their gruff camaraderie. But she wanted no part of that.

Mei determined from the time of her tragedy that no one would ever take the place of her family, and she has been true to that self-directive ever since. She doesn't want friends. Besides, jumpers aren't real humans anyway, not human the way people are human on the reservations. All jumpers have been modified to make their work easier. Most, in fact, were created to be jumpers. There are stocky, muscular wrenchers, narrow-bodied cable-jockeys, weasely pilots, and morosely exacting androne managers.

She found work with the Combine as a jockey because she is slim and has a head for circuit work. Jockeys have to ride cable runners into mine shafts and grottoes and hook up power units. She overcame her fear of tight places and got good at her job, because she didn't want to go back to the reservation or, worse, one of the colonies, where everyone thinks they're going to live forever.

Her job is exhausting, but it has made her strong, so terribly strong she doesn't always know what to do with her strength. That is why she was in the arcade in pastel mode when Munk found her. She needed midstim—direct magnetic stimulation of the amygdala in the midbrain—a sedating euphoria that drains away all restlessness and fatigue and leaves one with an empty body and a soul full of infinite care.

If she hadn't been on midstim and if she hadn't been surprised by Munk appearing suddenly in a nimbus of bleached colors, would she have come with him? If she had known about Mr. Charlie's plight beforehand, would she have elected to risk her life in a slingshot maneuver to go to him—an archaic brain locked in an ore processor and already claimed by another company? She ponders this at length and decides she should go, as if she has a choice now. She will go, because she has already stayed too long at Apollo Combine. She has become comfortable with her job and the indifference of the other jumpers—and midstim, illegal in the reservations, has become too important to her.

After Mei Nili dozes off, Munk patches into the onboard translator. He wants to hear again the segment of the archaic human's radio broadcast that he captured on Deimos, and he feeds the recorded signal to the translator. Most of it comes back as noise, and all he can summon up is a ranting excerpt:

Soul in my mouth, I begin. . . . I am a mind without a body. . . . Can you hear me? . . . I am dead and yet I live. . . . Past lives drift by. Can you hear me? Listen. A dead man visits you. Listen to me . . .

Munk plays the scraps of message repeatedly, listening for nuances. Is this human being still sane, or has the trauma of his revival broken his mind? *I am dead and yet I live.* How much of what sounds like madness is insanity and how much mistranslation? The mechanical voice he hears only approximates the radio signals that the brain has found a clever way to generate from the interior of the ore processor. How much is error? *Listen. A dead man visits you.*

Broken chunks of rusty static crowd the air, and Mei

Nili stirs from her fitful rest. "Is that him? Is that Mr. Charlie?"

"It is as much of his signal as I can translate into speech we can understand. The language he spoke in his first life has been dead for centuries."

Mei unstraps from her sling and drifts across the cabin to the flight bubble, as if propinquity to the warbly machine voice will clarify it. "Is there anything more?"

"Some, but just as distorted. No matter now. We are approaching Phoboi Twelve. I've plotted a course that masks our approach among waste clouds of nickel-schist debris, slag exudant from the processor. Ares Bund has only one vessel in the area, *Wolf Star*, and they haven't detected us yet. They are preoccupied with their salvage operation. I'm pulling in their radio signals."

"Radio?"

"Yes. Wolf Star is communicating with Mr. Charlie in his own medium."

"I don't understand. Why don't they just go in and unplug him?"

"Mr. Charlie has been too clever for that. He's found a way to rig the bore-drill explosives to detonate on his command. He's threatening to blast apart the whole of Phoboi Twelve unless he gets certain assurances. He says he'd rather die than be locked into a machine again."

"Incredible."

"*Wolf Star* is promising him everything he wants. They're sending in a psybot—a handroid with a neural mesh—to hook up to his brain, to serve as his eyes, ears, and limbs."

"Phoboi Twelve is an Ap Com processor. Don't we have access to all the master codes? If we want, can't we defuse the explosives?"

"I've already thought of that. All the codes for Phoboi Twelve have been uploaded to our console. We are now in complete control of the processor. But that won't do us any good so long as *Wolf Star* has their androne in place."

"They already have an androne down there? Can you tell who it is?"

"It's a demolition androne *Wolf Star* calls Aparecida. I've tracked her salvage-rights declaration to the Commonality expediter on Vesta Prima. She's already filed for Ares Bund to sell Mr. Charlie's hippocampal gyrus, parietal and occipital lobes, and neocortex to four separate companies for use as functional wetware. Mr. Charlie doesn't know it, but he's already been legally dissected."

"Then they're lying to him."

"Baldly."

"We've got to do something." Mei floats before the transparent curve of the flight bubble and sees only a few barbs of starlight among the tattered blackness of the waste clouds. "Look—Mr. Charlie's brain is still encased in the core chamber of the ore processor, and we've got all the codes. Can't we selectively detonate the explosives so that the core chamber is left intact? Then we can pluck Mr. Charlie out of space on our flyby."

"I can't do that."

"What do you mean? We have the codes—"

"Aparecida is on Phoboi Twelve now. If I detonate the explosives, she will be destroyed. It is illegal for me to offensively destroy another androne."

"Illegal?" Mei gives him a look of stupendous incredulity. "Munk, we're going rogue. You said so yourself."

"Yes. But my intent has never been to destroy anyone."

"How the hell did you expect to get Mr. Charlie away from the Bund?"

"He is a sentient being, Jumper Nili. I have always expected he would elect to come with us. That's why I needed you to accompany me—to woo him to us with your humanity."

"And the Bund? How did you expect to woo them?"

"I had hoped to get here before they docked. *Wolf Star*

is a goliath-class prospector. I thought it would take longer for such a bulky vessel to moor."

She levels a cold look at the androne and says, "So we've lost out to a silicon miscalculation, is that it? Well, what do we do now?"

"Mr. Charlie has not yet agreed to go with Aparecida. If you approach him, we may still be able to convince him to come with us."

"Forget that. Aparecida is a demolition androne who has already filed salvage rights. If I interfere, she can legally destroy me."

"You will have to be careful and clever."

"Me? Why don't *you* go in there and face down this demolition expert?"

"I am an androne." He slightly lifts his thick, blackly iridescent arms to his sides as if to reveal himself. "I cannot possibly be as persuasive to Mr. Charlie as you would be."

"Okay, okay—I have a better idea. Let me use the codes to explode Phoboi Twelve and liberate Mr. Charlie."

"If I give you the codes, I will be in violation of my primary programming. I can't do that."

"Can't—or won't?"

"For me, they are the same."

"Really? I don't think so, Munk. You're not some solder-seamed handroid like Aparecida, patched together by the Commonality. The Maat created you. You were just bragging about your contra-parameter program that fires you with human wonder and capacity. Remember? That's why you're here. That's why you dragged me out here. You have free will. Use it."

"I cannot."

"You can. It's either that or we forget about Mr. Charlie and go back to Ap Com. Is that what you want?"

"I must save Mr. Charlie. My C-P program insists—but . . . not this way. We must work together. There is no time for debate. Won't you help me? Go down to Phoboi

Twelve. Aparecida does not yet know we are here. When you are in place, I will break radio silence and inform Mr. Charlie that Ares Bund is deceiving him. Then you will reveal yourself to him, and he will come with you."

"And Aparecida?"

"Aparecida is three times your size, designed for destroying obsolete structures, not for pursuit. You can evade her."

"Right. And if Mr. Charlie won't come with me? What then?"

"I control all the codes to the ore processor from here. I will unclasp the mag locks that fuse him to the core chamber. He is only a brain, after all, and even with the plasteel capsule housing him and his glucosupport pump, he won't weigh more than three kilos."

Mei throws up her hands in disgust and swims across the cabin to the pressure hatch. What choice does she have? Having come this far without requisition or flight plan, she is sure to lose rec privileges, and without mid-stim, Apollo Combine offers her no solace.

After donning work boots and gloves and a clear statskin cowl that zip-seals to the collar of her flightsuit, she straps on a jetpak and moves to test the com-link under her shoulder pad. Munk dissuades her by holding up his blunt-fingered hand.

"Don't use the com-link till after I break radio silence," he warns. "*Wolf Star* will detect any kind of ordered flux. Also, when you exit, use the jetpak as little as possible. Stay in the shadow of the slag clouds until you reach the drop vector to Phoboi Twelve. Surprise is essential."

"Don't patronize me, Munk," she says, staring sternly at the androne. "I know what I'm up against out there. Remember, you got me into this. I'm counting on you to get me out."

Before Munk can reply, the pressure hatch winks open, and Mei jettisons into space. The sleek and perfectly black silhouette of *The Laughing Life* dwindles swiftly into the starry distance, and the vacuum cold prickles her flesh through the sheer filaments of her flightsuit.

Mei executes a slow body twist to orient herself. She is comfortable in the void, having spent much of her working life there, and she readily locates her destination. Phoboi Twelve is a small asteroid, two kilometers long, half that wide, blotting out a tiny portion of the spangled stars and barely visible among the obscuring tendrils of slag clouds that the ore processor has exuded. The sprawl of tenebrous vapors is what enables Mei to spot the asteroid so quickly, and she uses one short burst from her jetpak to send herself hurtling into the slag cloud toward her goal.

Her flight is dangerous. With her sight obscured in the smoke from the processor, she could strike a sizable rock, which, at her velocity, would rip her statskin cowl and expose her to the vacuum. Statskin, a micro-sandwich fabric that blocks radiation, admits visible light, and reclaims oxygen from exhaled carbon dioxide, was designed to enable people to work in airless environments but was not meant for long jumps through space. In the past when she had to cross wide distances in a cowl, she avoided blind trajectories or used a field projector to clear the way ahead of her. But she carries no projector, for that would expose her to *Wolf Star*.

In brief glimpses as she slashes through gaps in the slag fumes, she spots the prospector vessel. It is indeed large—a fifth the size of the asteroid itself—and luminous, guidelights and floodbeams shining from its bubble turrets, scaffolds, and conning towers, a huge phosphorescent arachnoid perched on the cratered and jagged rock. Then her flight takes her behind the asteroid, and with one tiny burst from her jetpak, her course deflects away from the mute stars and into the darkness of Phoboi Twelve.

She alights on the pitted surface and begins her search under the eternal night for a way in. Soon she finds a vapor duct and with a wrench from the utility tools stored in her jetpak removes the wire-mesh screen and drops herself into the lightless maw. The lack of vibration in the metal panels assures her the machinery below has shut down, and she descends swiftly.

By the glow of the light projectors she has activated in her statskin cowl, she moves toward the interior of the ore processor. She knows this factory well, having helped install scores of them during her tenure with Apollo Combine, and she nimbly makes her way among scorched, dormant furnaces and smelter chambers with their gargantuan cauldrons. Following command cables through a colossal bore tunnel, she approaches the nucleus of the ore processor, the core chamber.

A dull vibration in the rock alerts her to a presence approaching from behind. Urgently, she scans the rock-face, searching for the vapor ducts she knows must be nearby. She finds one thirty meters above her and claws hurriedly up the concave wall, employing the dim gravity to bound feetfirst into the opening.

Moments later the quaking intensifies, and the lightless tunnel below her brightens suddenly. Floodlights gouge the darkness, and with a rumble Mei hears through the rock, a lithe yet heavily armored figure strides into view. Six meters tall, outfitted with serrated appendages, rock-saw talons, and strap-blade tentacles, the spike-studded androne pauses directly below her and swivels its hammer-long head, alert to the heat trail Mei has left in her wake.

With a reptilian rasp, its tentacles score the wall she had climbed moments earlier, tasting her path. The floodlights dim, and only the ruby purple of its heat-seeker eyes shines in the gloom. A viper's hiss scalds the remnant nitrogen gas that the processor has used to lubricate the bore hole, and the demolition androne concludes it has detected relict heat lingering in the ducts from the recently shut-down factory.

Mei slowly and quietly backs her way through the duct. The sight of Aparecida has left her heart slamming in her chest, and when the duct opens above a large cavern, she leaps gratefully into the darkness. Knees bent, she floats downward, waiting for the bottom to arrive. She is glad when she lands in a soft, dusty mound that swallows her. This, she knows, is a soot dump, and after routing around in the heaped cinders for a while, she finds her way up the opposite rock wall to a conveyer chute that will lead her by an alternate path back toward the processor.

She ascends along the steep track, clambering over trucks filled with charred dross. An azure shine leaks through the darkness from ahead, and she kills the glow of her statskin cowl and edges forward crouching between the trucks and the rough-hewn rock wall of the chute. Ahead, the core chamber comes into view, a luminously transparent geodesic under a mammoth vault of groined stone.

Feeling the wall for vibrations and peering cautiously out of the chute without detecting any sign of Aparecida, Mei enters the huge vault and approaches the bright geodesic chamber. She goes directly to the access panel and uses her jetpak tools to begin loosening the sealing bolts. Peering inside as she works, she sees the gleaming twin towers of the giant power coils, dormant now but still radiant with seething energy. A gauzy aura of blue force illuminates between the towers the command pod, a compact, iridescent complex of fused mirror spheres, silver-gold vanes, and ribbon antennae. That is the nucleus of the factory, where Charles Outis is installed.

Mei turns the last bolt, but when she tries to pry loose the access panel, abruptly all the bolts spin back into place.

A mechanical voice shouts from the tiny com-link speakers in her cowl: "Halt! If you proceed any further, I will detonate the bore-drill explosives!"

"Mr. Charlie?" Mei calls and turns on the light inside her cowl so that her face can be better seen from outside. Arms outspread, she presses against the clear panel. "Can you hear me?"

"I hear and I see you." A psybot half her height trundles out from behind the nearest of the towering power coils, a swivel-turreted torso of green metal sliding toward her on tractor treads. Mounted atop the pincer-armed torso, two stalk-eye lenses watch her. Though the device appears crude, Mei knows otherwise, for it contains a neural mesh and psyonic receptor that allow it to interface with Charles Outis's brain, extending his senses into the environment. That Wolf Star would deploy such an expensive machine, which is usually reserved for clandestine work with dangerous rival companies, attests to their eagerness to salvage this wetware. "Are you Aparecida?"

"No." She glances apprehensively over her shoulder, afraid to be caught in the open by the demolition androne. "My name is Mei Nili. I'm here to warn you that Aparecida is not your ally. I don't know what you've been told, but she is here to salvage your brain for wetware. Do you understand?"

"Who sent you?"

"No one. We heard your transmission—that is, Munk did, the androne I work with. He's waiting in a magjet cruiser not far from this rock. If you broadcast that I'm here, he'll break radio silence and announce us."

The psybot stares silently at her with its faceted lenses. Though Charles is apparently controlling the machine, she is well aware that it is an Ares Bund device and will certainly respond to their commands as well. The hopelessness of Munk's scheme suddenly presses heavily on her, and she feels trapped between the Bund's psybot on the other side of the geodesic wall and Aparecida behind her. Nervously, she stares across the amply lit vault to the dark tunnel rutted by the passage of numerous drilling machines.

Munk's broadcast echoes dimly, like cricket noise, from her com-link. She distantly hears him declare the Bund's true intent and the willingness of *The Laughing Life* to take Charles away from here to Solis, where a new body may be cloned for him. Munk tells him about the Maat's C-P programming and how Mei Nili and the androne need the archaic brain to gain entry to Solis for themselves but says nothing about controlling the function codes of Phoboi Twelve.

This new input bewilders Charles, and he paces back and forth in the psybot. After so long in the virtual space of the ore processor's core chamber, he is grateful simply to be able to move about and see the grainy, blue-and-white images the psybot affords him. But right now he wants to close these eyes that cannot close and diffuse his consciousness so that he can think through what he has been told and decide how best to respond to this woman—the first human he has seen since he died.

But events are not waiting for him. At this very moment, *Wolf Star* is also receiving the news of their trespass, and Mei dreads the commands that will be sent to Aparecida. A grating sound commences from inside the tunnel, and as she is considering edging back toward the conveyer chute while Charles ponders Munk's message, the psybot swivels alert.

"I'm confused," the mechanical voice says.

"Of course," Mei replies in the most compassionate tone she can muster. "That's why I've come to you. I'm human, too. These others are androgynes—artificial beings. But I have lived on Earth as once you did. Please, let me in. If Aparecida catches me out here, I'll be killed."

The psybot's eye-stalks strain forward, practically

touching the transparent panel. "You're beautiful. Oh. I didn't mean to say that. I mean—I thought that—I . . . I didn't mean to say it out loud. I'm not used to . . . this machine."

"That's okay, Mr. Charlie. Everyone is beautiful now. It's in the programming of the vats that grow us. They will make you beautiful, too." The scraping sound grinds louder, and the mouth of the tunnel brightens. "Please, let me in!"

The psybot whirs backward. "I need time to think."

"There is no time!" Mei anxiously turns to face the clangor in the tunnel. "Aparecida is coming! Please."

"This is happening too fast," Charles complains. "I must get used to this machine first. You're confusing me."

Out of the tunnel, Aparecida appears, slouched under shoulder-wing torchlights, her slinky length spike-studded, sleek as a moray eel with a long, curved, genitally blunt head and a razorous brow ridge hooding lenses of molten embers. She slides closer. Glint-toothed tentacles lash the ground ahead of her like shock ripples in water.

Mei slaps on her com-link to *The Laughing Life* and shouts, "Munk! Open the core chamber's port-side access hatch! Now!"

Bolts spin, the panel slips aside, and Mei jumps backward into the geodesic chamber. Manually, she heaves the panel back into place.

"How did you do that?" Charles asks in a fright.

Before she can answer, the psybot whisks forward, and its pincers grab her legs and slam her to the ground. "Hey!" she cries. "Stop that!"

"It's not me!" Charles calls. "I'm not doing it."

The pincers jab at Mei's statskin cowl, and she twists and contorts, using a desperate agility to avoid their stabbing blows. With a mighty heave, she lurches free of her jetpak as the psybot seizes her collar and tears at her flightsuit. Her hands fumble with the ignitor, and the jetpak flares a blue burst that bangs Mei against the wall and knocks the psybot to its side, tractor treads running.

Charles squawks, "Stop it!"

Mei shakes off the stardust sprinkling her vision and, wielding the jetpak as a weapon, strides over to the psybot. With controlled spurts that make her flesh hop on her bones, she cuts away the androne's pincer appendages and lower body. Hoisting the upper segment of the psybot by a writhing eye-stalk, she bounds away as Aparecida's slashing tentacles smash the geodesic wall behind her into a blizzard of sparkling motes.

"What have you done?" Charles cries. "What have you done to me?"

"Munk!" Mei screams. "The command pod! Open the pod!"

Ahead, the mirror surface of the clustered spheres wrinkles, and a portal appears close to the ground. Mei throws the eye-stalk segment of the psybot before her, tucks herself around her jetpak, and somersaults into the command pod. "We're in! Shut the pod! Munk—hurry!"

Through the constricting portal, Mei glimpses Aparecida lunging toward them, tentacles thrashing, ax-edged arms whirling, jaguar body slumped in a full-tilt charge, a gaze of gorged fury in its slick metal face. The entry shrivels close, and a tremendous boom rattles the complex and the small bones in Mei's ears. Quake-force juddering trembles the ground.

"What is happening?" Charles asks out of the darkness.

"Aparecida is trying to break in. But she can't. This is a prestressed alloy no demolition androne can breach." In the glow from her statskin cowl, the severed psybot with its wavering eye-stalks looks like an exotic sea plant. "Munk, turn the lights on in here."

Static drizzles over the com-link, and Munk's voice comes in jagged chunks: ". . . evasion. *Wolf Star* has deployed . . . Repeat, can't respond, must execute . . . battle evasion. Will contact you again when—"

"Munk! Detonate the explosives! Munk, respond! Detonate the bore-drill explosives!"

"Can't. Programming prohibits—"

"Damn your programming! You're a rogue androne now. Use your free will. Save us, Munk!"

"Evading *Wolf Star* destroyers. There are . . ." Static fizzles into white noise.

"You have control of the factory," Charles realizes.

"Yeah," Mei admits, feeling through the dark for the switch box she knows is somewhere to her right. "This ore processor belongs to Apollo Combine, the company we work for. Or used to work for." By the slim light from her cowl, she finds the switch box and wrenches it open to reveal a colorful hive of circuitry. She probes the mesh of neon-bright conductors with a filament tool, and the interior lights up.

They are in a chamber of tall, intersecting crystal sheets—controller plates—that contain all the directives for operating every device and procedure in the ore processor. Beyond, Mei knows, through narrow companionways, are the vaults that store the repair supplies. She shoulders her way among the controller plates to a knee-high central frustum that houses Charles Outis's brain. It is made of the same translucent, crystalline material as the plates, and inside it she discerns a vague ovoid outline.

"Don't touch that!" the psybot commands.

"I'm sorry," Mei says, "but I must turn off your senses for a brief time. Everything we say is being relayed to Wolf Star, and we have no chance of getting away so long as they're spying on us."

"Leave me be!" the psybot shouts. "I don't want to go with you."

Mei ignores him, snaps open the top of the frustum, and lifts out the clear plasteel case with the brain inside it. The convoluted tissue is suspended in colorless gel and a chrome net, the support system that sustains it. Awe at the antiquity of the being in her hands and revulsion at its nakedness mix in her.

"This is *Wolf Star* speaking," the psybot says. "You are in violation of Commonality salvage-rights law. Your life is forfeit unless you immediately surrender the wetware with which you have absconded."

Mei places the plasteel case on the ground, grabs her jetpak, and fits its vent to the ripped end of the psybot.

"*The Laughing Life* is in violation of salvage-rights law," the psybot declares. "It is being stalked and will be destroyed. You have no means of escape. Surrender the wetware now, or face the—"

Mei fires a blast of the jetpak that lifts her toward the curved ceiling and shatters the psybot to spinning shards. She lands on her heels and dances backward with the inertia, crashing into the controller plates with enough force to knock the breath out of her. There is no sound in the virtually airless chamber, yet she hears with her bones the pounding atop the pod stop. An ominous silence pervades her. And in that palpable emptiness she feels suddenly tangential to life, fugitive to the world of sounds, to the living world, as though she brinks on the emptiness of a void greater than being, where the dead enclose the quick.

2

Remains of Adam

OVERCOME BY A SENSE OF UNREALITY AND AMAZED THAT HER LIFE is going to end here in the presence of an archaic human, Mei Nili picks up the capsule with reverence and stares through the milky plasteel at the brainshadow and the silvery net that sustains it. The idea strikes her that she can talk directly with this man using the electrodes in the net and the signal processors of the core chamber.

With a feeling of eerie portent, she returns the brain to the frustrum. She goes quickly to the switch box and, using filament brushes from the tool unit of her jetpak, connects the core chamber with her com-link. "Mr. Charlie, can you hear me?"

"Aye, yet strange you sound."

"It's the translator," Mei explains, relieved to hear a human voice again, no matter how comically distorted. "It must be having difficulty converting your archaic language."

"I be black in the kingdom of the blind!"

"I'll try and make some adjustments." She attempts tapping into the powerful logic boards of the controller plates, hoping she didn't damage them too badly in her collision. "I'm going to get us out of here, Mr. Charlie. But first I'm going to see if I can fuse the transmitter units in your support system with the translator mode in my comlink—my compact communications system. That way we can talk once I remove you from the core chamber."

"What heinous wickedy-split plans have you toward me?"

"I mean you no harm," Mei answers, tediously struggling to find the right pathways among the circuits. She subvocalizes her curses, not wanting the archaic brain to hear her frustration. "I'm taking you to Solis to grow you a new body—a whole and beautiful body—if we can get away from here."

"Much virtue in if," Charles says mournfully. "With broodful nod, proceed. What choice for a miser in a poor house?"

"Right." The pinhead bulb atop her filament brush flickers, then lights up, indicating she has opened a new pathway among the microswitches. "Okay! I think I've got it. Am I coming across more clearly, Mr. Charlie?"

"Yes, a lot clearer," a soft voice comes over her comlink. "You sound intelligible again."

She blows a satisfied sigh and slides to the floor. "Now all we have to do is get out of here without getting killed." She closes her eyes, reaching inward for the rageful strength that has carried her this far from the reservation. "It must seem ironic to you," she says quietly, "to have survived all this time only to wake up and discover your life is in jeopardy."

"It's not a happy feeling," the archaic mind admits. "I've been disoriented since I've woken up. Can you tell me what year this is?"

"Time isn't marked that way anymore, Mr. Charlie. I mean, on Earth there are still standard years, each with three hundred sixty-five and a quarter days. But each community has its own reckoning based upon its origin. On the reservation where I come from, we were in the year seven hundred forty-eight when I left."

"So I've been dead over seven hundred years," he says in a whisper so faint it is almost only a thought.

"Longer than that, probably. Our reservation was one of the most recent. What did you call the year when you lived?"

"I died in the twenty-first century. Does that mean anything to you?"

"No. I only know that the archaic age had its own reckonings for time. Religious ones, I think."

"Yes. Maybe you can tell me when the archaic age ended."

"I don't really know. I mean, I wasn't much interested in history. Do you know about the Maat?"

"No."

"Sometimes they're called neo-sapiens. They're what became of humanity after we mapped the human genome and amplified our intelligence."

"The next evolutionary step," Charles says with startled understanding. "The step we take for ourselves." Then, his voice rises to a puzzled lilt, "But why are you here? Why isn't everyone Maat?"

"Who knows? Maybe the Maat like diversity. Before they went underground, they founded the reservations, not just for people but for many life-forms. My reservation was one of the last they set up. I'm pretty sure they'd already been around for over a century by then. So you must have been dead for—well, for almost a thousand years."

Charles is silent, and Mei does not disturb his profound quiet for a long moment. During the interminable time he had spent locked in the virtual space of the ore processor's command core, he has had ample time to mull over his past and visit with the ghosts of those he knew in his first lifetime, now all long dead. He has no regrets about leaving them behind, where they had wanted to stay. But knowing how long they have been ghosts, how long he has lain dormant awaiting this vital moment, pervades him with an appalling sense of his own transience. He yearns deeply for the return of his senses so that he might grasp and smell and see the moment-by-moment reality he has traveled a thousand years to experience.

Mei's edginess becomes unbearable, and she must break the silence. "Do you wish now you hadn't frozen yourself?"

"No—no, not at all." He speaks in a hush, his awe palpable. "I knew there were great risks. I knew it might be frightful here. I—I wanted to see it for myself. I only wish now I had eyes."

"You will," Mei answers brightly. "And you'll have your whole body, too. The vats in Solis will shape you just as you were—or with modifications, if you want."

"Solis—where is that?"

"On Mars. Not far from here. It's a human community. They strive to maintain the old values. They'll appreciate an old-timer like you."

"But the gravity—it's only a third of Earth gravity."

"Yes. You and I will be in the minority there. Most have taller, less dense bodies. They'll find us quite exotic."

Mars! he thinks, simultaneously astonished and panic-stricken. It was because he had wanted to see Mars, to see the *cities* on Mars, that he arranged to have his head frozen upon death, to Van Winkle enough time so that he would wake to see its wonders. And now, right here in his blind presence, is a woman of this scary and marvelous future, his one tenuous hope for a new life. "Why did you leave Earth?" he asks, suddenly seized with a desire to know everything about her.

Mei hesitates, not sure what to say. She feels foolish telling him about the personal tragedy that impelled her off-planet, for this archaic mind is from a time when mortality was the common truth. Mute, she stares at her square-knuckled hands, and the visitor from the past must ask again, "Were you unhappy there? Has the Earth changed a lot from my time? Would I recognize it?"

"Oh, yes," she blurts. "You'd recognize it. The Maat restored the planet. The oceans and forests and grasslands are as they were before the sprawl of the city-states."

"But where do the Maat live?"

"Underground. The villages on the reservations are the only artifacts on the planetary surface. Factories are located in space or on the moon, and the mines are out here in the Belt. No one really knows what the Maat are actually using the raw materials for. I mean, there's no sign of them on Earth. I guess their subterranean cities take some of the material. And here and there, in desolate places—in rift canyons, deserts, and glacial peaks—you can find their crystals, big prismatic columns, a hundred meters tall. They're a mystery. Same with the Array. That's what everyone calls the Maat's massive project in trans-Neptunian orbit. It looks like some kind of pattern-less net, and it's built from the material that the numerous companies in the Belt and the gas planet systems garner for them. The actual construction is done by specialized androne, artificial workers created by the Maat."

"What do they look like—the Maat, I mean?"

"Anything they want." Mei stands up and starts probing the switch box again with a stylus from her tool kit. "I'm going to try to hail my partner and see if he can get us out of here."

"Won't the others hear you?"

"They'll hear the signal, but the codes in the switch box will scramble it." She speaks to the com-link in her shoulder pad: "Munk—are you there?"

"You're still alive!" Munk's signal comes back immediately on the secure channel. "*Wolf Star* declared that Aparecida had killed you."

"It's a lie, Munk. We're okay, for now. What about you?"

"I had to swing wide to shake the destroyers *Wolf Star* deployed. But I'm free at the moment. Do you have Mr. Charlie?"

"Yes."

"Can you get to the surface? I can pick you up in a drop-dead flyby. If I come in any slower, the destroyers will fix on me and there won't be any pickup at all."

"Aparecida has us locked in here."

"Take Mr. Charlie and break for the surface. I will position myself for the flyby now and execute the drop-dead in twelve minutes."

"It's too risky, Munk. Detonate the damn explosives. We're safe in the command pod."

"You know I can't do that, Jumper Nili."

"Let your C-P program do it! If you don't, I'll work this switch box until I figure out the detonating sequence myself."

"That will take too long. It'll be hours before you crack the code, if then. *Wolf Star* will have computed the codes for itself long before then. Make a break for the surface. I will pick you up."

"Munk, wait. Listen. There's something in you that's human. The Maat instilled that in you. I need that part of you to act for me—for Mr. Charlie—right now."

"Jumper Nili, I'm positioning *The Laughing Life* for the flyby. Break for the surface."

The secure line cuts off, and Mei disconnects from the switch box with a curse. "Damn that bolt-dolt!"

"What is a drop-dead flyby?" Charles inquires.

"It means he'll throw *The Laughing Life* at us and come in without any impulse power, engines dead, flying by momentum only. Because our ship is made from a substance called blackglass, it's virtually invisible in space. Without using the engines, the ship will offer no profile to *Wolf Star*. It will fly by undetected. All we have to do is be there to hop on."

Muttering blood oaths, Mei straps on her jetpak, stalks to the frustum, and removes the plasteel case. "Can you still hear me?"

"Yes." He has no sensation at all of movement. He is simply in blind space, informed only by the nerve-induced sounds from the translator in the case. "What are you going to do?"

"We're going to try to outrun Aparecida to the surface," she mutters sullenly, fidgeting with the switch box, setting a brief lagtime on the portal control. "Just be grateful you don't have eyes to see this."

She takes the ovoid case in both arms and positions herself at the egress point and waits, gnawing her lower lip nervously. Her fear angers her. What is there to fear? That she will die? Everyone she loves is dead. They died unknowing, believing the mercies of their age. At least she will die with her eyes open. What of Mr. Charlie? He died too, once, believing in the mercies of an age to come. But there are no mercies. She knows that now. And when the door dilates, she screams her bitter rage and fires her jetpak.

On the com-link, Munk hears Jumper Nili's defiant cry and begins his drop-dead flyby. Mars glides past the viewport; small with distance, its sharp rays cut the darkness like a star of blood. Its clear silence illuminates an uneasiness in the androne. What if Aparecida kills Mei Nili? The future becomes pointless then. Where can he go? Without the archaic brain, Solis will have nothing to do with him, and finding work in the Belt will be degrading, for none of the Commonality companies tolerate rogue behavior. To return to Apollo Combine or even Iapetus Gap where he began would mean certain ligature of his self-directive functions: His brain would be bound to a work governor that would inhibit all future independence.

That possibility is untenable to him, not after the pleasure he has derived from his anthropic studies, which he would lose once his C-P program is shunted by a work governor. But the other options available to him seem little better. The best he could hope for would be to wander the Belt, seeking bandit operations, salvage jobs that he could get to first before any company vessels show up.

Even then, he would have to rely on markets outside the Commonality to credit him for the materials he salvaged. Then he would have to transfer his credits to independent brokers among the colonies so that they could be converted to the power cells he requires to continue functioning. At any time he himself could be set upon by bandit salvagers or legitimate company crews who would be within their rights in dismantling him and brokering his components.

Of course, the Maat would grant him sanctuary from bandits and the Commonality companies in Terra Tharsis, their vast community on Mars. They would take him in, their creation hammered out of nothing. They would accept him as they accept all who come into their communal presence, and he would be changed, as all are changed in the grand thetic fields of their recondite being, changed and made anew, no longer Munk but Munk-of-the-Maat, naked before the infinite, at the foot of the dream that mind has named existence—and he would be made again mysterious even to himself.

Fear twines in him at that prospect. Is this some subprogram installed by his creators? Perhaps. He does not want to dwell on it. The Maat are too strange to contemplate, and he would rather live as a bandit in the void than submit himself to their unknowable whims.

For a similar reason, Munk has not dared consider

Jumper Nili's request that he override his primary programming and blow up Phoboi Twelve. If he does that, he compromises the only stability he has, the certainty of his own mental being. Carbon minds, having evolved from organic accidents, know madness. But the silicon mind is singular and thus secure from insanity. It is clarity itself, crystal become mind.

The androngs constructed by the Commonality are such truly pure silicon entities that they are incapable of defying their cybernetic natures. But a Maat construct, imbued with a contra-parameter program as he has been, is subject to the possibility of continual redefinition. Such randomness is the very threshold of madness.

Munk fears that. His primary program—to serve as a patrol and salvage androne for Iapetus Gap—was immutably altered by the activation of his C-P program—to acquire all the anthropic data he can. That diverted him from his work station in the Saturn ring system and brought him to Apollo Combine. Since then he has suffered flutter-gaps in his attention whenever he even so much as glimpses holo-images of the rings or hears data blurbs about the gas giants. Studying the anthropic psyche, he has learned that these attention gaps are experienced by people as pangs of remorse, guilt, nostalgia. Why, he has often wondered, have the Maat instilled such an inhibiting inefficiency in their creations?

Whatever the reason—if it can be called reason at all—Munk dreads all further deviation from his primary program. He has gone so far as to question the merit of his C-P interest in humans. Yet question is all he can do, since he is incapable of terminating his C-P file. As he cuts the magjets and commits *The Laughing Life* to its plunge toward Phoboi Twelve, he knows his fate is locked. Mei will either be there with the archaic brain, or she will be dead.

A tendril of fern floats by, and he plucks it out of the

air, enduring another flutter-gap in his attention. When he arrived in the Belt, this was the first bioform Munk saw. All the jumper ships are festooned with them—flowering lianas, crimson-leafed creepers, emerald bracken, and glossy jade plants. His initial lesson in human behavior was to learn that the human psyche relishes the presence of this early ancestor.

He takes the fern leaf between his digits and marvels again at its delicacy. The microvoltage of the phosphorylation of adenosine diphosphate to adenosine triphosphate in the cells' chlorophyll tingles his fingersensors when he feels for it. This is the photosynthetic process that has evolved spontaneously billions of years ago on Earth, releasing the free oxygen that made the evolution of respiring organisms possible.

How eerie it seems to him that this being appeared automatously out of the molecular frenzy of life. No creature manufactured it as he was manufactured. It emerged of its own accord, nascent, replete. As did the archaic brain that Mei Nili carries in the plasteel case. Mr. Charlie was not shaped in the vats. His genetic structure manifested without benefit of Maat or androne guidance. And that fills Munk with wonder as he tunes into the code-privileged band of the com-link.

He hears nothing, for Mei has shut down her link. The static that fills the enclosed space is the thin wind of the sun nagging at the electrons of the ship's antenna. It is a cold and unfailing sound.

Mei Nili fires her jetpak and, with a whooping cry, is flung through the hatch of the command pod and across the vault, Charles hugged tight against her. Aparecida, squatting atop the pod, lashes her spiked tail at the streaking figure and misses.

Shooting through the smashed gap in the geodesic dome,

Mei skids to a stop at the entry to the gigantic bore tunnel. A charred screech from the demolition androne sends Mei fleeing through the dark corridor, using short kicks from her jetpak to bound as far ahead as her cowl light permits her to see. She must find a vent that ascends to the surface. The plasteel case in her arms whispers through her com-link, "Mei Nili, Mei Nili, are you still with me?"

"Yes, Mr. Charlie, I'm here. Calm down. I can't talk now. Aparecida is after us."

Charles hates not knowing what is happening. He wants to help, to participate in his own salvation, and he rakes his mind for some worthy counsel. "Do you have a weapon?"

"No. Nothing that would stop a demolition androne."

Mei dares not even glance behind. Her full attention is ahead of her, among the numerous escapes in the riven rock wall—the vent holes and sludge chutes. Some, she knows, must be dead ends, terminating in dross bins and catch chambers. Very few will lead to the surface. Desperately, she strives to bring forward in her memory the bore-tunnel pattern that is the model for the ore processors she has helped install. But she has lost track of where she is in the tunnel.

Jarring vibrations quake the thin air with Aparecida's hammering stride, and the whipstroke whistle of her tentacles lashes its screeching echoes like a slicing siren. At any instant, Mei expects a shatter-blow to slam her into blackness. Stifling her terror, she fixes her gaze on a likely cavity directly overhead. A tight burst of the jetpak launches her upward, and she curls about in midleap and slides into the opening feetfirst.

Below her, she sees Aparecida lunge at the rock wall, talons biting into the stone, tentacles hoisting her along the sheered surface with weightless agility, her long head tilted back, fixing Mei with a pulsing, fireshadow glare.

"Where are we?" Charles asks. "What's happening now?"

Mei scuttles backward into the cavity, her fear coiling

tighter with the rapid pounding of the androne's pursuit. All she can hear is her panicked breathing.

"You're scared," Charles moans. "Tell me what's happening!"

"She's after us," Mei manages. As fast as she elbows backward, the opening before her crumbles and the androne's tentacles reach closer. The rock-cracking noise of Aparecida's frenzied approach jars the roots of her teeth, and she chatters curses in a fury of fear and rage at herself that she entered the duct backward, succumbing to the temptation to see her pursuer. Now the tight space prohibits her from turning around so she can use her jet-pak to propel her faster through the channel.

Though she is facing the wrong way, she fires her jet-pak anyway and shoots through the loops of the blind tentacles and out of the duct, streaking past the blunt face and spiked claws of Aparecida. A razorflash of tentacles loop and swirl after her, and she darts daringly into the blackness.

"What's that sound?" Charles presses. "Did we get away?"

Mei glances off the opposite wall and ricochets back into the darkness as Aparecida pounces swiftly on the space where she had been. Sizzling arcs of flogging tentacles drive Mei back and forth across the tunnel until her heart cannot pump oxygen out of her lungs fast enough and her strength no longer fits her muscles. With clambering, wobbly strides, she hauls herself up the broken face of the wall and heaves herself into the first opening she finds.

"Tell me what's happening!" Charles pleads, frightened by the gasping sounds of Mei's terrified exertion. "Where are we?"

Mei slaps off her com-link and tries to steady the raw fieriness of her breathing to get a grasp on where she is. The oblique angle of the narrow channel indicates it leads elsewhere than to the surface. A wrenching roar kicks her deeper as Aparecida's powerful limbs burrow a larger entry.

In moments the androne will have sufficient rock debris to fire projectiles. Skidding forward with boosts from her jet-pak as fast as she dares in the dark pipe, she roots her stamina in the hot current of her fear and finds the strength and clarity to push the plasteel case under her, down between her legs where she can clasp it with her ankles.

The first projectile whacks so hard against the case that her bones shudder, and she releases Charles. The plasteel case rolls backward down the pipe, but the next projectile smacks it back between her legs. Then the channel opens into a conveyer chute, and she tumbles out of the pipe.

Mei recognizes this chute as the same one she had fol-lowed earlier to the command pod. She releases a dis-tressed cry, knowing the chute only descends deeper into the asteroid. From here there is no chance of reaching the surface. Stabbing into the darkness with the light beam from her cowl, she begins the climb toward the core chamber and the command pod, gnashing her teeth in frustration. The regularly spaced ducts in the chute wall all lead back to the main bore tunnel, and entering them would be certain death, for Aparecida's heat sensors would spot her at once. Her only hope now is to return quickly to the command pod before the androne can cut her off and trap her in the chute.

Employing all the alacrity she can muster from her weary muscles, she climbs along the cable track. With conveyer trucks before her and cables looping above, her jetpak affords her no help. She fights to quiet her breath-ing so she can hear the danger ahead, while at the same time she demands fierce haste from her legs. Each sinewy second that she lags decreases her chance of getting out of the chute before Aparecida blocks her way.

A truck mounded with cinders appears out of the dark, and she cat-scrambles over it, vaulting the gap to the next truck. The plasteel case in her arms bobs cumbersomely, and she hopes that the blows it took in the pipe haven't damaged its precious interior. She considers flicking on her com-link to contact Charles but at that moment notices the blue glow from the power coils at the end of the chute.

Safeguarding her already wrenching heart from the excitement of making good her escape, she steadily keeps her alertness on her balancing leaps along the crests of the trucks. Her breath inadequate, her legs leaden, she won't relent, hoping she can reach the mouth of the chute and fire her jetpak. But as she reaches the last truck, her jouncing stride breaks at the sight of a blurred, groping tentacle.

Mei ducks behind the truck as Aparecida swarms into the conveyer chute, limbs thrashing. The truck whangs loudly with the impact, and the whole linkage is shoved deeper into the chute, knocking the plasteel case from her grasp. Tentacles scything above her, Mei ducks lower, her hands working furiously to uncouple the end truck. The pin jumps out, and she snatches the plasteel case from the ground and clutches it hard to her chest as she throws her jetpak to full throttle.

The force of the thrust hurls Mei, the cinder-laded truck, and the demolition androne across the giant vault toward the geodesic dome. Spewing ash, the jet-powered truck hurtles through the ripped gap in the dome, shoving Aparecida ahead of it and crashing violently into the towering column of a power coil. Lightning rigs a thundery harp between the smashed coil and the vault's dark peak, and clots of blue fire geyser through the chamber and crawl wildly over the naked ground.

Mei tumbles free of the collision and scrabbles with quavery legs toward the open portal of the command pod. Throwing off the dented truck, Aparecida leaps after her. A scourging hiss rips the air as tapers of steel claw the air at Mei's back. Flung forward again by her jetpak, Mei bounds with shock fright into the command pod, drops the plasteel case, and throws herself at the switch box.

The portal wrinkles shut before Aparecida's flailing blades narrow close enough to find flesh, and Mei collapses in a quaking heap. Three hot raps vibrate through the pod, and then there is silence but for her frantic breathing. She gropes for the com-link in her shoulder pad and splutters, "Mr. Charlie?"

"Mei Nili!" Charles is agog with fear. When she cut him off, he was sure Aparecida had killed her and he was on his way to the dissector. "I—I thought . . . Are you all right?"

"Yes," she gasps.

"What happened? Where are we?"

"We're back—back in the pod."

"What about Aparecida? Is she still after us?"

"Yes. My escape—I couldn't get away. I had to come back."

"We're still trapped?"

"For now." Mei pushes herself to her feet and leans against the switch box. Her fear-buzzing fingers steady only under the greatest concentration, and she manages to transmit a hailing frequency to *The Laughing Life*. But there is no response. From that she knows that the cruiser is either destroyed or maintaining strict silence because it has drifted within striking range of *Wolf Star*. "We'll have to wait a while before Munk can contact us again."

"What are you going to do?"

Mei picks up the plasteel case and notes the smudges where Aparecida's projectiles impacted. An open, lonely feeling—a tender sense of vulnerability—replaces the dazed and jangled aftermath of her terror-stricken flight. This remarkable being—a man from a lost era a thousand years gone—has been reduced to this—an object of barter, useful as an ore-factory controller or a shield—a *thing* that she has risked her life to steal. "You've got your ears, Mr. Charlie. Now I'm going to give you your eyes."

"You can do that?"

"I think so." She places the case back in the crystal

frustum and returns to the switch box. By channeling to Charles the input from the light sensors in the ceiling that monitor the interior of the pod, she opens for him a rainbow-tinted vision.

"I can see! It looks like I'm floating above you."

"There are ground-level light sensors, too," Mei says. "I'll connect you to them as well. These are what the jumpers use to scrutinize the controller plates by remote."

"Yes! I've found the reflex. I can will it myself now."

"There are also light sensors outside the pod. If you try . . ."

"There it is," he says in a cold whisper. "Is that Aparecida? She's huge—grotesque—"

"What is she doing?"

"Squatting in front of me. She's got these thick, barbed cables waving slowly around her—and her face, it's—"

"I know. We've met."

"How long can we stay in here?"

"Not long. *Wolf Star* will break the codes soon and then usurp control of the pod."

"What are we going to do?"

Mei smiles, and the sensation is so unfamiliar it startles her, opening her lungs to a giddy sigh.

"Why are you laughing?"

"Mr. Charlie, you said 'we.' I just think it's funny that we're in this together—me and a thousand-year-old man."

"Actually, Mei Nili, I'm scared shitless, as we used to say in my time."

"I am too, Mr. Charlie. I am too. And for a long time I wasn't." She settles to the floor and leans back against the jetpak. "For a long time I really didn't care if I lived or died."

"You were depressed. Why?"

"That doesn't matter. It would sound silly to you—a

man who already died once, who lived in a time when everyone had to die."

"You lost someone you love," Mr. Charlie surmises.

"I lost everyone I love. They weren't supposed to die. No one is supposed to die where I come from."

"That doesn't sound silly to me. I tried to escape death myself. But after what I've been through—crammed in here, forced to work as a machine slave—I would rather die than go back to that. Cowardly as that must seem, that is what's happened to me. Really, though, at bottom the only courage that is demanded of us is to go on living."

"For what? Simply to exist?"

"No. That's vile. But look at you, Mei Nili. You *are* beautiful. And you've told me that everyone is beautiful now. Disease, old age, distortion are done with, and at last, humanity attains the physical dignity that before we could only claim in spirit."

"That was the spirit I left Earth to find. Physical dignity is not enough, Mr. Charlie."

"No, I suppose not. Much as I hate to admit it, the old philosophers were right. We sing best in our chains. Even so, I would love to taste some of the freedom humanity has won in the thousand years since I had a body. Is there any hope we can get away to that place you told me of—to Solis—where they will shape a new body for me?"

Mei shrugs disconsolately. "Only if we can convince Munk to override his primary programming and detonate the explosives."

"Patch me into *The Laughing Life*. Let me talk with him."

"He won't listen to you. He's an androne."

"Yet when he first contacted me he introduced himself as something more—a rogue androne with what he called contra-parameter programming installed by the Maat. He's capable of free will."

"Not if he can help it," Mei says with a gleam of anger.

"Then we have to make it necessary. We have to give him no choice but to use his freedom."

"I don't understand."

"Mei Nili, you gambled your life to save me. I know that serves your self-interest. You need me to gain entry to Solis for yourself. Yet if you want, you can surrender me to Aparecida this minute and your life will be spared. You can go on living."

"I didn't come this far to give up. If I have to die now, at least I won't be running away from life—which is what I was doing before."

"I'm glad to hear you say that. There's a chance, then, that we can get out of here. But we'll have to gamble our lives. Are you willing?"

"What do I have to do?"

"Let me talk to Munk."

Mei pushes to her feet. At the switch box, she finds that the transmission circuit is already active, and Munk's voice is droning, ". . . hear me? Respond, Jumper Nili."

"Munk! We're back in the pod. We couldn't make it to the surface."

"Jumper Nili, I was ready to believe you were dead."

"We will be soon, Munk, if you don't help us."

"Jumper Nili, don't ask—"

"It's not me this time that's asking."

"Munk? This is Charles Outis speaking. Can you hear me?"

"Who?" the androne asks. "There's noise in your transmission I can't decipher."

"This is Mr. Charlie. Do you hear me?"

"I hear you, Mr. Charlie. I regret we have not been able to liberate you just yet."

"You can liberate me, Munk. Detonate the explosives immediately."

"I can't do that, Mr. Charlie."

"You can—and you must. Mei Nili is going to open the

pod entry now. If you don't detonate the explosives at once, Aparecida will destroy us. Do you understand?"

Mei's heart surges, and she turns with shock from the switch box.

"Jumper Nili, do not do this. I will swing about for another drop-dead flyby. Try again to evade Aparecida and get to the surface."

In her astonishment, Mei says nothing. This is it. The clarity of Charles's decision penetrates her, and all the lorn and muddied raging that had carried her from Earth to this lifeless rock in the preterit void lifts away. Tears come quietly to her eyes.

"Jumper Nili!"

Mei blinks away her tears and nods toward the sensors, holding Charles's gaze and not quite smiling. "I'm setting a ten-second lag on the pod entry, Munk. If Mr. Charlie and I are going to survive, it's entirely up to you."

"Jumper Nili, I will use the codes to countermand your portal control."

Mei tugs a small pliers from her tool kit and inserts it into the switch box with a deft twist. "I've cut the code link to the portal. You can't stop it now. It will open in ten seconds. Our lives are in your hands, Munk."

"Don't do it, Jumper Nili."

Mei sets the timer and retreats down the aisle of controller panels. She removes her jetpak and sets it beside her on the floor. "Get us out of here, Munk."

"Help us!" Charles calls.

In *The Laughing Life*, Munk pulls away from the command console abruptly, as though it has become white-hot. He stands erect, suspended by his conflict in a bitter, utter stillness. Ten seconds for a silicon mind is ten eternities in which to dwell on the permutations of the future. Munk locks into a frozen logic loop: If he does nothing, Mei and the archaic human will be lost forever—yet if he detonates the explosives, he will have defied his primary programming, and he will—forever after—endure the claims of insanity, of loss of guided control, of uncertainty in his own behavior.

There are no feelings to guide him. If he trusts his C-P programming, he will detonate the explosives and destroy not only Phoboi Twelve and Aparecida but also his identity as an androne. If he does not act, there will be no grief, no remorse, no sadness at the loss of an archaic human. He will go on, a rogue androne, salvaging errant mining equipment to earn the credits necessary to replenish his power cells. Eventually, he will meet other jumpers, add their interviews to his developing anthropic model, and so continue to fulfill the inner directive of his creators.

In the tenth second, Munk decides to leave his primary programming intact. The uncertainty of existing without it is the most puissant emotion he has ever experienced, and he crouches over the command console and turns *The Laughing Life* away from Phoboi Twelve.

Over the com-link he hears the shouts of Jumper Nili and Charles Outis as the portal opens and Aparecida comes for them. The wildness of their anguished yells pierces deep into his C-P program. He adds that to his anthropic model. And then he hears the gusty roar of the jetpak. Jumper Nili has launched it ahead of her. He can tell, for it dopplers away from her shimmering cries, thuds loudly, and whines to a stop. She has struck Aparecida with it, driven the androne back a few paces, and purchased herself two, maybe three extra seconds.

Such resistance is absurd, he thinks, and realizes, of course, such absurdity is the very source of being human—to live and strive simply to live and strive, even for a few extra seconds, to go on living and to make the laws according to which one lives, to program oneself—

which, to the androne, is madness and yet something more, a willful desire to set one's own limits in a universe where there is no real edge to anything, where the interpenetration of cosmic energies and molecular flow and accidents creates an eternal flux despite all programming, all structures, all the crystallizations of the silicon mind, even those seemingly impenetrable sanctuaries of purpose, identity, and safety created by the Maat.

And all at once, Munk's plight ends. Though he still does not understand, he comprehends why the Maat put a human heart inside his androne bulk. They never intended him to be human, only to be as free as a human—as free and as absurd. Without hesitation, he generates the firing codes for the bore-drill explosives and sends the detonating signal.

Mei Nili is hunched among the controller plates, gawking in horror with Charles as Aparecida casts aside the crumpled shape of the jetpak and springs toward them. Her prodigious head slung forward in a gaze of flame-cored mineral intensity, tentacles slithering ahead of her steely, clacking claws, she is death itself.

A searing flare of white fire bleaches the androne to a skeletal silhouette and consumes her in a wincing radiance blind as any darkness, and she vanishes like a tattered shadow into the wraith world of all nightmares.

The portal reflexively squeezes shut under the blast. The brunt of the shockwave tosses Mei against the far wall with a sickening thud, and she slumps lifelessly, a cast-adrift body in the reduced gravity.

"Mei Nili!" Charles bawls, and then, "Munk! Munk, are you there? Mei Nili's hurt! Hurry!"

Munk receives the distress signal from nearby, where he has watched the silent holocaust billow into fiery tatters. He steers *The Laughing Life* into the infrared haze to recover the scorched command pod. Resorting at once to his primary programming, he ignores the emotional valence in Charles's message and calmly guides the cruiser through the debris of the explosion. The heavily damaged *Wolf Star* has swiftly retreated, dwindling to a bright star in the galactic haze, leaving behind pewter shards of fused blackglass, twisted finjets, mangled hull plates, and melted shapes of plasteel among the rapidly cooling dust cloud that is all that remains of Phoboi Twelve.

The command pod itself has separated into several heat-tarnished spheres whirling doomful and mute as absolute rock among the cosmic dust. Munk gently docks *The Laughing Life* against the sphere emitting Charles's signal. The controller plates recognize the company vessel, and the pod mates its portal to the cruiser's pressure hatch and accepts Munk with an inrush of heated air.

Charles, unprepared for the sight of the bulky humanoid with the chrome hood and featureless faceplate, utters a weak groan. "Munk?"

"Yes," the androne replies, hurrying to Mei's body. "Have no fear. The danger for you is over, Mr. Charlie."

Munk checks the oxygen content and pressure of the air mix in the pod as well as the temperature to be certain that they are adequate to sustain human life, and assured of that, he unzips Mei's statskin cowl. His thick hand hovers a centimeter above her face, not only attempting to measure her rate of respiration but also at venture, daring for the first time to touch human flesh.

His sensors can detect no gas exchange at all. His first contact is to the side of her neck, trepidatiously feeling for her carotid pulse. None. "She is dead."

"No!" Charles cries. "She's not dead. Not yet. It's only been a few minutes. You've got to start her breathing. Do you understand?"

"How?" From his memory-allocation files, Munk filters

cardiopulmonary therapies. He retrieves the first-aid-for-humans program that his makers installed in the earliest andrones and that persists in him at a low level of his operating system as a kind of racial memory.

"Force air into her lungs," Charles calls desperately.

Swiftly, the androne positions her under him on the deck, his fist placed over her nose and mouth, his finger pistoning air into her lungs. A vigorous thoracic massage follows as he pumps her rib cage with his fingertips, feeling her bones stressing to their breaking point. He considers applying a small electric jolt, when her heart thumps back to life and she gasps for breath.

Mei shudders alert, peering up blearily at the crimson lens bar in the black faceplate, and she feels the bright magnetic touch of his living metal against her flesh. Alertness jams into place as he lifts his electric presence from her and she takes in the intersecting crystal plates and mirror-gold concavity of the pod.

And then, quite unexpectedly, she finds herself blinking at the kneeling androne with tears welling in her eyes. It is as if everything she had ever refused to reckon with, the sadness and loneliness, is trying to rise within her involuntarily and all at once, overflowing from her as much in release as in pain. Awareness of the blackness that has relinquished her under the androne's ministrations taps into the very source of her grief.

To Munk's amazement, she begins to sob. He finds it incredible that this molten grief could have churned inside her for so long without finding a way out, that she had to literally die before it found relief. In the formless nothing where she has just been, the androne realizes, everyone she had ever loved had gone. And now she has been there too—and come back.

"Welcome to the club," Mr. Charlie says with quiet exultation. "Welcome to the survivors' club."

In the wash of air from *The Laughing Life*, strands of

fern and a white blossom have drifted. Munk sweeps them into his grasp and presents them to Mei. "To life."

She accepts the bouquet with a quavery smile. "To Solis."

Installed in the flight bubble of *The Laughing Life*, Charles sees and hears through the ship's sensors. While he scrutinizes the interior of the vessel, amazed to be alive *inside* a magjet cruiser, even more amazed at the ambit of his own hazardous destiny that has delivered him from the darkness of the machine, Mei and Munk talk. Vaguely, the thousand-year-old mind listens to the androne and the woman struggle with their relief and the joy of their success while they discuss what lies ahead—the brief flight to Mars and how it will be necessary to abandon *The Laughing Life* in a high orbit. The cruiser is the property of Apollo Combine, and the only way to avoid the company's legal claim on them is to leave it behind. They will all go down to Mars in the pod and will slow their entry with a jetpak rig they'll hook up from the ship's stores.

While they carefully plot the immediate future, Charles gazes at the macramé of vines and roistering ferns spilling from ceiling nooks. He is quietly astonished to see them dangling here among the mysterious alloys of the transparent hull, wavering with the vent breeze in the aqueous glow from the crystal devices of the console. To him, the plants are weary and beggared life-forms, sufficing on the merest offerings, yet noble in the poverty of radiation, thin air, and meager dirt that sustain them. Of course they would accompany humanity into space. From their cellular struggles, human life slowly and violently evolved and stands before him now as this beautifully pale and dark-haired woman chattering gratefully. By comparison, the androne beside her, holding her steady in the empty gravity, seems a divinity, silvery black and ceremonial, a faceless apparition of a higher order, a more ideal actuality, that has emerged from her even more distinctly than she emerged from the genetic turmoil of the plants' early lives.

The archaic human stares at them tirelessly, scrutinizing these three orders of reality arrayed before him—ancestral, human, and noetic—and as the fourth, the ghost witness of the past, an obscure soul without a body, he experiences for the first time in this calamitous and unreckonable future some emotion other than fear.

Charles stares ahead through the prow's sensors at the swelling vista of Mars. The awe that had begun for him when he first woke from his long, cold sleep steepens at the view of the orange-red deserts and rows of dead volcanoes. As the cruiser glides closer to the rimlands of smeared lava flats and scoria, he sees the famous veins of dried riverbeds that he remembers from the *Viking* photographs of his former life a millennium ago. The rumor of floods chamfering the rusty plains, grooving the reddish black slurry floors with the toilings of water, fans out and melts away into the dark amber glass of alien mantle beds.

And suddenly, there it is, in the chancre of a crater surrounded by burned-out cinder cones—an immense and gleaming city! Astonishment expands to a worshipful feeling in his archaic brain, for here is the justification of his gamble and his suffering—the triumphant faith of the vision he had died and been reborn to see. Set like a strange jewel in the barren plains and stark promontories of the dead planet, the city is woven of radiance. Its gold-and-onyx spires twinkle with sunfire and emerald spurs of laser light, its dazzling foundations sunk in the bedrock of the future's hewn and ancient-riven altar of Mars.

3

Terra Tharsis

CHARLES OUTIS IS A BRAINSHADOW ENCASED IN AN EGG OF CLEAR plasteel. Psyonic pads designed to read and induce brain-waves cap both ends of the capsule and connect it by com-link to the console and the sensory array of *The Laughing Life*. Through the prow sensors, Charles watches Munk floating in space, the galaxy like mist behind him. The androne uses mag-lock clips to attach jetpaks to the mirror-gold hull of the pod.

"You only have four jetpaks," Charles notices. "Will they be strong enough to brake our descent?" Under ordinary circumstances, Charles prided himself on his observational abilities; now, survival has made him hyperalert. He notices the microchipping of the rover's hull and the thin feathers of electric fire around Munk as the androne aligns the jetpaks and magnetically locks them into place.

"These won't brake our entry," Munk answers frankly, indicating the circle of puny shoulder packs with their tapered jets that he's fixed to the hull. "But I'm not going to drop us to the surface. I'm aiming for Terra Tharsis, the city you saw on our last flyby. The jetpaks will help steer us to where scouts can pick us up as we go in."

"I still say there's enough lift on this cruiser to make a dunefield landing," the jumper calls from the helm. "Terra Tharsis is too dangerous. Let's go directly to Solis. Put us down in the Planum, on one of the sandy verges near the settlement. We'll hike in."

"The landing is too risky," Munk says. "The dunes veil rock reefs, and this pod isn't designed for an impact entry. We have no choice but to seek sanctuary with the Maat, unpredictable as they are. Which is better—to take a chance on incalculable physics or on an unguessable psyche?"

Inside the flight bubble of the ship, Mei is washed out by the pelagic glow of the console. Monitoring near space in the view scanner, she advises the androne, "We've got only a few minutes left. Two Bund ships and an Ap Com transport are closing fast."

"All right, then," Munk responds, "lock the helm and get into the pod."

Awe, fear, exultation at basking in the brown glow of Mars fuse inside Charles to a wide-staring intensity, so that he feels more alive now than he ever had in his former life. "What's going to happen to us in Terra Tharsis?" he asks.

"I don't know," Mei admits without much sympathy. "Terra Tharsis belongs to the Maat, not the Commonality. We'll have to find our way as we go."

Charles fixes his attention in the pod's external sensors and watches the planet view floating below, Mars rising splotched and enormous against the starsmoke. The winy mist of the atmosphere shimmers thinly against the black depths of space, and the blister-peeled and coagulate surface of the world shines with ectoplasmic wisps of dust and frost vapors.

The jetpaks fire soundlessly, the mute flares of blue

exhaust standing before the stars like votive flames on the gold rim of the pod. Snug in his plasteel case, a husked brain devoid of even the primitive sense of vertigo, Charles does not feel the tug of acceleration. Instead, he surmises motion by the swelling vista.

Charcoal scrawls of shadow resolve to fault lines, nacre blotches expand to vast sandy verges, and the horizon becomes serrated. The barren vista of oxide deserts and crenulated mountain ridges swims closer, aslant in the yawing descent of the pod. Scalloped dunes spring from the mutant sands, warped and quaking as the thin atmosphere buffets the plummeting vehicle, and Charles wants to blink, to shunt even for a moment the incoming vantage of wind-rowed buttes and stress-cracked rock.

The planet's rancid colors blur through the lens of the pod's thermal bowshock. Munk mutters some command that Charles is too distracted to catch. Below, a jagged shadowline of flint-faceted mountains looms as the pod's ultimate and calamitous destination, and a delirious howl whirls through Charles. Before Mei disengages the plasteel capsule from the ship's console and steeps him in darkness, he sees the sharp peaks veer away, and through a rocky draw in the broken horizon, Terra Tharsis rears, her crystal towers swarmed in reefs of reflectant haze and star-barbs and carats of unearthly radiance.

"Mr. Charlie, wit you wise?"

The voice comes from all directions, and Charles Outis groans groggily awake, unable to remember where he is. His last recollection is of a supernaturally beautiful city of gleaming spires.

"He be witful. Spark his eyes, say I."

"Where am I?" Dim red embers worm in the darkness. "I can't see anything."

"The translator needs adjustment," a basso profundo voice declares.

"Yes, it does," a softer voice replies. "I've just tuned it. He can understand us now."

"Good," the voice of thunder says. "Mr. Charlie, will you acknowledge that you can hear me?"

"Yes, I hear you. Where am I? I can't see anything. What's happened to the others? Where's Mei Nili—and Munk?"

"Calm yourself," the rumbling voice commands. "In a moment your sight will be returned to you. But first, listen to me. You are now in the custody of the Maat Pashalik. Several claims of ownership have been laid against you, and you are on exhibit before the Moot to settle this question of proprietorship."

"Wait, I don't understand. I don't belong to anyone. Where am I? Let me see where I am! Mei Nili? Munk?"

"Activate Mr. Charlie's vision," the heavy voice orders.

Wincing rays of hot color pierce Charles painfully before relaxing into the panoramic vista of a marbled cream floor slick as a mirror extending toward distant ivory tiers of swerving architecture strange as turtle bones and manta-ray hoods. A massive plate-glass wall reveals the glittering city of onyx arcs and silver-gold needle-towers he has seen from *The Laughing Life*. The copper-and-quince tones of Mars are visible on the horizon, the dark amber of mountains above the red skin of the desert.

"Mr. Charlie," the thunder calls him, and he notices two figures emerge from the glare where noon light stands on the gleaming white expanse. One is no more than a ruby staff topped by a manikin face, a mask on a broomstick. The other is bulkily draped in floating black scarves and an amethyst mist, and the humanoid face gazing from under the stammering flame that wreathes his faceted head is a dark metallic gray with black eyes impenetrable and empty as a shark's. "I am the Judge," the bulky one says with the voice of thunder. "And this is the Clerk."

"You're androns," Charles gripes wearily, stifling a momentary swirl of dizziness at the strange sight before him.

"We are agents of the Maat," the Judge intones, "and you are in the Pashalik of the Maat where our authority countermands all other judgments."

"Where's Mei Nili?" Charles asks, fighting his panic. "How did I get here?"

"Mr. Charlie," the Clerk says in her suede voice, the lips from the manikin face unmoving, "you shall not address questions to the Judge—only to myself. You are, after all, an exhibit and not a plaintiff in these proceedings."

"What do you mean?" Fear fists so tightly around him he thinks he may pass out. "I'm Charles Outis. I'm a human being, dammit, not some—thing."

"You are speaking nonsense," the Clerk warns in a gentle tone. "Our memory survey indicates that you are fully aware of your demise. Your remnant and relict survival, objectively speaking, is solely as a thing. The only question to be resolved by the Moot is to whom do you belong."

"I belong to myself!"

"That makes no sense, Mr. Charlie. By universal convention, a legally dead person has no claim upon anything, physical remains or otherwise."

"But I'm not dead!" he cries desperately. "Can't you see? You're talking to me, for God's sake."

"We're talking to you only because your dead brain has been reanimated at a measurable expense and for an expected return," the Clerk patiently explains. "You were dead for many terrene years and would be dead now otherwise."

"That's absurd!"

"That is the law."

"You mean I have no rights at all?" He looks away from the bizarre apparition of the magistrate and his puppet, stares past the veering geometries of Terra Tharsis, and sinks his gaze into the primal horizon—the ruddy vista of Mars—hoping to calm himself.

"There are important property rights that do pertain," the Clerk quietly admits. "Because you were stolen from the Commonality archive by lewdists, this demonstrates negligence of protectorship on the part of the Commonality. The case may be made that the Commonality has thus forsaken any claim to you. As you were afterward stolen from the lewdists by the Friends of the Non-Abelian Gauge Group and subsequently recovered from them by the Commonality, you may claim to be property of public domain. Then, ownership rights will devolve to those who salvaged you."

"Why are you doing this to me?" Charles moans.

"The law requires the Judge and the Clerk to examine all exhibits prior to presentation in the Moot." The Clerk floats backward into the glare of noon light. "Unless the Judge has further questions, I believe our examination is concluded."

"The exhibit is found whole and without defect," the Judge decrees, the amethyst vapors around him fluorescing brightly, the flaming halo vanishing. "It shall be admitted to the Moot and herewith subject to all pending arguments for final and absolute proprietorship."

"Hey, wait a minute. Please!" Charles pleads. "Where's Mei Nili? Where's the androne Munk? How did I get here?"

The Judge retreats into the sunfire, and in the next instant blackness swarms over Charles Outis.

Mei Nili and Munk sit in the alcove of the Moot, awaiting their turn to testify. Munk's faceless aspect stares out the transparent walls at the supernal ramparts of Terra Tharsis. He is livid inside with fear. So, this is the adytum of the Maat. And here he is at the foot of the dream, far beyond the parameters of all his programming. His hope, however improbable, had been that the flyers who intercepted the incoming pod would deposit them outside the city. But they didn't, and now here they are in the midst of the Maat's creation. An incestuous anxiety possesses him: This is the place of his maker, the very trespass he most dreaded.

The Maat's hand is everywhere apparent, from the artificial terrestrial gravity to the blue tint of the filtered sky. When, in the grip of the flyers' magravity net, the pod touched down on the summit of an onyx tower eight kilometers tall, Munk expected some kind of encounter with his creators. Instead, only a faceless androne on a skim plate awaited them. It ignored all their questions, removed the plasteel capsule with Charles inside, and floated across the rooftop among a panoply of prisms and mirror vanes. They followed, and the mute androne led them a long way down a spiral ramp of abstract chromatic mosaics to this enormous chamber of sun-shot glass and ivory.

"You are in the Moot of the Maat Pashalik," a genderless voice softly advised them out of nowhere after Mei seated herself on a transparent bench. "Please wait here until you are summoned."

"How long have we been here?" Mei asks curtly. She has refrained from berating Munk verbally for their predicament, but he can see by her eyes that she thinks the dunefield landing would have been better.

"Two hours and thirty-seven minutes," Munk replies meekly. Within the first few seconds of entering the chamber, he had already measured its domed ceiling, glass perimeter, and 2,853 viewing loges tiered in midair in the vast space surrounding the amphitheater of the central court. The sleek hoods of the loges are an evanescent blue shading along a lateral line to a hue subtle as the bronze tint on a mushroom, lending them an eerily organic look, like hovering skates or devilfish. Afraid to examine these odd structures too closely and too embarrassed by their predicament to engage in taciturn conversation with Mei, he turns inward and focuses on listening to the communications of the numerous andrones in the vicinity. Their code logic does not match his, and because he does not understand anything they're saying, he must remain content with their music.

Mei paces about the sterile alcove, returning repeatedly to the window bay to gaze at the surreal skyline. The teetering spires and hyperbolas loom so tall their lower stories disappear below in a haze of ramparts and sparkling viaducts and spans that meld with distance to a golden ether.

Who lives here? she wonders. In the arcade on Deimos, she had once seen film texts of the multitudinous types into which humanity has diversified in the colonies—the morphs, clades, and plasmatics, to name just the three biggest groups. None are permitted in the reservations on Earth, not even the Maat, and in her job with Apollo Combine she had met only morphs, people morphogenetically adapted for specific tasks.

Here in Terra Tharsis, however, she knows there are clades, new branches of humanity that would barely be recognizable to her as human, and the plasmatics, those who have genetically transcended anthropic anatomy altogether. Perhaps this chamber itself is a hive, and the organic loges floating overhead belong to a plasmatic class . . .

"Jumper Nili?" a smoky voice calls. "Androne Munk?"

A tall, sinewy youth with ethereal cheekbones, cumin complexion, fire-blue eyes blacked with kohl, and red hair glittering with pixel-gems and braided in a long rope down his back shows the palms of his tapered hands in colonial greeting and bows curtly. "My name is Shau Bandar. I represent *Softcopy,* a local news-clip service for the anthro commune. The Moot is allowing one of the twenty-six anthro news services to interview you pre-hearing, and I got the luck of the draw. If you don't mind, I'd like to introduce you to our viewers."

Mei has encountered reporters like this before, when she was a novice jumper and considered mildly news-worthy for wanting to leave the reservation in the first place to take up such risky work. This reporter, like the others, exudes that same blue smell of serenity—a sedating olfact used by journalists to put their subjects at ease. For that reason alone, she decides she wants nothing to do with him. "Look, Slim, why don't you go find out for us how long we're going to be kept waiting here—"

Munk quickly steps between Shau Bandar and Mei. "Excuse me," he says deferentially. "Could you kindly give us a moment?" Then turning his broad back to the reporter, he whispers hotly in a voice pitched for Mei's ears, "For hope's sake, don't speak too hastily, Jumper Nili. This reporter may prove helpful. He is, after all, like you, an anthro."

"Put it away, Munk. That's your C-P program talking. Forget your anthropic model. Can't we just get Mr. Charlie and find our way to Solis?"

"Has it occurred to you yet that Solis is four thousand, three hundred forty-five kilometers from here?" Munk whispers. "Have you given any thought as to how we're going to cross that much open terrain? The anthro commune may be able to abet our journey. Come on, now. Let's be logical and cooperate with this man."

Mei accedes with a reluctant nod, and Munk faces the reporter, beckoning him closer. "Excuse our ignorance, Shau Bandar," Munk says solicitously, "but this is our first time in Terra Tharsis. Perhaps you can inform us as vitally as we can you."

The reporter makes an adjustment to the microcontrols on the cuff of his purple dress coat, and a small blue light comes on in the collar of his short mantle, where he carries his sensors. "I'd be glad to help. Softcopy can connect you with both the anthro and androne naturalization projects—"

"We're not staying," Mei cuts in. "We're bound for Solis."

His brown, angular face lights up. "Even better! That trek has endless appeal to our viewers. You know, I've never covered it myself, but I'd like to. I imagine the archaic brain you recovered from Phoboi Twelve will be your entrée?"

"You know about Mr. Charlie?" Munk asks with surprise.

"Of course. It's in the court records. The news clips are already touting him as the Chiliad Man."

"Chiliad?" Mei frowns.

"The Thousand-Year-Old Man," Munk translates.

"What our viewers want to know," the reporter continues, "is what will you do if the Judge awards proprietorship to the Commonality?"

"Is that what's being decided here?" Mei asks, miffed. "They can't do that. Terra Tharsis is independent of the Commonality."

Shau Bandar nods sympathetically. "In principle, you're right. But the import of archaic remains has little precedent. That's why *Softcopy* is monitoring this case. The anthro commune is unhappy with the legal but inhumane exploitation of anthro remains by the Commonality. A copy of Mr. Charlie's radio distress broadcast is among the most popular clips in the contemporary index. In fact, the renowned Troupe Frolic already has a skit clip out based on the broadcast, called 'Wax Me Mind,' that's been both enraging and entertaining the commune since yesterday."

"When will the judgment be passed?" Munk inquires.

Shau Bandar regards the iridescent facets set in his

cuff. "Initial arguments will be heard in about—oh, seventeen minutes. After that, judgment will be withheld pending further data for the minimum cycle required for a property case. That's one year—six hundred and eighty-seven martian days."

"What?" Mei's cry sends annulate echoes fading into the ivory distance.

"Am I right in assuming that neither of you has arranged to transfer credits here before going rogue?" the reporter queries.

"We had to respond immediately upon detecting Mr. Charlie's distress signal," Munk answers, somewhat defensively. "Regrettably, the credits we have accrued with Apollo Combine have been forfeit."

"Then after the initial arguments," Shau Bandar says, "I'll connect you with the naturalization projects and you can find work and begin to make yourselves at home here in Terra Tharsis."

Mei sits grumpily on the transparent bench, crosses her legs, and rests her chin on her fist. "This is just great. We risked our lives to salvage Mr. Charlie. He's ours, dammit. No one has any right to take him from us."

"Would you like to tell the viewers of *Softcopy* about the risks you took?" Shau Bandar says, edging closer.

Mei casts him a sidelong scowl. "What? Are you going to pay us for this?"

"Now, now," Munk intercedes soothingly. He places his heavy arm lightly on the reporter's shoulder and guides him away from the sulking jumper. "Come, let us talk. I am interested in asking you a few questions as well. Are your viewers aware, for instance, of contra-parameter programming in Maat-construct andrones?"

The Judge, in a sheath of amethyst fog and black fluttering scarves, stands at the center of the amphitheater beside the stick-mask of the Clerk. Between them, on a frost-green pedestal, the plasteel capsule is displayed. A score of loges float nearby, their galleries packed with spectators. Shau Bandar waves from one of them, and though he is talking, his voice is absorbed in silence.

Munk waves back, but Mei Nili offers nothing, staring straight ahead as the transparent bench she shares with the androne skims over the marbled cream floor.

In his stentorian voice, the Judge announces, "The argument for proprietorship of the revived remains of Mr. Charlie has been conducted for the Common Archive by Sitor Ananta. As this argument has been laid before the Moot from Earth, the communications lag of six minutes forty seconds has been edited by the Clerk. The compressed argument presented here remains true in form and content."

The air beside the Clerk wobbles, and there appears a holoform image of a morph with slant-cut brown hair and long, Byzantine eyes, dressed in the loose, red-trimmed black uniform of the archives. "The archaic brain on display was uncovered at Alcoran site three by Commonality archivists twelve terrene years ago," the image declares. "The full records of discovery have been forwarded to the Moot. The remains date from the late archaic period, and though no chronicle of a prior life is extant, a direct cull was made of the dendritic memories and proof positive obtained that this individual experienced a full terminal episode before encephalic separation, glycolic perfusion, and immersion in liquid nitrogen. Though the definition of death has changed over historical time, this archaic brain was in fact declared dead by the definition of his own time. This is shown in the records of the dendritic cull, which have also been forwarded to the Moot."

The Clerk's slender voice pipes up, "Discovery and memory cull records on display."

Above him, for the benefit of the loges, calligraphic smears of color squirm through space: coded spectra to be translated by the spectators' sensors. Mei ignores them, but Munk records the full display and determines by correlation to the data in his anthropic model that Mr. Charlie had been interred in the archaic province of Californica in only his ninth decade. The primitive brevity of his existence—for such can hardly be deemed a life—stirs pity in the androne, and he determines then and there that this man, who through a misweave in the weft of history has escaped the utter obliteration of his age, shall know the abundance of life the human spirit deserves. Fear of what he is about to do swarms like static through him, but he overrides his panic by focusing on the prime directive of his C-P program, to treat all people humanely—even if it means his own destruction. Mr. Charlie is human, and he will no longer be treated as an object, if Munk can so help it.

Sitor Ananta continues, "The exhibit, revived by standard archival procedures—"

"I have seen enough," Munk declares, rising. He hears the music of the nearby androne shift tone, sensing his threat. Fear mounts again in him as he expects the Maat to intervene and scatter him into a tenuous blowing of atoms. But nothing happens.

The Commonality agent continues talking: ". . . exists in its animated form today only because—"

"No judgment will be passed on this human being," Munk declares, "unless it is the judgment of life and the concomitant freedom that humanity has wrested from the accidents of creation and history."

". . . of the efforts exerted by the Commonality Archi—" The image of Sitor Ananta shrivels away.

"Be seated, Androne Munk!" the Clerk commands. "You are in contempt of the Moot."

"Yes!" Munk confesses, amazed and emboldened by his

defiant survival in the temple of his makers. He can hear—sense—all the other androndes in the chambers and corridors of the tower, each one a cell in the metabody of a grand silicon mind. He feels their animus. Yet none act. Are his makers restraining them? Can there be any other explanation? "I *am* in contempt of you." He points a squared finger at the magistrate and sweeps his hand toward the loges. "And I am in contempt of all of you who dare pass judgment on a human being who has broken no law, committed no crime."

"Sit!" the Clerk brays.

"No." Munk steps toward the Judge. The loud music of the foreign code logics from the androndes in the court crest with rageful intent, but no threat appears. "I have been created by the Maat and contra-parameter programmed by them to study and respect *homo sapiens*. I am an authority. And this archaic brain I recognize as human and alive. I cannot permit you to pass any other judgment but life and freedom upon him. Do you understand?"

The fiery halo above the Judge's faceted head flares hotter. "I understand that you are in contempt of the Moot and will now be removed—forcibly, if necessary."

"The Maat have created me to withstand the gravitational tidal forces of the Saturn system," Munk loudly informs the court. "Unless you intend to destroy yourselves, the exhibit you presume to judge, and this entire chamber, you dare not try to stop me."

This, of course, is a bluff. His makers, who possess his signal codes, could turn him off in an instant—or, if they desired a more vehement display, he could be sheathed in a confining field and his body dissolved to atoms. He knows the Maat could do that. But they do not, which is all the approval he requires. He seizes the plasteel capsule and dashes in a blur across the expansive courtroom. At the plate window, he dives, his cowl shattering the wall of glastic to a blizzard of molecular motes.

Mei Nili, who has watched Munk's rebellion with slack jaw, rises weakly to her feet and gapes at the gashed hole where he has disappeared. Overhead, in the loges, the spectators mill excitedly.

"The Moot judgment on the proprietorship of the revived remains of Mr. Charlie is hereby suspended pending the recovery of the exhibit," the Judge announces solemnly. "The Moot is now adjourned."

Munk's silver-black cowl distends, and with Charles tucked firmly under one arm, he banks into a thermal updraft and rises against the glittering onyx skyline of Terra Tharsis. Earlier, talking with Shau Bandar, he acquired the signal codes for the reporter's com-link, hoping to stay in contact with a representative of the anthro commune. Now, he realizes, it is his only means of finding his way back to Mei Nili.

He listens briefly to the gentle internal chirping of the com-link to be sure it works. Satisfied, he disconnects and puts his full attention on the magnificent city around him, the brave dream of the Maat. Magravity—the conversion of magnetism to the acceleration force of artificial gravity—enables the celestial heights of these prismal turrets, skytowers, and aerial domes. He hears the deep, oceanic drone of it underlying the crystal music of all the andrones in this region of the city.

He turns down his internal sensors—a heavy silence reigns at these heights—and dips lower to avoid the spark-glint of flyers appearing in the hazy distance among the spires. No one was hurt in the commission of his property crime, and he hopes that not much of an effort will be made to apprehend him. Space-weathered as he is and with his power cells at nearly full capacity, he could cause far more destruction than the wetware tucked under his arm is worth.

Wide, interwoven balconies and ribboning prome-
nades appear below, bridging the cathedral spaces
between cupolas and minarets. A mere dust mote among
these immensities, Munk glides through the gap between
derricks, astonished at the graceful heights rising from
the crystal-cut shadows below. Unsure of where he is
going for the first time since his creation, he lets the
eddies of heat swirling from the behemoth structures
carry him.

The fear he feels in the titanic presence of his creators
is mitigated somewhat by his cargo. The Maat would
want him to save Mr. Charlie from those who would use
him as wetware, indifferent to the fact that this relict
brain was yet a man even though his bones had melted
long before in ancient Californica.

Down Munk drifts into the deep gorge of Terra
Tharsis, past mammoth-winged buttresses and laser-lit
parapets, confident that his makers are pleased with him.
After all, why else would the neo-sapiens who manufactured him have put a human thumbprint on his heart?

Shau Bandar misted his sinuses with a max dose of
dégagé olfact, calming his tripping heart. How could he
not have anticipated that this rogue androne would defy
the Moot? *Too much olfact,* he berates himself and holds
the thumb-ring mister to his nostrils again. But the over-
load is tripped, and he has to make do with the placid
action already soothing his excited brain. *Too much olfact,
Shau, and not enough edge—or common sense.*

With the other reporters in the journalists' loge natter-
ing excitedly around him and the timpan-com whispering
urgently in his inner ear from the copy office insisting he
get to the chamber floor before the other correspondents
corner the jumper, Shau Bandar stares mutely from the
gallery. He notices that the morph, clade, and androne

loges are nearly empty. They have little interest in a small anthro dispute over relict wetware. Below, the jumper sags on the witness bench, which is carrying her slowly backward out of the amphitheater. Her features are slack with that grim look people who do not use olfacts have when they are shocked.

The loge, too, is pulling away from the amphitheater, and the correspondents are filing toward the exit. But Shau Bandar stays at the gallery rail, waiting to see what, if any, response will come through from the Commonality. The holoforms of the Judge and the Clerk vanished immediately after adjournment, but he expects that the startling turn of events will elicit a reappearance at the six-minute forty-second mark. He stays at the rail even as the loge settles and the journalists exit. A few minutes later he adjusts the microswitches in his cuff to monitor the amphitheater. The Clerk flicks on and meets the incoming holoform from Earth—the archive agent, Sitor Ananta.

"This is not just a property crime to the Commonality," the agent says for the court record. "As duly reported, Mr. Charlie was absconded with and held by the revulsive lewdists and the anarchistic Friends of the Non-Abelian Gauge Group and is classified an insurgent, which is why he was exported off-planet in the first place. He may yet be a tool of those radical elements. Now that your negligence has permitted him to go rogue, the Commonality is charging you to upgrade this crime from property theft to abetting insurrection against established order with potential threat to human life. You are most strongly requested to recover this tainted resurrectant and return our property to us so that this potential threat to the Commonality may be obviated. Give this top priority."

Sitor Ananta vanishes, and the Clerk's response, if any, is coded and undetectable by Shau Bandar's sensors. His colleagues will read about the Commonality's ire in *Softcopy* and are more interested now in the jumper's reaction. He sees them below, moiling around her in the waiting alcove. Still, he doesn't hurry. He has a way to have her all to himself.

Mei Nili shoulders through the small crowd, growling, "Get off me. I've got nothing to say. Bounce off."

Her ire—so rustic and raw—engages the reporters' interest all the more. They claw her with questions: "Where will you go now?" "Say something about the androne. Are you angry?" "Do you now regret going rogue from Apollo Combine?" "Will you apply for asylum with the commune here in Terra Tharsis, or are you going back to the reservation on Earth?" "Will you use olfacts to manage this emotional bruising?"

She bumps into Shau Bandar, and as she irately shoves past him, he whispers, "I can take you to Munk."

She fixes him with a hot stare, and he takes her arm and pulls her to his side. "I've got an exclusive here," he says loudly to the others, and when a captious cry goes up among the journalists, he says to her, "Tell them. It's the only way they'll bounce."

"Yeah, yeah," she says morosely. "He's got the exclusive."

Shau Bandar smiles lavishly at the dejected reporters. "You'll find out all about it in Softcopy."

"Where's Munk?" Mei presses as soon as the others dissipate among the ivory colonnades. "Did he tell you he was going to do this?"

"I don't believe he knew himself," Shau Bandar replies, guiding the jumper toward the exit arches, "not until that creepy archivist took off about memory-culling Mr. Charlie. That must have triggered a response from Munk's C-P programming, don't you think?"

Mei nods her head, heavily. "Mr. Charlie and I changed

Munk on Phoboi Twelve. We forced him to override his primary programming. He's unpredictable now."

"I don't think so. He's an androne. He told me that the Maat contra-programmed him with an abiding interest in humanity. He's committed to Mr. Charlie now, and we can predict he will act to preserve that archaic brain."

"You said you could take me to him."

Shau Bandar stops before a droplift set in the base of a pilaster and uses his journalist's passcode to open the alabaster portal. "Come on. I'll tell you about it on the pavé. But let's not talk about it in here. Security."

They step into the indigo buoyancy of the droplift, and the sinuous magravity whisks them as if motionless toward the ground. In the close space, they study each other. She is put off by his bold eyeblack, precisely ruffled silks, and gem-pleached hair. He is intrigued by her raffish lack of olfacts, her musky savor matching the crude physicality of her square-knuckled hands and the facet cuts of her muscles apparent even through her flightsuit.

The droplift opens on the pavé, the hilly ground of Terra Tharsis. Each knoll is the gargantuan anchor base of a skytower, the slopes landscaped in a mazy complex of boulevards, villas, geometric plazas, and dome-roofed neighborhoods strewn with green splashes of trellised commons, tree haunts, and parks. Sunlight falls in wide swatches among the soaring towers that cast vales of umbrous shadow on the motley hillsides.

The enormity of the city daunts Mei, and she looks hard at the blue centers of Shau Bandar's panda-black eyes. "Where's Munk?"

"I don't know," he says and adds quickly, "but we can lead him to us whenever we want. He has my com codes. I gave them to him so he could reach me if he needed anything."

"Call him."

Shau Bandar shakes his head. "Not yet." As they stroll

on a tessellated pathway under heliotropic arbors beside a skim route where cars slash by in a soundless blur of magnetic propulsion, he tells her what he saw of Sitor Ananta. "That agent thinks Mr. Charlie may be tainted by the radicals who originally stole him from the archives on Earth. The Commonality are fanatics about control and accountability. You must know that. You worked for them. To preserve his own career, you can bet Ananta will do everything he can to hunt down Mr. Charlie."

They come to a beverage stall in the niche of a brown-stone wall scribbled on by lichen. "This shop has old-style ginger mead. Want some?"

Mei declines with a frown and gazes out at the undulant sprawl of bubble-top cottages and swirling roadways. "I'm not thirsty."

Shau Bandar sits at a vine-hung stall anyway. "When's the last time you ate or drank—or slept, for that matter?"

Mei doesn't hear him. Her gaze is lost overhead in the skyways and viaducts webbing high out of sight among the monoliths and casting vaporous shadows on the pavé. A clutch of smoke-haired morphs trundle by yakking in a dialect she doesn't recognize, their spindly arms gesticulating like egrets in a mating dance. The olfact wisps that trail off them fill her with an ice-blue sensation of midwinter. She shivers.

"Jumper Nili," Shau Bandar gently calls, "aren't you hungry?"

Mei turns from the busy cityscape and zips open the sleeve seal of her flightsuit to reveal a swatch of nutriment patches. "I've been on these since my last assignment. They're good for a couple more sleep cycles."

"Your alimentary tract doesn't mind the neglect?" he asks. "I mean, you're not morphed for your work, so your bowels must need some input."

Her eyes slim. "Hey, this is just another story for you. I didn't come here to talk about my intestines."

Shau Bandar puts a hand over his eyes and peeks at her sheepishly. "I'm sorry. I've never met a jumper, let alone an anthro jumper. I was just curious. Really."

Mei shakes her head and slides into the stall so that she faces him. "On long assignments I swallow a few ingesta tabs. They make up for bulk and keep my insides healthy but quiescent. Now, how are we going to find Munk and Mr. Charlie?"

"Right." He uses his journalist credit code to open the faux wood cabinet at the end of the table and removes two warm vials of ginger mead. "The Moot knows I won the draw in the anthro pool to interview you and Munk, so we have to assume they're watching us because I may have information where Munk is—and besides, I'm with you. If we call Munk now, there could be a conflict."

Mei disregards the steaming vial and asks, "Can't the Maat simply find him wherever he may go in Terra Tharsis?"

"In an eyeblink—you can bet." He sips the mead and closes his eyes to savor its sour shades. "But I don't think the Maat care at all about Munk or Mr. Charlie. It's the Moot who'll send their security to seize that archaic brain, if they can find Munk." He gestures to her beverage. "Drink up. The copy office is paying for it."

She pushes the vial aside. "Look, I thought the Maat created Terra Tharsis."

"Sure. However, they don't manage a damn thing here. That's all left to the communes, most of which are run by andrones. The Moot certainly is. They're strong about upholding what law they have—which isn't much in this city, to the great chagrin of the Commonality. That's why you came here, right?" He clicks his vial against hers and swigs again, draining the vessel. "It's a free city. The fact that an androne stole some wetware whose ownership is already disputed wouldn't be news if you weren't from the reservations and the wetware a thousand years old. Even so, it's still just a side clip."

Her stark gaze tightens. "Then why are you so interested?"

"You might have noticed even a side clip is worth enough credit to draw a small crowd of journalists. It's a free city, but it's not the reservation. Nothing is really free here. I have a comfortable abode. It's no aerie suite and it's a little rundown, but it still requires a lot of credit. And small as it is, I like it a lot better than sleeping in the park. I've lived with the park people, and I know how rough that is." He takes her vial. "If you're not going to drink it—" He sips and nods. "The park people work with the androphones for each meal—gardening, masonry—real work."

Mei gives a stern laugh. "You want to learn about real work and rough times, talk with Mr. Charlie about life in his day. Not even the park people have to cope with the grief that was the common lot then, real grief even for the most rich. I don't want to hear any of your big talk. It's all a game for you people. Live long enough in this day and age and even the dreamers in the park get lifespan credit and a nice hillside cottage maintained by androphones. You want to see reality, you find me Munk and Mr. Charlie and come with us to Solis."

Shau Bandar sucks at the vial, outraged at her haughty superiority. With a spray of dégagé from his thumb ring, his pique passes. Her fieriness is good, he realizes, and he feels foolish for the flash of umbrage he felt. Her time in the Belt has clearly toughened her for the trek, and here, at last, is his chance for a real story. On the synergistic surge of mead and olfact, an idea crystallizes for a true-life adventure series, a sequence of clips that will earn him his aerie suite after all.

"Okay, jumper," he says in a mounting seethe of ambition. "*Softcopy* will like this. There hasn't been a good trek story in a long time. I think we're going to make news."

• • •

Munk stands in tigerish shadows under overarching branches, staring across a spacious parkland of green sward and the flat of a pond molten with midday glare. Beyond the hedge fringe, the hills of Terra Tharsis look soft in the mauve shadow of a huge tower, while on farther hills the skylights of pavilions reflect the sun in hot motes.

Fish rise silently in the pond. Vivid, tiny birds spurt from a stand of white birches and stream away over tussocks of feathering grass. At the far end of the sward, a loose cloud of people swirl, playing some kind of ball game. Small figures, some as couples, most in bunches, drift among the quilted shadows of the tree-lumped fields. A forlorn music fritters from players in a distant grove.

Through his receptors, Munk listens to the crystal music of the city's silicon mind. He can hear the alien code logics chittering around him, and by their noise he has successfully located all androne in the vicinity and avoided them. Satisfied that none are near now, he tunes into a bramble of communications from the cars he sees twinkling on the causeways. They talk of games, foods, credits, raptures, meetings, morphings, rivalries, olfact recipes, music, humorous anecdotes, clade branchings, and barters. No mention of him or Mr. Charlie. Very little commerce is discussed. Perhaps that is all conducted in the skytowers, which are opaque to his sensors.

Tiny millions of lives are held in his gaze, he sees, scanning the hazy distances. Why have the Maat created so many lives? And so many kinds of lives—all of them human yet virtually none that would be entirely recognizable to the human in the plasteel capsule at his feet. Mr. Charlie had lived in a society of gonads and ovaries, adrenals and dopamine receptors. What will he make of this Maat creation, where sex, fear, anger, and pain have mostly been morphed away?

This man must live. He must be brought to the vats and have his body restored. To fulfill these imperatives, Munk believes the Maat installed in him the anthrophilic C-P program, which, since his escape from the Moot, has been gauging his options. He must leave Terra Tharsis as soon as possible, he knows. But first he has to find Jumper Nili—not out of any personal sense of loyalty. He feels none for her. She fulfilled her role in his plan on Phoboi Twelve, liberating Mr. Charlie from the deceptions of Ares Bund. If she still desires to go on to Solis with him and Mr. Charlie, then it is her responsibility to locate and come to him.

Yet Munk is certain Mr. Charlie will want to see Jumper Nili when he is next brought to consciousness. After all, she is the first truly human being he encountered since his death, and Munk's anthropic model assures him that significant bonding between the two has already occurred. Somehow, he must find transportation for them across the wilds of Mars. Without the jumper, he could simply walk with the plasteel capsule in hand . . .

"Excuse me, androne," a frail voice calls from the shrubs behind Munk.

A tremor scathes the androne with the disturbing awareness that he has been surprised. His internalized focus had locked up his alertness and left him inattentive to his surroundings. In the fraction of a second before he locates the source of the voice, he anguishes at this attention lag, indicative of the reduced capacity of his primary programming.

"Help me, please," a large, sandy-haired man says from where he lies doubled over in a bilberry bush. He is wearing a chamois strap-jacket and brown cord trousers with scruffy blue boots.

"I . . . I fell . . . long ways."

Atop burdock and vandal sprays of nettle far back in the hedgework, virtually hidden by the banked shrubs, gossamer wings lie torn and tangled. The shredded membranes are dissolving into iridescent fumes among the sun's bright coins. Already no more than coils of smoke, the straps from the fragile glider dangle where the stranger freed himself. Munk reads the dark track in the tufty grass from the man's strenuous effort to crawl into the bilberry bush, and the androne is appalled to realize that he has been standing beside this unconscious figure the whole time unawares.

"Who are you?" Munk asks, crouching over the fallen man.

"My name is Buddy." He looks up at the androne with a tight-sewn grimace. "Help me up. Please."

Munk scans Buddy's stout body, running his spatulate hands over the cramped muscles and detecting no broken bones. But there is a staticky sensation from numerous burst capillaries. "You are injured."

"No, just bruised." He swings an arm onto the androne's cowled shoulder and painfully unfolds upright. "I'll be all right."

Munk holds the powerfully built human steady and feels none of the microvoltage perturbations in the body's ultraweak soma field that would be indicative of profuse internal bleeding. He splays his hand over the skull and senses the slow, majestic theta rhythms of profound sleep or trance. "Your brain . . ."

Buddy pulls his head back and stares at Munk with a square, careworn face, vague eyebrows sad-slanted on a thick brow above large, tristful gray eyes. "I feel— stunned."

"What happened?"

Buddy brushes his thin blond hair back with the trembly fingers of both hands. "Stupid mistake. I took night wings out for a day glide. The membranes burned up."

He rubs his dented jaw, and his pale, thin lips smile wryly. "I could have killed myself. Stupid."

"A nearly fatal blunder," Munk concurs politely, regarding the purplish silver wings shredding to vapors. With his sensors he sees that they are a film of polarized monocolloidals, a sheer and nearly transparent material that cannot reasonably be mistaken for solar-sturdy fabric. These wings had to have been purposively selected. And yet, his internalized anthropic model assures him, humans do have monstrous attention lags, not unlike what he himself just endured wondering about his destiny with Mr. Charlie. Sometimes, he knows, humans have their most fatal lags when they unconsciously desire their doom. "Are you unhappy?"

Buddy stops rubbing his jaw and leans closer, looking at him with a peculiar intensity. "You're—different. For an androne."

Munk regrets questioning this man. The androne's primary program has already been committed to carry Mr. Charlie to Solis, and he wishes now that he could turn off his C-P impulses, which are coaxing him to interact with this human before him. Despite himself, he says, "I'm Munk, from the Saturn system. The Maat have installed contra-parametrics that inspire my interest in people. That is what brought me here. And that is why I am talking with you."

Buddy gives a slow nod of understanding. "Munk, can I lean on you? I want to try to walk." With the androne's help, he manages several tentative steps. "The thermals are strong today. They slowed my descent. And I steered for the trees to break my fall. I am an unhappy man, Munk—but not ready to die. At least, not consciously."

Munk's primary program feels he has heard enough and must remove himself so that he may fulfill his initial objective. But his C-P incentive insists on more data. "What saddens you?" the androne asks, letting the bruised man try a few wobbly steps on his own.

Buddy shrugs, offers a plaintive smile. "I don't know. This all seems so pointless sometimes. The usual plaint."

"Don't olfacts mitigate your plaint?"

"I'm an old one, Munk. I've been here a long time. Even olfacts have their limits." He lowers himself achingly to the grass and notices the plasteel capsule in a root cove of a nearby tree. "What's that?"

"An archaic brain. I am taking him to Solis, to the vats there. His name is Mr. Charlie."

Buddy groans as he leans closer to peer at the capsule. "I see him. All the goods are there. Brainstem, too. How old?"

"At least a millennium."

Buddy blows a silent whistle, sits up, and wipes the sweat of his exertion from his broad brow. "I thought *I* was around a long time."

"How old are you, Buddy?"

"Damn old—but not that old. Where'd you find Mr. Charlie?"

"I have already told you too much," Munk acknowledges, finally supressing his C-P compulsion with the awareness that he is threatening this man. "I am in violation of the Moot. Further association with me may put you in danger. Since you seem recovered from your fall, I will leave you here, Buddy."

"Don't go yet. Finding you has been a great stroke of luck for me." Buddy squints at Munk with a querying and pained expression. "Do androns believe much in luck?"

"No. My anthropic model includes luck as a vital faith that people have experienced throughout human history, but I believe such superstition demeans people."

"Yes." Buddy sighs and with his heavy hands strokes the grass as if it were fur. "The old ones have said that luck is the child of mystery and fear. But I subscribe to it anyway, fool that I am." His wide face flexes with pain as he leans backward on his elbows. "Tell me your story,

Munk. I accept full responsibility for what may come of it. Please."

The plangent expression in the man's blond face quiets Munk's anxiety, but he can find no reason to confide anything more. "I must go now, Buddy. Be well."

"Wait, Munk." In the sunslant through the branches that strikes his ginger-haired and freckled head, Buddy's eye-sockets look dragonish. "You said you're on your way to Solis and you've violated the Moot. Security may be looking for you. I know the city very well. I can help you avoid them. I can take you to a discreet egress where you can enter the wilds without being observed. An androne of your obvious durability can make the famous trek on foot." His sketchy eyebrows bend more sadly. "Please, tell me your story. I can help you."

Buddy's plangent voice reactivates Munk's C-P program, and for a full second the androne struggles with this decision. In that time, he calls forth the new data he recorded in the Moot when Charles's memory-cull records were displayed in coded spectra. Among those thousand-year-old memories are ideas that inspire Munk to transcend his primary programming yet again and trust in the creative—what he had always called the unexpected—to find for him new ways through the veils of the world.

Imagination, Munk tells himself within his capacious one-second arena of contemplation. Around that one word he constellates useful information from Charles's memory cull, which tells him that imagination is the psychic process that transforms the pain and limitations of the purely physical. "Man has no Body distinct from his Soul." Those are the words of William Blake, a poet Charles admires.

In the all-inclusive imagination, where circumference does not exist, uncertainty is renovated and becomes sacred, indivisible, impenetrable, unified with all that his primary program usually rejects, with everything ugly, fierce, and cruel. This unity of opposites, of matter and imagination, primary programming and uncertainty, beauty and ugliness—this, the ancient memories inform him, is where mind reabsorbs reality into a new wholeness. Then the fiery expenditure of energy that is our imagination and that makes us creative enables us to endure uncertainty, to tread emptiness, to be—human.

The crimson light in Munk's lens bar brightens, and as one soul reaching out to another, he tells Buddy his story.

Shau Bandar leads Mei Nili away from the beverage stall and the busy skim route and along an oak-cloistered promenade past water groves and hanging gardens and squat cottages behind flowering hedgerows to a cobbled lane. The lane climbs beside a curkling water rill through red-gold beechwoods, where other bungalows peek out. Staring up, Mei sees the stony trail wending ever higher toward bosky obscurities of pine and fir and the onyx immensity of a skytower.

"Here's my place," the reporter announces, stepping past a gnarled mimosa tree and opening a blistered wooden gate rhombic from wear. A flagstone path snakes among walnut trees and a billowy mass of frangipani to a grassy shelf and a lean, high, gabled house, ramshackle and nearly grown over with rock roses and creeping juniper. "Actually, it may not be mine much longer. I owe more on it than I make, and I'm probably going to have to give it up and live in the cells for a while. Unless, of course," he winks at her, "the copy office buys our trek series."

They pass a birdbath choked with dead leaves and a sundial knocked askew, climb slanted, creaking steps, and enter a dark, musty interior. Filament lights woven into the sagging ceiling flicker on, illuminating bare cubicles with buckled, water-stained walls. A hammock hangs in one corner, a tatty magnification of the cobwebs else-where in the room. In another corner tilts a splintery wardrobe.

Shau Bandar reads the uneasiness in Mei's open face. She is such a blatant provincial, he feels no embarrass-ment and admits, "I don't merit this house. It belonged to a renowned composer who moved up to a grander niche and left his place to friends. I eventually came to it through a friend of a friend of a friend. It sucks up all my credits and leaves nothing for me to maintain it. But it's haunted with music, and I like that."

He lifts a shroud from a low table beneath an oval rose-glass window and exposes a palm-sized oblong bubble packed with bright chromatic sections of data wafers. "This is the communications link to the copy office. Seen one of these before? It's a total immersion hookup, so it'll seem as if we're actually at the copy office while in fact we're still here. Try not to move around too much or you might walk into a wall. I'll tune us in, and we'll make our pitch."

With a wave of his hand over the bubble, he activates the linkage, and suddenly the shabby room is gone and they are in the ice-pale clarity of *Softcopy*'s editorial suite. Under a dome of champagne-tint glastic overpeering the glittering gorges of the skytowers, people in multihued scapulars mill around cube screens meshing together seg-ments for the next news-clip feedout. The full-view screens display the usual fare for the anthro commune: interactive neighborhood tours and encounters, sport synergies, gardening tutors, and the big mainstay of the agency, midstim fantasies, which appear as abstract pas-tiches of sculptural colors. Mei recognizes those from the dream den in the recreational arcade on Deimos and feels a pang of yearning for the neural dream-swatches that each brain tailors to its own desires.

"Bandar, this is not a good time for hashout," says a big-boned woman with silver wing-braided hair and bold streaks of feather paint on her cheeks. "We've got a fast run on a scootball tournament, and I haven't got ten seconds. Hey, isn't this the rogue jumper?"

"Jumper Nili, this is my editor, Bo Rabana—"

"Sweet!" Bo Rabana says, displaying her pudgy palms, then swirling about inside her solar-yellow smock, talking over her shoulder. "I'll open a cube for you, and we'll get your clip out on the next run."

"Bo, she's not here for an interview. We're pitching a trek. Solis."

"The scootball's on a fast run," Bo says, pivoting on the balls of her bare feet. "We'll talk later."

"We need a go now, right now," Shau Bandar insists, sliding closer. "Moot security is looking for the androne the jumper came in with. Remember?"

"Right, right. The Chiliad Man. Great clip. It had a strong run. We can replay when they catch him."

"Wait, Bo. Listen. The androne's going to take the Chiliad Man to Solis with the jumper. They're falling out now, as outlaws. I want to cover it. It'll be a hot series. Give me the go." Bo Rabana settles onto her heels, her cherubic face looking suddenly heavier. "Bandar, are you serious?"

"I know it's high risk—"

"You can *die* in the wilds!" Bo Rabana's pale shatterglass eyes grow wide. "I don't want that on me. Do the interview."

"It's not on you, Bo. It's me. I need the credits—"

"Get a Pashalik job and triple your credits," the editor says, backing off. "Don't throw your life away."

"Bo," he says with a dark change of voice, "if *Softcopy* won't back me, I'll plug in to *Erato*. They'll snap up a trek story."

Rabana's shoulders sag and she steps closer, a stern crease between her startling eyes. "You don't know what you're asking." She turns her fierce gaze on Mei. "You look like a hard-knuckler to me. Have you tried to tell this pastry puff what it's really like outside the bakery?"

"I don't give a damn what he does," Mei says in chilled, flat tones. "He has the link to the androne I came in with. Make him give me that, and I'm gone."

"I'm going on this trek," Shau Bandar insists. "It's a big story. It'll have a long run, and I want those credits. Do I get your go or not?"

"Once you leave Terra Tharsis," Rabana reminds him with a taut stare, "you can't come back."

"Sure, I can, Bo, if you give me a journalist's pass."

Bo Rabana lifts her dimpled chin defiantly. "I can't give you a pass, wise guy, until I file your assignment—and once we file, Moot security will be on to your plan to help the rogue androne. You'll never get out. The only way you can take this trek is cold—no pass."

The reporter gives a hapless shrug. "You can file after I leave."

"There's no guarantee that will be accepted," Bo retorts sourly. "You may never be able to come back—even if you survive the wilds, which I doubt, pastry puff. Do the interview. We'll hash out other assignments for you. You'll make your house payments." She turns away and bobs off, calling behind, "Stay sweet as you are, Jumper Nili. I've got a hot run going on the scootball. We'll touch up later."

"I'm doing the trek, Rabana!" Shau Bandar shouts, though inside he's trembling. "Do I get the go from you, or do I plug into *Erato*?"

"It's your scrawny ass, Bandar," the editor yells without looking back.

"Top credit? Full series?" he calls through a triumphant laugh that carries off his initial fright.

"If you live to collect," she shoots back.

•   •   •

From the prospect of the knoll where he crashed, Buddy stares at the dark towers. Wide and mingled as mountains, with sunny windswept pieces of sky squeezed between them, they fill space majestically. In their vitreous black depths, laser lines streak the paths of droplifts. Silver-spun threads of skim paths tangle around their bases, and flyers star-glint in the pellucid air of their heights.

Of course, he is thinking that those are the heights from which he has fallen—and within those vitreous black depths are the spaces where he has lived with the deathless ones alone together. Closer, Munk is telling of *The Laughing Life* and the viperous Aparecida, and how Jumper Nili gambled her life on his C-P program. And though Buddy is listening, he is listening deeper to the freedom of his nightmare, the fright dream that strapped him in to night wings for a day glide and that sent him plummeting into the incalculable abyss.

Buddy looks up at Munk and nods at the courage that it took for this androne to be here in the trees' quiet drizzle of sunlight, telling his story so matter-of-factly, his silicon mind wrapped around memories of near-death and madness as if oblivion and chaos shared a neutral equality with life and reason. He nods. Overhead, in the lordly blue distances, flyers spin on rings of wind, milling the emptiness.

4

The Avenue of Limits

WHEN MUNK FINISHES HIS STORY, BUDDY STANDS AND CASTS A long, sweeping look at the parkland with its willow manes, hackled reeds, glassy pond, and, all around them, wheels of sunlight riding among the trees. "After a lifetime in space, this must all seem very strange to you."

"Not at all. My C-P program is packed with terrene images I downloaded from the archives." He listens for the crystal atonalities of the city's silicon mind, and satisfied that the androns he detects are not near, he tastes the air with his sensors. The wind-woven and complex organic chemistries of heather, leaf rot, pond mulch, and lawn dew mingle the stoichiometry of their busy atoms in his mind's eye. But he ignores that and focuses instead on the bird raptures in the ferny holts, the cygnets gliding shyly across the pond, the solitary and strung-out clusters of people strolling along the mown fields. "It is beautiful," he declares, feeling a soft elation at actually being here in the leafy, loamy moment.

"Take this beauty with you," Buddy advises. "This is

the Maat's jewel, cut and polished by them. It doesn't get any better."

"Where are we going?"

Buddy juts his jaw to the side as he ponders this. "Now that I know about Jumper Nili, it's clear you can't just take Mr. Charlie and march across the wilds to Solis." He sinks his mind into the spangled sunlight on the pond and makes a decision. "I'll take you to the exurbs of Terra Tharsis. From there, you can contact Jumper Nili when she leaves the city. Come on."

Munk follows Buddy up the chine of the hill, past the last chrome wisps of the dissolving night wings lacing the shrubs, and they enter a thick grove where daylight dims to dusk. The cushiony leaf duff beneath their feet silences their passage, and Munk looks through the gloom of hawthorn and oak moss for the park. Heraldic sun shafts gleam like spectral crowns high in the forest canopy, but the radiant threads that pierce the dense undergrowth reveal only confounding reaches of bracken, vetch, and dodder vines among the pillared trees.

Ahead, the cold, crystal chimes of the silicon mind grow louder. "Buddy, there's an androne ahead."

"Yes," Buddy confirms, not looking back as he shoulders among the clatter and scarves of dried branches and vines. "There's security at every droplift that exits the city."

"Security?" Munk stops in the gray light pooling among the trees. "I don't dare confront security andrones. They will try to take Mr. Charlie."

"Yes." Buddy turns around in the burdock and nettles and holds out his arms. "Give him to me."

"Why?"

"The plasteel capsule is disputed property," Buddy says, leaning through the weeds. "You removed it from the Moot, and security will apprehend you if they find you with it. But, since it's not stolen goods, there's no crime in my taking it out of the city. You follow after me."

"I don't understand." Munk scans Buddy for signs of prevarication, increased bloodrush, sweat scent, blink rate, and voice-pattern stress and detects none. "Won't I be arrested?"

"Security won't stop you if you don't have Mr. Charlie. You committed no crime."

"Obstructing a legal proceeding, threatening violence, absconding with evidence, destruction of property—" Munk's voice drones nervously in the blurred shadows of the estranged sun.

Buddy shakes his head. "The fault lies with the Moot for placing an androne of your capability in the presence of property that the court took from you. I know the law. The court misjudged your C-P program and can't condemn you for being true to yourself."

"Then I am not a criminal?"

"Of course not. Give me the capsule, and let's get out of here."

In the instant's wide theater of decision, Munk twice reviews everything he has learned from Charles. His imagination, true to its natural duplicity, counsels trust and suspicion simultaneously. He wants the human experience of trust but cannot shake his wariness. Who is this man who requires his trust? Is he, in fact, a security agent sent to connive Mr. Charlie from him? Perhaps. Escaping with Mr. Charlie had been a supreme risk from the start. Perhaps it ends here. Or not. If Buddy is his ally, Munk must trust him. *If*—there is no way to know. *It is time to tread emptiness again,* the androne realizes in a flush of dread and excitement. *Time to endure more uncertainty—to act human again.*

Munk passes Charles to Buddy. "Thank you for helping me preserve him."

Buddy holds the capsule to his chest, and in the ruined light his expression is warped with sadness. "You're good to trust me."

"I detect no prevarication from your body's signals," Munk admits. "And as the archaic poet Blake wrote, 'There is no Soul distinct from the Body.' I trust your soul."

Buddy's small smile flares briefly in the shadows. He pushes through a tattery gap in the veil moss hanging from the groping boughs, skids down a dirt track on a steep, tree-clenched bank, and brattles through a cane brake. With the canes clacking, he runs directly toward the icy tissues of sound that Munk knows are the unreadable codes of another androne.

He follows, sick with fear. If the security androne challenges him, he knows he will not submit. He doesn't want to kill anything ever, ever again. Aparecida's silhouette slouches out of the liquid shadows of the tufty canes. No, it's the flutter of an attention gap—fear usurping his imagination. The silhouette is the thermal halo from a covey of birds seeking shade and insects.

Munk stares up at the underbellies of the trees, and the internal faces he sees cut in the leaf patterns convince him to shunt his imagination and revert to simple motor programming. Quickly, he crashes through the canes, closing the gap between himself and Buddy, until he is running in precision tandem a few centimeters behind the man.

When he exits the thicket in this alert, neutral state, Munk sees without any emotion the security androne guarding the droplift. The sentinel resembles an armorial statue, a human figure in transparent cuirass with a turtle-browed, mirror-flat mask. A hanging garden of rocky outcrops and flowery cascades rises above the droplift, a marble cupola in a grove of black, tapered poplars. The billowy indigo shine of the droplift glosses the marble ramp and even glows on the dewy sward where the sentinel stands unmoving.

Without hesitation, Buddy walks across the lawn and

past the   guard toward the droplift. Munk stays in close lockstep, until they reach the security androne. He pauses, unable to move. No physical force holds him. It's his own deep-level fascination that's immobilized him.

He snaps out of simple motor programming and realizes that he has stopped because some part of him recognizes this androne. A swift search shows that Charles encountered andrones much like this one when he was first revived on Earth. Their masks carried watery reflections of faces.

A face now appears in the flat pan of the mask—the soft, roguish features of Sitor Ananta. "You are in violation of Commonality law, Androne Munk. Return Mr. Charlie at once to the Commonality agent in Terra Tharsis."

"Munk!" Buddy calls. "Let's go."

Munk hurries to Buddy's side. "Sitor Ananta came through that androne."

"Ignore him," Buddy says and strides over to the directory, a glastic cube balanced on one point. Ice-green vapors spiral at its core, faster and brighter at the touch of his hand and the plasteel capsule. "The Commonality has no jurisdiction in Terra Tharsis, Solis, or the wilds between them."

Munk reads the code lights in the cube and sees that Buddy has ordered a short droplift, up and over the wall. Reassured by this simple route, he follows the man into the indigo light of the cupola and hears no more the thriving, brittle music of the city's silicon mind.

Shau Bandar leaves his credit cuff on the lacquered table in the narrow house haunted by music. The cuff is useless outside the city. He looks around a last time at the faded walls with their pastel print of lobster pots and cacti. Someone else now will have to make sense of that or redecorate. No one is allowed to hold property in Terra Tharsis if they leave, even temporarily, and though he's unhappy about giving up this house, he's excited by his decisiveness. He is finally making something grand of his life. He tells himself that when he returns he'll have enough credits for a house twice as large and each room replete with the most expensive shapeshift furniture.

He bounds down the cricketing steps of the skinny house without looking back and meets Mei Nili among the walnut trees, where she's been waiting while he spent his last moment with the house. "Are you sure you want to do this?" she asks gruffly. "I have nothing to lose, but I'm not so sure about you."

"Never more sure of anything," he answers and briskly leads the way along the sinuous flagstone path. He salutes the skewed sundial and clogged birdbath and barges through the crooked gate. On the walk down the stony lane beside the creek, he explains that *Softcopy* has arranged for a droplift to the Outlands where a skim car will take them to the caravansary. All expenses are covered. "There's always credit available for an insider willing to risk everything on the outside. Even a lazy, impoverished lichen like me will get a big run in the news clips."

"Especially if you die," Mei points out.

The journalist agrees with a fatalistic shrug. "It's the biggest thrill of all—the shadow of death."

On the walk through the oak cloisters down to the pavé, Shau Bandar talks nervously about what lies ahead, recounting news clips of caravans eaten by sandstorms and shreeks, voracious, bristle-fanged biots created in the vats of Solis to scavenge the wilds and discourage pilgrims.

Mei only half listens, attentive to the supernatural beauty of the hills. She has had to relearn the future too often since she last felt beauty. She has no idea where or even if she will be tomorrow, but for now, the heavenward towers and the shafts of sunmist on the hazy, cluttered hillsides are enough.

Autumnal shimmers of wind sweep the pavé with smoked brightness and a radiant chill. Mei is still staring up at the gusty heights of sparkling onyx when Shau leads her into a tight alley. In the dark, a boast of indigo light breathes.

The city's vallation is a four-kilometer-high rampart, twelve spans deep. It rims the caldera brink of Olympus Mons, enclosing the great skytowers of Terra Tharsis and their hillside purlieus. The barrier has the seamlessly smooth and black-green luster of jasper but is composed of a Maat alloy impervious to sensors. The mirror-vanes atop the encircling parapet serve as both detectors and signal scramblers so that from outside the vallation contact with the city is impossible.

Despite this isolation, an extensive community thrives outside the city under the stupendous wall. Sustained by the gravity shadow of Terra Tharsis, which provides near-terrestrial conditions, exurbs sprawl across the broad slopes of the extinct volcano in a coruscating expanse of solar mills and antennae. The mills amplify the weak sunlight that bleeds through the perpetual cloud banks churning in the penumbra of the city's magravity field. The Maat weather system stores heat and moisture in this surrounding area, and so, while there is no dearth of water for the Outlands, energy must be milled from the thermals and the wan sun.

Shau Bandar explains this and more to Mei Nili on the long drive through the skimways outside the city. Displacing his anxiety about the safety he has abandoned for this rich adventure, he points out the gigantic, androne-managed farms on the watery horizons. He has been out here on assignment before and knows the names of all the districts: Sky-Bowl with its power factories, the agrarian pastures and fish hatcheries of Willow, the congested thorpes of Britty, and the elegant estates in an opulent district called the Honor of Giants.

"Where do all these people come from?" Mei wonders. Even in the cool interior of the rented car, the air smells of swamp and thunder. Mountainous blue clouds hang in eerie stillness above the chain of hills and their clusters of hamlets and silver-foil roofs. "They aren't protected here by the Maat, are they?"

"No. They live in jeopardy of their lives, all of them." The car drives itself, preprogrammed for their destination at the very fringe of the exurbs, and Shau stares disconsolately at the smoky hills and the heat ripples on the skimway. "Actually, two hundred years ago—over four hundred terrene years ago—the exurbs were much larger. That was during the frantic Exodus of Light, when millions came here from all the colonies literally wanting to die in the rarefied air of Mars. Death passages were all the rage back then. The population here are remnants of that weird faith that got It, the idea that consciousness is light liberated into a glorious and rapturous field state called the tesseract range when the physical organism dies. Bizarre, huh?"

"Lately, it's living that seems bizarre to me," Mei mutters, pressing her fingertips to the cool glastic dome. She touches the speed-blurred images of the low stone houses with their shiny roofs and asks, "Why do these people live here? What do they want?"

"Most have come from the Commonality range towns on Luna," the journalist answers, stifling a yawn. "They believe the work is easier here. And they're probably right. You know how tight the labor strictures are in the Commonality. Also, work here affords each of them the chance of admittance to the Pashalik."

Among vegetable plots and sodden, sunken fields, roundhouses in unrendered concrete slip past. "Do many actually get in to Terra Tharsis?"

"If they accrue enough credits and an insider like myself leaves."

Mei hears the edginess in his voice. "Do you regret leaving? You know you can go back now. Just call Munk for me."

"Go back to what?" He crosses his lanky legs and clasps his hands over his knee. "You saw my elegant house that I'm about to lose unless I go to work for the Pashalik monitoring andrones. No. I want adventure—and credits. This is what I want." He puts his olfact ring to his nostrils, then presents it to her.

She declines by turning her attention from him to the pastel roundhouses with their foil roofs and red-dirt gardens. "How long have you lived in Terra Tharsis?"

"I'm forty-two."

"Mars years?"

He nods, distracted by the electrical nearness of the purple clouds with their flutters of lightning. "You'd think with all these hopefuls teeming out here to get in the city, they'd shut down the vats."

"The Maat have a life-type agenda."

"Is that what they believe on the reservation? Ha." He looks at her naked face, smells her sweet-sour body odor, and feels once more his sorrowing astonishment at her rustic mien. "The Maat have no agenda. If the commune didn't insist on racial parities, the whole city would have gone plasmatic centuries ago. The Maat don't care."

With violet tremors in the piled clouds and trundling thunder, a dazzle of rain sizzles toward them on the skimway and pummels the clear top of the car. "Have you ever had an encounter?"

"Nope. And all the encounters I've followed up for *Softcopy* were bogus. The Maat are so far inside now they're not even bodies anymore. That's what I think. They have no more truck with us than we do with apes in the aboriginal forests."

Veils of rain smoke off the hot rooftops and steam along the empty road. For a long while, they ride in silence, Mei worried about Munk and Mr. Charlie, Shau still debating the merits and dangers of the impending trek. In the blue darkness, under the hammering rain, the world draws closer.

Buddy, holding Charles Outis in his arms, stands with Munk in a grassy verge under the giant vallation of Terra Tharsis. The droplift that carried them out of the city has deposited them on a hummock overlooking low, tinsel-roofed cities strewn brightly under toppling clouds. The androne glances up at the indigo blur of the vanishing droplift vortex, relieved that his creative willingness to trust this stranger has indeed delivered him from the city of his makers. The noise of the city's silicon mind has vanished entirely, and he senses no other andrones using Maat codes nearby.

"Where do we go from here?" he asks, scanning the cluttered plain. On the steep horizon, lizards of lightning squirm among the mauve thunderheads of an isolated storm.

"I think I know, Munk." Buddy hands Charles to the androne and removes his chamois strap-jacket. "If the jumper you came in with wants to make the trek, she'll have to start from the Avenue of Limits. We'll go there." He slings his jacket over his shoulder and wades through the tall grass.

Munk cradles Charles in the crook of one arm but does not budge. He senses waftings of ozone from the storm and the distant chatter of thunder. "You have kept your word, Buddy. Show me the direction to the Avenue of Limits, and we can part here."

Buddy stops among the feathery grass. "I'd like to come along," he says, almost apologetically. "The Avenue of Limits is at the fringe of the Outlands, on the edge of the wilds. It's a big place and a long walk from here. But there's a skim station in Sky-Bowl, not far away. From there, we can ride to the Avenue of Limits and you can use the reporter's codes to contact him. What do you say?"

Munk regards the man for a full level second, playing various motives though his anthropic model again and again, until finally he must admit, "I don't understand why you should care at all about me."

"It's a new one for your anthropic model, isn't it?" Buddy's strong face with its imprint of sadness nods once. "Anomie."

"A psychic state of isolation and disorientation," the androne recites. "That is the unhappiness you confessed to me."

"Yes. That is my unhappiness." His strong face looks weak, and he says with a slow, aching solemnity, "I belong in the wilderness now. Can I go along with you?"

"To die?" Munk asks ingenuously.

Buddy gives a vigorous shake of his head that scatters his sweat-wrung hair over his eyes. "No. I don't want to kill myself. I want to test this life. To make it stronger."

Munk absorbs this, and it prints in his silicon brain as something heard before. He plays back words from Mr. Charlie's broadcast: "We all live by our fictions. We create stories in order to fill the emptiness that is ourselves. And because we must create them with strength from nothing, they make us whole."

"We will go together then," Munk decides, glad to participate in yet another human being's story.

"Good." Buddy winks. "We'd better get going before the rain gets here."

In the oblique light slanting through the storm clouds

onto the immense vallation of Terra Tharsis, the weather displays massive and strange contours, and the androne feels very small among the powers of the world. He follows Buddy through the feathery grass toward the wide, cluttered horizon of human life.

Mei Nili and Shau Bandar arrive at the Avenue of Limits with the rush of night. The oblate and gaseous sun shudders among the cindercones and black volcanic hills on the serrated horizon like demonland's burning portal. Shau takes the yoke and slides the rental car onto a terminus bed along the shoulder of the skimway. The doors wing open on the sultry, incandescent dusk.

"Why are we stopping here?" Mei asks.

"I want to record the sunset over the Avenue of Limits. It's a good bridge shot for the first clip." He steps out into the simmering evening.

To one side, in the direction from where they have come, the citadel of Terra Tharsis dominates the highlands, the breadth of its vallation dark as a ruby in the long sun shafts, the skytowers silver-veiled and dazzling with laser points of gemlight. In streaks, flares, and fiery globes, the scarlet-plumed sky hoards the last of the day's sun, and the rooftops on the lava slopes shimmer with purple flames.

In the other direction, the wilds of Mars catch the twilight in gleams of amber glass and crimson smears of slurry, a dim and barren badland that stretches away into darkness. Shanty sheds crowded among behemoth warehouses and industrial barns front the wilderness. Lux wires and torch globes pour light like magma through the tight lanes and burrows at the very brink of the hungry darkness.

"This is the Avenue of Limits," Shau announces, fortifying himself with a sniff of ergal from a pinky ring. The stimulating olfact makes the stifling heat seem more bearable, even invigorating. With an expression of determination, he looks to Mei, who has gotten out of the car and strolls away from him. "From here, the journey to Solis really begins. Rabana's been in touch by cable phone to the local copy office in Britty, and they've relayed her messages on my timpan-com. She says *Softcopy* has data on three caravans lading for departure from here to Solis. But two are sure losers, religious fanatics from the Outlands who expect divine help in crossing the wilds."

Mei listens absently. She stands at the edge of the terminus bed, staring down the slope of the skimway to where the concrete-block walls and derelict buildings begin. No people are in sight. "It looks abandoned."

"It is," Shau says, stepping alongside her and pointing into the distance to where a devastated swatch of debris breaks the shoreline of packed-together sheds, ricks, storeyards, and longhouses. "A fallback took seven whole blocks out a short while ago. The magravity border fluctuates. It usually extends into the wilds about a kilometer beyond here. But sometimes it falls back, and when that happens, whole sections of the Avenue are ripped apart by the abrupt gravitational shift. The clips I've seen are really spectacular—whole buildings launching into the sky and breaking apart. Some of the debris has been found a hundred kilometers away."

Shadow shapes stir within the crepuscular fields below, but when Mei looks closer they are only cane-grass stirring in the wind among piles of old scantlings. "What about the third caravan Rabana found—is that a more reliable group?"

The reporter juts his lower lip dubiously. "The trek captain is some kind of entrepreneur, but he's also an extraordinary mechanic. He's run a wilderness-tour service out of Britty for years. A wealthy eccentric from the

Honor of Giants has hired him to captain the trek and is putting up the credits for the equipment. She wants to donate all her energy and assets to Solis and is determined to get there in one piece. With her backing and his expertise, this caravan is our best shot. *Softcopy* will pay our passage in exchange for the exclusive news-clip and drama rights."

"Someone's down there," Mei says, pointing to the junkyard below them. "They've been watching us."

"I don't see anyone."

Mei fixes her focus on the ruddy yellow lux wires gridding the Avenue of Limits and with her sharper peripheral vision spies figures crouching through the scrub of the eroded hills. "They're coming," she says, backing from the edge of the terminus bed. "Call Munk."

"I don't see anyone."

Mei slips into the car. But she has no credit codes to activate it and hops out again. "Come on, Bandar. Let's get out of here."

The reporter approaches the vehicle casually, orgulous with the olfact sparking in him. "I've been here before. There's nothing to be afraid of. If you saw anyone, it's probably the traders who lurk around the storehouses, wanting to barter."

"Just get us out of here."

Shau eases behind the yoke and taps his cuff onto the credit plate, but the car doesn't start. He adjusts the microswitch insets in his cuff and tries again. But the control panel remains dark. "I don't get it," he mumbles.

"Call Munk, dammit."

The reporter fidgets with his cuff switches and is shaking his head bewildered when the first figures shamble up the embankment. Against the sky's last opal cracks of light they are hunched, hooded silhouettes wielding pipes and clubs. Their sudden shrieks snap Shau's fixation with his cuff controls, and he rears back in fright.

"Damn! They must have cut the power cables to the skimway."

Mei reaches across him and pulls down his door, slapping the lock into place. "Get Munk on the com-link, Bandar. Do it!"

Shau complies with trembling fingers. "Munk! Munk! Androne, are you reading?"

Ten big mongrel morphs leap about the car, slamming their clubs on the glastic dome. With the third blow it cracks, and with the next one it shatters into a splash of molecular dust. Whoops and hollers flap into the night, and large, splayed, four-fingered hands reach in and yank the passengers from the car.

Mei tucks her knees and kicks out with all her might, pushing free of her assailant. She twists to the ground and scuttles on all fours. But two other morphs seize her arms, and she's hoisted upright to see Shau flopped face-down on the hood of the car, the hulking bandits tearing off his jacket and his rings. His mouth is wide with pain and fear, his teeth black with blood. One of the morphs grabs the reporter's long braid of hair and jerks his head back. Another slides a curve of blade under Shau's straining throat.

"No!" Mei screams.

Delirious hollers carom shrilly into the night, warbling into howls at the sight of the slim jumper writhing between her captors.

Beads of dark blood appear under Shau Bandar's jaw, and his eyes swivel wildly in their sockets. He groans in thick guttural bursts, pleading for his life.

Up from the embankment where the morphs first appeared, a silver cowl rises, cloaking a darkness with no face. "S-ss-s-t!" the androne directs a hypercompressed packet of sound waves at the morph holding the knife, and the blade wrenches free and clatters into the car.

"Let them go," Munk commands in a thunderous voice.

The morphs drop Mei and release Shau, then rapidly scatter, dissolving into the darkness with tattered whines and aimless cries. A moment later, a pipe wings out of the dark, slashing toward where Mei has risen to one knee. The androne bounds forward in a chrome streak and plucks the projectile out of the air less than a meter from the jumper's head. With a deft wrist snap, the pipe whirls whistling back into the night and finds a mortal shriek.

"I came as quickly as I could," Munk says, helping Mei to her feet. "I heard your distress on the link."

"Help Bandar," she says. "He's been cut."

"I'm okay," Shau declares tartly. He holds a shred of his shirt to the superficial cut at his throat and glares wrathfully into the dark where the morphs retreated. "They slashed my dignity more than my flesh. Gruesome things! They're distorts, not people. They must be destroyed."

"Who are they?" Mei asks, rubbing feeling back into her wrists.

"I tell you, they're distorts," Shau croaks with anger. "There's no real law in the Outlands. Rogues run their own vats out here and morph gangs of homicidal brutes—distorts—to protect their territories. Sometimes the distorts range wildly. The posses that hunt them down are always a popular run in the news clips."

Mei puts a hand on the plasteel capsule under the androne's arm. "Munk, where have you been? Why did you run away?"

"You know why I fled with Mr. Charlie."

"I know," she says, drearily. "Your C-P program."

"Yes. Since Phoboi Twelve, I can actually hear my imagination as loudly as my primary programming. I could not bear to imagine what Sitor Ananta wanted to do with Mr. Charlie. I know it would have been clearly inhumane."

Shau thumps his sandaled foot against the skim plate of the car, irate that he lost his jacket and recording mantle and with them his chance to report on an androne with a human spirit. "Now look! I have to get a new link. I lost everything!"

"Do you at least know where we're going?" Mei asks testily, approaching him. She peeks under his jaw to view the wound and sees only a gray smear of blood in the dark.

"Of course I do," he answers defensively and nudges her away with some annoyance. "Raza's. It's just down the bluff. But we can't ride there. The distorts cut the damn power cables. And even if they hadn't, we can't operate this car without the credit patch in my jacket."

"Buddy has a rental car," Munk suggests. "I met him in Terra Tharsis. He helped me to get out. But I had to leave him behind when your distress call came. He couldn't move fast enough."

"Where is he?" Mei asks.

"About sixty-three kilometers down the Avenue of Limits."

"You ran *sixty* kilos from the time I called you?" the reporter asks.

"I can move much faster than that," Munk replies modestly, "but there are structures to avoid on the Avenue. And it is warm here. My coolant system was nearly overtaxed."

"You must have spent a lot of power," Mei notes. Despite herself, she can't help admiring the androne's spunk, at the very least.

"Yes. I depleted fifty-two percent of my power cells to get here quickly. But the expenditure was required."

Shau heartily agrees. "I'll say! They were going to kill us."

"But how are we going to charge your cells?" Mei places a concerned hand on the androne's breastplate and feels the dew-chill of it. "We have no credits."

"Get me to a link," Shau says, "and we'll see what *Softcopy* can do."

"I have already contacted Buddy," Munk acknowledges. "He says he will meet us at Rey Raza's garage. It's only a few kilometers from here. I will carry the two of you."

"And me without my damn recorder!" Shau kicks the car's skim plate again. "This would have been the perfect lead-in!"

Munk spends a moment adding this behavior to his anthropic model. Mr. Charlie had declared that we all live by our fictions, and here is a bleeding man who grieves for the story he has lost. Mei Nili herself has an incredulous look on her face, as if she is convinced a life can be overremembered.

The androne regards them both with quiet satisfaction, proud that he has preserved two dewdrop lives from the void. Staring at these human creatures his strength has kept whole, he feels right. He knows this feeling is the cyberkinesis of his C-P program, his own subjectivity, but that doesn't seem to matter.

He feels a mutual kinship with Jumper Nili's cool detachment and the reporter's hot ambition. He yearns to see Mr. Charlie, the ancestor of his maker, whole before him. And yet—and yet, he is an androne. His yearning is the calm fury of his maker.

He remembers floating in the delicious cold of farside Saturn, tiny in the penumbra of the gas giant, knowing that he knew he was a programmed being. He experienced an echo of that humbling smallness under the immense vallation of Terra Tharsis. And now here, again, he knows he is becoming an accident, like everything else.

Jumper Nili has seen something become nothing when her family died, and he almost saw that tonight. He has never witnessed a human death. The very thought oozes with unhappiness and makes him recall that there are light-years of silence surrounding him. That fact mutes his sadness.

Once again, he determines that he will defend these frail residues of human life with all the strength in his power cells. That pleases him, or at least makes him less unhappy with his smallness under the tumultuous sky and the slowness of time.

Clutching Charles Outis between them, Mei Nili and Shau Bandar ride in the embrace of Munk's arms. They bound over the main artery past hip-roofed sheds, gaunt storage towers, oxide-stained corrugated fences, weathered warehouses, a graveyard of rust-gutted drums, and desolate crossroads grimly empty under the blazon of lux wires. At the reporter's command, they stop before a wide garage with a pyramid of latticed metal on the roof and a circular sign hanging above the open port announcing: RAZA'S TOURS OF THE WILDS.

Within the tall port of the garage are three big sand rovers, painted a glaring white with REY RAZA stenciled in red on the vent-ribbed runners. Slender laser cannon mounted under the eaves of the garage swivel aggressively, and Munk turns his reflectant cowl toward them.

"State your business!" a gravelly voice exclaims over a speaker system.

"Rey? This is Shau Bandar from *Softcopy*! We're here for the trek."

"Sorry," an unamplified voice says. "You can't be too careful on the Avenue of Limits."

A wiry, falcon-faced man with a shaved head, tiny mustache-tips at the corners of his wide grinning mouth, and green splashes of face paint under his eyes strides across the port. He's dressed in scarlet and gold clothes, a magnificent fullness of pleats and panels and intricate braiding, baggy as a bright, rackety kite. "I am Rey Raza," he proclaims boisterously, through a gleeful smile. Wrinkles of merriment seam his face, but his small, hooded eyes regard the world with a mean squint. "*Softcopy* said you were coming. Where are your recorders?"

"Distorts jumped us," Shau says, stepping out from behind the androne. "Munk here saved our lives. The distorts probably still have my jacket. If we act quickly, we can use it to help target a posse."

Rey Raza tosses a thick laugh at the reporter. "You've seen too many news clips, Bandar. There are no posses on the Avenue of Limits. Here we are ruled by the one and true law, the natural right of primacy itself."

"What about justice?" Bandar complains.

The tour guide shrugs. "Justice, moral right, equity, and due consideration to the weak have no value whatsoever here or in the great and terrible land beyond these limits. You'd better get that straight now, Mr. Journalist, for there will be no turning back once we are away."

"Sand rovers will take several days to make the crossing to Solis," Munk notes. "Are there no flyers available?"

"You are clearly from a far and distant system, Munk," Rey Raza observes chidingly. "You're a Jovian deep-space patrol-class androne, I'd judge from your looks. And those legs have been augmented, haven't they? Must be unbearably hot for you around here."

"I am from Iapetus Gap in the Saturn system. My legs were fitted for me by Apollo Combine on Deimos. And, yes, I find this heat enervating. Most of my power is spent cooling my systems."

"Didn't you tell them anything, Bandar? Flyers—really." Rey Raza waves them inside. "It's not a good time of day for street talk. Will you join me for some refreshment? Munk, I don't think I have the right power amps for your kind of cold-body cells, but you're welcome to look over my equipment. As for flyers—well, Terra

Tharsis and Solis just don't permit flyers anywhere near them. Ah, here is the archaic brain." He presses his forehead to the plasteel capsule. "He's dreaming. Maybe of Earth. I'll bet he feels more awake now than when he wakes next among us, eh?"

The interior of the capacious garage smells acridly of lube oil and lathed metal. Behind the three sand rovers, a wire-mesh partition isolates a machinist's pit, engine hoist, and a tool-and-die shop. Raza admits Munk to the generator deck and leads Mei and Shau past the dimly lit work areas to the back of the garage.

A sheet metal door slides open on a radiant room with the clean redolence of woodwork. Blue straw mats cover the floor, and yellow paper screens, like vertical louvers, section the suite. Between the screens, strips of a kitchen and a sleep cubicle are visible, both with wooden furniture—floral-carved pantry, painted cupboard, swivel stools, a trestle cot, and lacquered side tables.

A blond wood table and fanback chairs in the front room squeeze Mei's heart, and a tear startles down her cheek. She lowers her face to smell the spray of wildflowers in the table's centerpiece, trying to hide her emotion.

Rey Raza places an airy hand on her shoulder. "You're exhausted. I can see the fray light around you."

Shau, surprised, starts to explain, "Rey's from a strong-eye clade. He sees some infra and ultra, bodylights—"

"It's the wood," Mei manages to get out, feels stronger for it, lifts her head and wipes her eyes. "I haven't been close enough to smell and touch wood since I left Earth. I didn't know how much I missed it."

Shau puts a fist to his forehead, regretting again the absence of his recorder. He's convinced that these are the moments that will make his clips run. "Rey, I've got to call in."

"Use the cable phone by the cot." Rey points the way, then says with mesmeric softness to Mei, "You must sleep. Tomorrow Grielle comes. She is the woman on the death passage. Like all passagers, she's eager and will want to leave at once. So we will skip the refreshments and let you rest now. You may have the cot, and Shau can sleep in the rover. I have more work to do in the shop and will stay there. Good night."

Before she can demur, he exits through the metal door, and she is left alone to touch the satiny wood and, for the first time, the palpable distance from her origin. She feels rent from her past, her family, and she rends herself from the table. She doesn't want to think about that now. On Phoboi Twelve, in the black moments when she was actually dead, she learned release. She is appalled that she will have to learn it again.

In the cubicle she finds the reporter sitting at the edge of the cot, brushing the off-pad on the cable phone. His smile, for all its meekness, is warm. "I'm sorry about the distorts," he says. "Rabana just scolded me for stopping. I should have come straight here and skipped the damn sunset."

Mei's eyes lower to meet his, then swing up, weary and burned by tears. "We're alive. That's enough for me right now." She sits down on the cot and unzips her boots. "Is *Softcopy* going to take care of you?"

"They're sending me a new link and a recorder mantle." He thumbs the lux pad, and the cubicle lights dim. "I'm going to wait outside for the courier. What I wouldn't give for a whiff right now. Oh, well, I won't see that ring again. Ease, Jumper Nili. Ease and the countenance of dreams."

A slat of dark blue light glows dully from the latrine. She strips off her flightsuit and throws it in the sanitizing hamper. While it's running, she unpeels the nutriment patches from her forearm, all of them spent, and drops them in the disposer. The sonic shower dispels her last resistance to the fatigue she's been feeling since Terra

Tharsis. She retrieves her clean flightsuit, zips it on loosely, and collapses onto the cot.

Pulling onto the concrete apron of the tour office lot, Buddy kills the electric engine of his black and bulky rental car. He waits under the gaze of the laser cannon until Munk appears with Rey Raza and Shau Bandar. The androne, still holding Charles, introduces Buddy, and the stocky man removes a credit clip from his jacket and passes it to Rey.

"Round trip?" Rey asks, backing toward the garage.

"One way," the man with the quiet eyes says.

"A passager?" Rey inquires.

Buddy shakes his head. "No. Just a traveler."

"Not all travelers are admitted to Solis, you know," Rey points out as he takes the credit clip inside to book passage. "A one-way trek both ways is expensive."

"Whatever it costs," Buddy replies.

"Munk called you an old one," the reporter says as they stroll into the garage port. "Are you filed with *Softcopy*?"

"Yes," Buddy admits and adds with a gentle, mysterious patience, "But I don't want you pulling it up, if you can restrain yourself. I don't want that with me on this trek."

"I don't think I *can* restrain myself, Buddy," Shau confesses, again wishing he had his mantle, which could access old clips immediately. "I'm a reporter, and what you've just said is far too tempting. Why would an old one go on a trek—unless it's a death passage?"

"It's not," Buddy answers and looks to the street, where a courier van has pulled up.

"We'll talk," Shau promises and hurries out of the garage.

Munk asks Buddy, "What was that about?"

"Most of the old ones have files with the news services." Buddy shrugs. "I'm no different. But my past is.

Where most of the old ones were intent on working with the Maat and building great worlds, I feared the strange new breed and worked mischief against them. It was a short-lived insurrection. But a Maat and some other people died. I was apprehended and reconditioned. Now I feel indifference where before I was hateful."

"The Maat forgave you," Munk says.

"No." Buddy's small smile carries no malice. "They altered my brain."

Shau approaches with his arms full of bubble-wrapped packages. "It's all here," he exults with exaggerated enthusiasm. "I am again the eyes of millions!"

Rey returns Buddy's credit clip and helps Shau unpack. The recorder jacket and mantle are desert-ready, tailored in sturdy canvas, dark brown and sere. The reporter slings it over his shoulders, and a delighted Rey assumes his most ingratiating air for the camera and takes Shau on a tour of the shop.

Munk stands in the port, staring out into the Martian night. Buddy pats him affectionately on the arm, then crawls back into the rental car to sleep. The crystal music of a silicon mind chimes from farther down the Avenue of Limits, too far away to be a threat just now. Nearby, he hears the journalist's recorder whispering to itself. Then it, too, is silent. Soon everyone is asleep, their brains as disengaged from the continuum of actual events as is Charles's in his plasteel sleep.

A jeweldust of stars gleams in galactic vapor trails over the black horizon. There is much for Munk to add to his anthropic model and review, but before he does, he tracks the night sky. In the heavens' swirling turbulence, Earth's silver-blue star stares over them unblinking.

At the first smear of dawn, a skim-flight truck pulls up before Rey Raza's garage and mindless loader handroids begin depositing large high-impact crates. A mocha-skinned woman with long eyes and short black hair braided in tight designs on her pattern-shaved head emerges from the cab. She is dressed in a slinky green gown of firepoints that fluoresce like auroras as she walks forward under the tracking laser cannon. Standing before Munk, she places her thin fingers on Charles.

"Dear man," she whispers to the archaic brain, "we meet going in opposite directions. By the grace and acts of light, I will get you to Solis, and you will be the last of the first men with whom I speak."

"That is a touching sentiment," Munk states.

The angular woman cocks a fine eyebrow. "What does an androne know of sentiment?"

"Enough to recognize it when I see it. You must be Grielle Aspect."

Her dark, elongated eyes assess Munk calmly. "I've liked you from the moment you defied the Moot. I believe we will be famous friends."

"How do you know of me and Mr. Charlie?"

"I watch the news clips," she says, turning her chin to her shoulder, revealing a clean, haughty profile as she peers into the garage. "I'm leaving this world, dear androne, not my mind. Knowledge still is power—as it was in Mr. Charlie's time. As it ever will be."

Rey emerges from the floodlit ranks of sand rovers, his scarlet, satiny loose suit like a gray cloud around him in the dusky light. "Grielle! All is in readiness for this happy, happy occasion."

"Fine, Rey." She waves wearily at the mounting stack of crates. "I have decided to bring a larger offering to the good workers of Solis. Lux tubing, psyonic core units, semblor parts—"

"Psyonics?" Rey shakes his bald head. "No, no, Grielle, we can't have that. Essentia won't stand for it. We'll have fanatics *and* pirates all over us. It's going to be hard enough with the shreeks and the devil storms. We don't need psychopaths intent on destroying us."

Shau Bandar hurries out of the garage, pulling his recorder mantle over his desert jacket. "*Fanatics?* Come on, Rey. *Softcopy* viewers regard the Anthropos Essentia favorably. Maybe you can soften your tone for the clips." He shows his palms to Grielle Aspect. "So you're the passager funding this trek. My viewers would love to hear your—"

"Turn that thing off," Grielle snaps. "My passage is not some curiosity item for a damn news-clip service."

"Hey, *Softcopy* is helping fund this trek, too," Shau retorts indignantly. "The anthro commune respects what you're doing, Outlander Aspect. How about a little respect for them?"

"Why should I respect people who live redundant lives?" She tilts her head back as if peeking at something very small. "They're never going to experience revelation coddled in their commune. The icky mess of a caterpillar in its cocoon. The light is out here, Bandar, shining on the world as it is. The truth of the world is in its suffering. Now, turn that thing off, or I'll scratch your corneas."

"Save the speeches, Aspect," Shau goads her as he steps closer, the small blue recorder light shining from the collar of his mantle. "What *Softcopy* wants to know is how you amassed your fortune. Is it true that you run zombie vats and staff your farms with distorts?"

Grielle lunges at him, and he dances backward with an angry laugh, crowing, "Another act of light, Outlander Aspect?"

Rey steps between them, deftly catching the journalist by the pleat of his jacket while stopping Grielle's attack with one knurled finger touching her firmly between the eyes. "You," he says sternly to Shau, "will refrain from recording the passager, or I will have to put my penury aside and cancel our contract. And you," he levels his mean squint on Grielle. "Our contract says nothing about exporting psyonics to Solis. I won't allow it."

Grielle stands taller, adjusts the flounce of her gown. "You will have to compromise, Rey dear. Elsewise, I will make other arrangements."

"With whom?" he asks archly. "I am the only wilds runner you can trust to get you there alive. Unless, of course, as you *are* on a death passage, Grielle, you don't mind dying in the wilds."

During this minor fracas, Buddy pulls himself out of the electric car parked on the concrete apron and stands rubbing the sleep from his eyes.

"Who the hell is he?" Grielle gripes.

"He's an old one, Outlander," Shau says from over Rey's shoulder. "You know—the icky mess inside the cocoon."

"What are you doing here?" Her eyes are star-webbed in the floodlights, and her glossy face, with its feline hollows and sharp planes, looks carved of dark wood. "Are you a passager, too?"

"No, lady, I'm not." Buddy casually shows his palms and nods. "My name's Buddy. I'm going to Solis to broaden my horizons—make more room for meaning in my life."

"No matter how broad your horizons, Buddy dear, it's still the same mess, just more of it. You may have been around a long time, but clearly, you've not yet seen the light. Open your eyes." Not waiting for a response, she puts her arm over Rey's shoulders and steers him into the bright garage for a private conversation.

Shau confronts Buddy. "I viewed your file last night. You were a real hitter in the good old days. Would you comment on that for our viewers?"

Buddy yawns. "I've changed."

"You sure have. Cortical surgery qualifies as quite a big change, I'd say. Even in Mr. Charlie's time, lobotomy was considered cruel. Do you honestly think your punishment is just? I mean, given the heinous nature of your crimes?"

"It's not a punishment."

"Then you've become completely passive, is that it? You accept yourself wholly as you are?"

"I'm not a sociopath anymore, if that's what you mean." Buddy drifts away toward the empty avenue and the weedlots beyond, where dawn shines in laminar streaks, like a sky-wide agate above the desert.

"Last night Buddy told you not to read his file," Munk says to the journalist from where he stands motionless, conserving his power for the arduous trek ahead. "Why did you disregard his explicit wish?"

"Come on, Munk," Shau says, focusing his recorder on Buddy's retreating back. "Use your C-P program and tell me."

"Your empathic capacity is atrophied from a lifetime of self-centered development," Munk supposes. "Buddy's desires matter far less to you than your own."

Shau looks to the androne with a vexed moue. "My desires serve the commune. I want to know what the people want to know."

"And individual rights?" the androne asks. "What of those who wish to stand apart from the commune?"

"Spare me the sociophilosophy," Shau says, walking back to the shop. "If people were always good or always anything, we'd be andrones, wouldn't we?"

Munk stands alone in the dawn, considering the psyonic core units in their high-impact crates. Those are pieces of the silicon mind. Dormant now, but when they are assembled and activated, they will think, feel, and have the capacity to imagine as he does. He hears Grielle and Rey softly arguing about the units.

"I tell you," the man rasps, "the Solis cults will target us if we take those crates."

Grielle sniffs derisively. "We're a target for them anyway with that androne along."

"Munk is Mr. Charlie's guardian. The Anthropos Essentia can understand that. We're conveying an archaic brain, for Maat's sake!"

Munk's archive files produce no information on cult activity in or around Solis. But the Anthropos Essentia are famous. They are the zealous anthros who several martian centuries ago founded Solis. Originally, their settlement was entirely divorced from the Maat and the silicon mind. It makes sense to Munk that they would oppose importing psyonics.

Of course, since the Exodus of Light two centuries ago, when the planet became crowded with death passagers and their hangers-on, Anthropos Essentia has been a minority even in their own stronghold of Solis. Munk is glad when Rey grumpily agrees to convey the psyonic units. The anthros' genetic purity is a fiction of the past. Mind is wider than life and should not be hindered by animal fears.

Munk directs his attention to the dawn, the stellar fire that long ago initiated the journeys of carbon and silicon to this moment. It seems to the androne that everything is woven of that light. The carbon creatures arguing about utilizing pieces of the silicon mind and the stars dissolving in the brightening air are a living tapestry of light.

For three-tenths of a second, Munk indulges himself in these thoughts. He stops listening warily for other andrones, stops caring what the people around him are saying, and fills himself with the biggest plausible thought in his mind: Everything really is made from one fire, the fire of all the stars. In that furious light, the stars forge the elements, strew them into the black void, and then stand around and watch the frantic atoms huddling together at the cold limits, sharing their small heat and enormous dreams.

5

Nycthemeral Journeys

MEI NILI ROUSES FROM A DEEP BLACK SLEEP TO THE SOUND OF voices and the mute drone of engines. She slides off the cot and shuffles into the latrine. Sitting there, she suddenly realizes how much she misses her old habits and routines—the dream den with its ineffable midstim, her solitary jumps in the company of mindless andrones, the simplicity of nutripatches. Her old life required no thought, only mechanical reasoning and decent reflexes, but this new life is nothing but thought, weighed possibilities, wearisome gambits. *No use looking back now*, she scolds herself. She hears her stomach growling louder than the engine purr outside. Someone shouts her name, and without hurrying, she dips through the sonic shower in her flightsuit.

Through the morning's startling brightness, she catches sight of Rey Raza's hulking sand rovers. They fill the bleak avenue in front of the garage with a pageantry of blackglass viewdomes and brilliant white hulls. Already a small crowd has gathered around them, people covered head to toe in colorful scarves, peering through the dark slits of their headwraps at the large flex-treads with their traction belts of polished gold.

Farther down the road, a sturdy dune climber with giant blue tires and a silver tarpaulin pulled tightly over its contents waits, watched over by Munk. A few of the locals have gathered there too, waving their iridescent scarves at the unusual androne.

"Come on, Mei," Shau Bandar calls impatiently from the sunny apron of the garage. He has the gold-foil hood of his desert jacket pulled up and is wearing wraparound reflectants across his eyes. "Raza says everything's ready. We're leaping into the wilds!"

In the center of the garage, a topo map has been projected on the concrete floor. Rey and an angular woman in desert togs and clear statskin cowl wade through the holoform, discussing the journey ahead. A burly fellow with no face paint sits on a chrome faldstool under the chain loops of an engine hoist, arms crossed, his blond face closed around a melancholy ease, as if he's seen all this before and is resigned to its dire outcome.

"Thank you for joining us," the woman facetiously greets Mei. The long, carved eyelines in her shrewd face seem indifferent, but there's no ignoring the haughtiness of her aloof stare. "I am Grielle Aspect."

Mei shows her palms. "And I'm—"

"Mei, dear, the androne and the nose from *Softcopy* have told me all about you. Have you met Buddy yet, the old one your androne brought with him from the city?"

Mei and Buddy perfunctorily show their palms. "What does that mean—old one?" she asks.

Grielle wags a silver-nailed finger at her and points to where Shau paces, recording them with the blue lens in his shoulder harness. "Stand over there, dear. You're in time to hear the details Rey and I have worked out."

Mei walks through the ruddy ghost image of the martian landscape and sits on the bench.

"As I am the founding sponsor and major contributor to this trek," Grielle says, speaking to Shau's recorder, "I have the privilege of directing our passage to Solis. In all practical considerations, I defer, of course, to our pilot, Morphë Raza. Among the numerous tractor paths that diverge from here and converge on Solis, the pilot accepts my choice of Nebraska Trace. I've chosen that path because it passes through the ruins of Sarna Neve, where the Acts of Light first became dogma."

Mei pipes up, "But is Nebraska Trace the safest and most direct route to Solis? Munk and I want to get Mr. Charlie to where he can become a whole man again as quickly as possible."

"That's entirely irrelevant," Grielle sniffs and adjusts the olfact setting under her cowl to maximum calm. "You're here to listen, Mei dear. I have already explained, I am the director."

"Nebraska Trace adds three days to our crossing," Rey interjects, kneeling in the topo map, bent over with his flat nose almost touching the lucid craterland. "But the weather looks very good. And I see no major shreek migrations in that area."

"What about the psyonic core units?" Shau asks. "Are you still concerned they'll attract marauders?"

"They might," Grielle concedes with a wary nod. "That's why the psyonics will be conveyed in a separate dune climber well away from the caravan. If there are marauders, we will have to defend ourselves, not machine parts. For that same reason, I have directed the androne Munk to travel apart from us."

"That's not smart," Mei objects. "He's Mr. Charlie's best protection, and we'll all be a lot safer if we stay together. Where is Mr. Charlie? Munk isn't carrying him."

"I installed him in the second rover," Rey answers, "where you and *Softcopy* will ride. I'll pilot all the vehicles from the lead rover. The dune climber will take the point. And the androne can scout ahead—"

"You installed Mr. Charlie?" Mei asks, standing up. "You mean, he's awake?"

"I suggest you sit down, dear, and listen. These will be nycthemeral journeys, that is, each will be a day and a night long. We will stop at dawn to affirm the Acts of Light, as has been done since the first pilgrims . . ." She stops talking as Mei walks out of the garage, then glares at Rey. "Find another cosponsor. I don't want to travel with this rude jumper."

"It'll take days," Rey mumbles, crawling on his hands and knees with his face grazing the planet's blighted surface. "And we won't find anyone with deeper pockets than *Softcopy*. Besides, the weather is clement now. Later in the season—" He looks up with a dubious frown. "The dust storms from the south make it tougher."

"Don't go away miffed, Mei dear," Grielle calls with mock concern.

The jumper ignores her and walks into a solar frenzy of hard radiant light bounding off the desert floor and sparkling sharply from the scarves of the crowd. She steers herself toward the glare of the second rover and slips among the onlookers without acknowledging their keen stares and friendly waves.

Clambering up the tread-guard, she pulls herself atop the runner and climbs the inset steps in the hull among the tinted viewdomes to the bridge. There, standing at the taffrail, she waves at Munk. The androne raises both arms and shifts the reflectance of his cowl to catch the morning sun in a wink of starfire.

"Come on in," a muffled voice calls from below. "The hatch is unlocked."

Mei dilates the hatch at her feet and drops through the companionway into the forward cabin's aqua-lit interior. Pellucid daylight washed of glare filters through the blackglass dome and mingles with the watery glow from the console.

"Good morning, Mei," a cheerful voice says.

"Mr. Charlie?" Mei calls. The bright cabin appears empty, until she sees the plasteel capsule bracketed by platinum clamps under the console.

"Grielle Aspect is hauling a couple tons of psyonic parts to Solis," Munk's voice comes out of the dome speakers, "and Rey used some of those components to hook up Mr. Charlie. We've been talking to each other over the rover's com-link."

"It's a great talk," Charles Outis says enthusiastically. "I'm learning about the death passage and its impact on modern society. And the sky—I see the sky through the rover's outside sensors! It's bright—and pink!"

"The thin atmosphere carries dust right into space," the androne says. "Most of the particles are less than a thousandth of a millimeter, the most effective size to scatter red light." From his post before the dune climber, Munk turns his empty face toward the jumper. "I have been hearing a firsthand account of the archaic bonding practice called family from Mr. Charlie—from his childhood! Can you imagine? Neonatal memories. How very rare."

"Mr. Charlie," Mei sits down in the gray, form-fit hug of a deck chair. "Did you hear about Terra Tharsis and the Moot?"

"I heard it all," Charles tells her. "I spoke with everyone while you were sleeping—Rey Raza, Grielle Aspect, Buddy—"

"Aspect is acting like we're baggage," she complains. "And she's lugging us three days out of our way for some damned religious observance."

"Don't be upset," Charles says brightly. "We're on Mars! We got away from the Judge and Sitor Ananta. I met the Judge, and he didn't seem very favorably disposed to my plea for freedom."

"Mr. Charlie," Munk cuts in. "I must tell you that I saw Sitor Ananta in the facepan of a sentinel androne."

"What? Wait a minute," Mei asks. "Who is Sitor Ananta?"

"The Commonality agent who tortured me," Charles replies. "A maladjusted hermaphrodite."

"Probably a morph," Munk says.

"Morphs, clades, anthros," Charles sounds perplexed. "It doesn't make any difference. Trust me, Sitor Ananta is dangerous."

"At the Moot he charged that the Friends of the Non-Abelian Gauge Group tampered with your brain," the androne says. "I don't have much on them. They're a faction of clades, aren't they, Jumper Nili?"

"I think so," she replies through a morose frown. "Maybe, yes. The name is familiar. There are so many reservations, I can't remember them all. Ours was exclusively anthro, but we'd heard of the clades."

"Can someone please explain—" Charles begins.

"Clades," Munk hurries to elucidate, "branches—genetic variants on the human genome, not just morphologic changes like the gender shifts and body-shaping of morphs, but whole new neurologies, new biokinetic paradigms, new species—like the Maat."

Mei ignores the sadness that talk of Earth stirs in her and adds, "The Maat are the most successful of the clades. They're the branch that has expanded its intelligence the furthest. Other branches have grown in different directions. The Friends, I think, are factions of an adrenal or parasympathetic clade. I don't remember exactly. But they hate authority of all kinds and live with what seems to us anthros a peculiar passion for certain kinds of mathematics."

Charles remembers the humanoids with four-fingered hands, delicate, glass-faced beings who used him to teach their young. "My torturer told me that the Friends are rebels or something."

Munk's voice enters assuredly, "I have here what you

recorded in your broadcast: 'They're enemies of the Commonality—anarchists, a selfish cult intent on usurping the law.' "

"The Commonality are full of themselves," Mei says bitterly.

Charles asks, "Who exactly is—"

"The Commonality?" Munk anticipates him again. "They are a cartel of all the anthro and morph colonies on Earth, Luna, Mars, and the Belt who were set up by the Maat to help collect materials for neo-sapien projects."

"They throw their weight around a lot," Mei adds. "I think they feel the Maat have gone on to another reality and left this one for them."

"Well," Charles says, "all I want to know is whether or not Sitor Ananta is coming after me."

"The Commonality thinks you're a weapon," Munk responds, his voice lively but his body motionless in the brash sunlight. "We have to get you to Solis. That's a neutral settlement."

As Mei and Munk talk, Charles uses the desert rover's external cameras to direct his attention to his surroundings. *It's enough,* he tells himself, staring through the seething air above the red iron desert. *It's enough to have lived to see Mars.*

The 360-degree vista displaces his dread with wonder. The surface looks pretty much like a desert, but the Avenue of Limits is as alien a scene as he's ever imagined. He sees the sleek, multitiered contours of the other rovers parked in a row and behind them the imposing skyline of silos and warehouses with their odd architectural character, looking to him like a queer blend of Chinese and art deco. The people, too, are both seen-before and utterly singular, swathed head to toe in multicolored mummy windings, bobbing in slow rhythms like tribal dancers, polishing the air with their glittery veils.

A feeling of awe and unreality pervades Charles, and he says earnestly, "It's enough that I've lived to see people on Mars."

Shau Bandar has chosen to ride alone in the third rover so that he can better record the dramatic start of the trek. Sitting on the rover's bridge above the swarming crowd, he adjusts his reflectors to play back an earlier interview with Rey Raza, queuing it for a leader to explain what he is going to record next.

Rey stands in playback blue before the open bay to his garage five minutes in the past. In the background the locals bob-dance, tatterdemalion garb floating around them like kelp, handkerchiefs dazzling blessings over Grielle and Buddy, who are making their way toward the shining rovers.

"The leap start," Shau begins feeding lines into his recorder, "is perhaps the most famous part of any desert trek from the Outlands, Rey. How do you plan to use it for this crossing to Solis?"

"Routinely," Rey answers, his bright splash-painted face grinning solicitously. "Raza Tours has been leap-starting for more than thirty years. Spectacular as these jumps are, for Raza Tours they're purely routine."

"Could you tell Mr. Charlie," Shau says, "and our off-world viewers who may not know about leap-starting, what it is?"

Rey's bald head gleams like a dolphin's in the false-color playback. "Okay. See, when properly constructed vehicles cross the perimeter of the city and pass from terrene to martian gravity, the abrupt downshift in acceleration sends them flying. We've all seen the tragic consequences of magravity fallback here along the Avenue of Limits. Whole blocks of warehouses exploded across hundreds of kilometers. Well, we harness that powerful force, and with the aerokinetic design of our desert rovers we fly deep into the wilds. Raza's Tours has been doing this for thirty years. It's a great attraction for day trekkers. The physics is very accurate. The thin martian atmosphere and the sixty-two percent dimmer gravity are exploited to keep our vessels aloft long enough to reach specially prepared landing strips . . ."

Satisfied, Shau turns off the playback and pans the crowd with his recorder. The swaddled onlookers stir excitedly as the rovers begin gliding forward.

"Get in your cabin now, Bandar," Rey calls over the com-link.

The reporter shows his palms to the scarf-fluttering bystanders and descends the companionway, constricting the hatch after him. In the aquamarine glow of the forward cabin, he removes his reflectors and sits in a deck chair, its flexform contours hugging him securely. Anonymous storehouses drift by, and the vehicles bank off the road and slide through the weedlots with little sound and no vibration.

The shimmering foil roofs of the Outland thorpes rise like star clusters above the blunt skyline of the Avenue of Limits. The horizonwide expanse of Olympus Mons shines flamingo-pink, and a mauve band of knobby clouds in strict procession sail a wide circuit, trawling slack, blue nets of rain. Among the walloping weeds, a narrow orange-gravel road appears, running straight toward the shattered buttes.

"Okay. Everybody push back in your seats," Rey calls over the link. "We're going to leap."

Shau's flexform chair tightens, and he has to lift his chest to keep his recorder focused through the viewport. Ahead, the big blue wheels of the dune climber are a blur as the heavy vehicle hurtles down the runway and flies up the long, curved ramp at the far end. With a clangorous peal of thunder, the dune climber shoots high into the tangerine sky. Then the rover in front of Shau accelerates, and he hears the engine under him churning more powerfully.

Another boom of thunder, and the rover that shoots up the ramp ahead of them dwindles instantly into the cloudless void. The ascending roadway swoops before them, the broken shards of the desert floor tilt away, and with a force that yanks a gasp out of the reporter and presses his face flesh tight to his skull, the sky jolts closer.

Munk watches the dune climber and the first two sand rovers catapult into the martian sky. Shau Bandar's rover shoots down the road after them, bounces up the ramp, and fires into the blue, leaving behind a sonic burst that shudders with the other echoes across the horizon. The androne follows the arcing speck until it vanishes over the distant reef rocks. Then he dashes swiftly down the runway and up the incline.

Gravity sheers away in a giddy heave, and the buttes, pinnacles, and fins of the desert spread out before him. By distending his cowl and catching the upsurge of heat from the warming rock floor, he lifts higher. In the woven distance, mountain peaks merge into one another and melt like clouds in the thermal drafts.

One glance behind reveals the giant sprawl of Olympus Mons and the violet mass of boiling cumuli ringing the caldera. Terra Tharsis catches the morning light in wet reflections of layered air, a mirage that amplifies the crystal depths of the city in fractured glints. The androne hears no sign of the silicon mind from there, and the diadem city wavers silently in the transparent veils of heat.

Munk ascends, soaring toward the purple heights, relishing the cooler temperature. None of the generators in Rey Raza's garage were adequate to recharge his power cells, and he is grateful for every opportunity now to conserve energy. The trek across the 4,345 kilometers to Solis will take seven days, the tour expert has estimated, and Munk feels that with the cooler conditions and lighter gravity, his power cells will keep him active for the entire trip.

Feeling optimistic, the androne gazes down benefi-cently at the elemental fire reflecting from the bronze gravel flats. Among vast splash-petals and widening rip-ples of henna sand, he spots the drop spots where the dune climber and the sand rovers have landed. The dust plumes downwind, and Munk stares through it until he is sure all the vehicles have landed safely.

The task assigned him by Rey is to fly ahead a full day and night's journey, scouting the territory for threats. Apart from sandstorms, which are atypical this time of year and which the topo map would warn about, he is to watch out for shreeks and marauders. Munk is eager to see a shreek, for they are catalogued as the most ferocious of biots—bioforms eco-adapted to scavenge the wilds and thrive off each other and any other life-forms they can apprehend. They look fierce in the archival infoclip, whose verbal description begins, "Imagine a three-meter-long, four-meter-tall tropical fish half a meter wide and transparent as glass . . ." Their snicking, grotesquely nim-ble, transparent mouth parts scissor their prey apart with slow deliberation. But they are mindless and less danger-ous than the marauders.

Sweeping the rusty ridges and rocky pleats below, Munk detects no life-forms at all. In the sepia distance are the three Tharsis volcanoes, each ten kilometers high and evenly spaced seven hundred kilometers apart on the buckled horizon. Like the shawled, hunched bodies of the three fates from archaic mythology, they will watch over the caravan from portside the entire trek, and Munk finds himself pondering what judgment they will pass on the pilgrims at the limits of this world before he catches himself and turns off his imaginal subprogram.

Then, gliding down in a widening spiral, he listens deeply and hears far off the tiny noises of the caravan's silicon pilots. Among that distant chirping is the psyonic hookup that reads and translates Charles Outis's brain-waves, and the androne is calmed knowing that the archaic human is alert again and aware that he is on his way to a better life.

The wide, cratered land narrows toward a labyrinth of torture monuments: rock racks and toppled blocks, tilted stone benches, needle spires, and eerie hatchet arches, all a morbid green-black and trembling like flames in the reverberate air. Taking last advantage of his loft, the androne turns into the wind, swivels upright, and walks down the air's invisible steps toward the floor of the wasteland.

With the dune climber in the lead, the caravan churns across the desert flats at thirty-five knots, flagging streamers of dust behind it. For all the available daylight hours, they travel without stop, flares of shadow over the sands. From the lead rover, Rey Raza takes advantage of Charles Outis's curiosity and Shau Bandar's attentive recorder to flaunt his knowledge of the wilds. He identifies the thorny silver-green beach balls clustered in the shadow gulches as zubu cactus, the first biot to thrive on Mars. He also points out the three giant cindercones on the blighted planet rim—the Tharsis Montes.

"It's no coincidence that these huge volcanoes are the same height above the datum surface—the sea level," He nods to Charles's camera eye. "It's the maximum height a mountain on Mars can build to before the planetary crust breaks under it and lava spills over the land. We're on the smooth ride of one of those spills now."

Charles stares disconsolately at the melted hills. Since his salvation on Phoboi Twelve, wonder persists in a hushed, distant corner of his soul. But nearer, dread mounts. He is afraid, though at first he is not sure of what. Mars is eerily beautiful, and he is inclined to think that the calamitous landscape with its pocked craters among strange liquid-looking bluffs disturbs his earthly expectations, especially with the console's computer noise clicking and whistling around him like whale music.

But that's not it. After a few moments' reflection, as Rey natters on about types of lava, Charles narrows the source of his nebulous dread down to one face—Sitor Ananta's. Munk's news that he has recently seen that cruel visage in the facepan of a sentinel androne has been working on Charles. Evil pursues them. The bitter memory of the pain-raked eternity that Sitor Ananta inflicted hardens Charles's fear to a brittle panic.

Dwelling on that, he feels that his mind could snap. It is difficult enough to be bodiless and at the mercy of this unguessable future without a terror of helplessness and torture to overcome. He reaches for a deep breath to calm his fright and teeters at the brink of his disembodied emptiness, lungless, limbless, boneless, virtually nonexistent.

An immeasurable longing displaces his fear. He wants to be whole again. Passionate courage rises from this longing, and he determines that he will not be afraid anymore.

Outside, through the rover's cameras, he sees welded boulders the color of whisky glide past. And the blighted landscape shimmers with untouchable veils.

At sunset the craterland blazes blood-red, and the rovers shift to infraview, their cooler engines running faster through the spectral landscape. The desert's vaporous plant life is easier to see in the long light. Ghostly blooms of thermal shadows billow from the nooks and crevices of the crater outcrops, each species a different shade of fire.

"At night it becomes obvious why this track is called the Nebraska Trace," Rey announces. "Mr. Charlie, later you can tell us about Nebraska, the archaic land where the flora here originated. All these scrawny plants you're seeing shining in the dark are biots of terrene species and carry their names with their redesigned genes. That pink smoke in the graben to our left is prairie cordgrass, and that skeletal shrub among the boulders is yarrow. Tansy and purple clover grow in abundance on the lee of dunes. And if you stare off there to the far right ahead of us where the tableland begins, you can see a whole mosaic of foxtail, gayfeather, and prairie sage."

In the sudden darkness the sky crackles with stars. Bioluminescent insects zag in the darkness. Rey, who sleeps less than twenty minutes a day, continues his colloquy with Charles Outis on the features of the two moons. He explains how the smaller moon, Deimos, rising full in the east at dusk will still be a brilliant silver tuft in the eastern sky when the sun rises, because like someone walking down an up escalator, it travels against the planet's rotation.

The oblate moon, Phobos, on the other hand, ascends in the west on its eight-hour sprint across the sky, displaying all its waxing phases but never reaching fullness before it plunges into the planet's shadow. Rey begins relating a folktale about the frustrations of Phobos, until Grielle, who shares the front rover with him, feels compelled to tell him to shut up. Buddy and Mei Nili have already fallen asleep in their flexform recliners, wearied from a day spent getting acquainted with one-third gravity and talking about archaic times with Charles Outis.

Alone in the third rover, Shau Bandar records the night through infraview, tracking the undulant wraiths in the smoky light. Gradually, the sedative olfacts in the air supply put him to sleep too, and after a while the recorder in his mantle automatically shuts off.

A moment later the midstim begins, and the animal gods, full of their resolutions and silences, awake in a dream. Shau becomes a tree with quarrelsome branches. He lives underwater in a tide rip that is breaking him into pieces. But instead of vital fluids spilling out of his broken parts, he bleeds music.

Lavender creases of dawn unfold as the caravan comes to a stop on a shelf rock above a vista of desolate craters. Munk's silver cowl glints below, where he stands on a sandstone anvil overlooking the couloir that cuts the most direct path through the rings within rings of cratered waste.

Rey tells the androne to wait down there, and Munk makes no objection, for the hike up the slope would cost a tenth of a percent of his remaining power. The temperature is a sultry minus fifty degrees centigrade, and he needs to conserve strength for the torrid hours to come. He climbs down the dark side of the anvil, squats between two zubu cacti, and listens and watches through his com-link with the reporter.

The rovers have backed together, and crablike handroids from under the chassis quickly erect a transparent pavilion. Protected by the warm air pressure of the tent, the pilgrims frolic in the fainter gravity. Shau Bandar whirls triple somersaults in the air, and Rey lifts the back end of the dune climber with his bare hands to check the wheel bearings. In the orange shine of the thermalux at the center of the pavilion, Grielle Aspect opens her long-sleeved arms and beckons the others.

"I am the Light," she chants. "Stranger to nothing. I stand against the ancient life of remembered darkness and summon all of you to yourselves. The body is a drug.

It deforms consciousness with its hormones and secre-
tions. I am here to tell you to drop the body. Let yourself
go. Become the light you are."

Buddy sits on the runner guard, looking groggy. Mei
Nili jumps from the back of the rover and with two prac-
ticed leaps crosses the enclosure and is standing at the
clear wall gazing down toward Munk.

"Good to see you again, Munk," she whispers on her
link line to the androne.

She can't see me in the dark, Munk knows. *She wonders
what I make of this odd human behavior.*

"Are we supposed to be doing anything?" Charles asks
over their link. "I mean, are we participants?"

A laugh bursts from Grielle. "Whether you know it or
not, you are all participants." She swivels about, pointing
fingers at each of them. "Rey Raza wants the credits and
thrills. Shau Bandar wants credits and fame. Mei Nili
wants escape. Buddy wants escape. People, you are all
participants. Even you, Mr. Charlie, even you want a
body and a future."

"What about Munk?" Mei asks. "Isn't he a participant?"

Grielle snuffs the thermalux. Sheets of fire hover in the
sky over the dark, riven terrain. "All consciousness is
light." She wheels around in the ebb shadows, her arms
outstretched under the blazing sky. "But the body
deforms us with its chemical powers. It addicts us to its
hungers. The body is a drug. Let the body go."

She dances up close to Shau and says directly to his
recorder, "Wanting is not the way. I invite each of you to
become the Light that you are but do not know."

"What do we have to do?" Charles Outis asks.

Rey rolls his eyes, and Buddy rests his forehead in his
hand.

"There is only one path to the absolute freedom of pure
consciousness and light, dear Mr. Charlie," Grielle says,
pointing her body toward the rover where he watches

through the sensors. "One path—but not the path you've taken, Mr. Charlie. Not more wanting. Not more organic life. The one path is death."

"You really think there's consciousness *after* death?" the archaic man asks.

"Let's get this ritual done," Rey almost whines. "We've got a long way to go."

With a flourish of her robes, Grielle shifts her attention to the reporter, who is still bounding among the rovers, flipping and twisting with clumsy vigor through the air. "Bandar, dear, educate our archaic guest, will you? Show him an infoclip or something on consciousness and light. Ignorance is such an ugly trait."

Grielle disappears into the back hatch of the lead rover, and Rey follows. Immediately, the flat, crablike handroids emerge and begin disassembling the tent. Shau back-flips into the rover and conks his head sharply enough so that he collapses to his knees and retreats with a sheepish grin. Mei waves to the residual darkness in the canyon below where Munk waits and then joins Buddy in the second rover.

"There may be consciousness after death," she tells Charles, plopping into a deck chair, "but no one who's died is talking."

"That woman Grielle is a fanatic," Charles mutters. "Religion doesn't seem to have gotten any less irrational in the millennium I've been gone."

"Actually," Munk comes in over the link, "the Acts of Light is not a religion. They don't postulate a supreme being, nor do they codify human behavior—apart from their willingness to terminate their lives. Most of their belief system is actually founded in science. Close empirical observation has shown that consciousness is not a state or function of the brain, nor does it interact with the brain."

"How can that be?" Charles asks.

"It's true," the androne asserts. "Memory, reflection, planning, learning, choice, and creativity all take place regularly in the brain without consciousness. Unconscious brain activity guides these functions. They're all automatic brain processes. Consciousness itself is nothing more than a witness."

"Where does Grielle's 'light' come in?" Charles inquires with an audible frown.

Shau snorts. "Even in your time, science knew that matter and energy had equivalence. That all matter had once been energy at the time of the Big Bang—"

"But there's more," Munk submits. "If consciousness is not a function of the brain, as science shows, then it may well be, as the Acts of Light decree, a standing wave pattern in a wider dimension, the tesseract range. When any neurology—carbon or silicon—gets complex enough, it receives the standing wave, which is there all along. In that way, consciousness enters life and suffers the indignities of physical limits until death liberates us."

"Then what?" Charles asks.

"Then the Guest is free!" Grielle Aspect announces over the link. "If you live long enough, Mr. Charlie, you will feel the rightness of this. Life is a physical phenomenon. Consciousness is not!"

Dust devils tilt over the red land. Sand blooms swell on a distant horizon like giant sorrel mushrooms. Ball lightning bounces over cobbles and the solemnities of boulders under a perfectly clear, pink sky. Strewn over the gritty terrain at unexpected intervals are the remains of earlier caravans smitten by dust storms—flex-treads twisted in the sand like molted snakeskin, crazed pieces of blackglass embedded in roan dune drifts, and bleached bones scattered like so much debris across the gravel under the blast of heaven.

Charles Outis is surprised to see human skulls among the shattered ribs and femur bones protruding from the coagulated red sandstone. He interrupts the lively discussion among the other pilgrims to ask, "Is there no respect for the dead anymore?"

"Not in the wilds," Shau Bandar replies nonchalantly. "What happens out here simply happens."

"It is my suspicion that the isolationists of Solis strew these bones to dissuade travelers," Grielle Aspect says, to which the others respond with grouchy mumbles.

Dune lemurs scurry along the gully of an ancient streambed. Suddenly, from behind them, a gleam of air shimmers like a pursuing will-o'-the-wisp.

"Shreek!" Rey Raza calls. "Shreek on the portside!"

Virtually invisible in the sunlight, the transparent predator appears at first as a blur. Then one of the big-eared, tufty-furred dune lemurs is plucked from the scattering bunch, and the carnal face of the thing reveals itself as the lemur is macerated in midair.

"It looks like a huge angelfish," Charles remarks, observing the airborne beast's thin protoplasmic body and whirring fins.

"But," Mei Nili adds, "with the face of a piranha."

With a jaw-thrust blur of teeth, the shreek swiftly bolts down the lemur, the prey's shredded flesh and crushed bones becoming a mere shadow in the clear bulk of the carnivore. And then, in a ripple of caught sunlight, the beast is gone.

"Good heavens, what was that creature it ate?" Charles asks.

"Dune lemur," Rey answers.

"A biot," Munk adds over the link from where he rides on the dune climber. "They were templated from a hybrid of the Gila monster and the mongoose."

"Weren't there wild animals in your time?" Shau inquires.

"Of course," Charles responds, "but nothing like that. Most predators in my time lived in game preserves."

"Not unlike the reserves the Maat have provided for anthros on Earth in our time," Grielle says, her sarcasm palpable even over the com-link. "We're wild animals to them. And we're on the loose."

Mei ignores her and asks, "Mr. Charlie, what do you miss most about your old life—apart from your body, that is?"

"It was an avaricious and desperate time," Charles mutters, reminiscing. "I don't miss much. Just the people I knew then. My wife. My friends."

"Your wife," Shau's voice comes over the com-link. "What was she like?"

"She was a playwright. She wrote for children—and the child in adults. She kept getting younger the more she wrote."

"Was she frozen, too?" the reporter inquires.

"No," Charles replies sadly. "Everything she learned, she learned by heart. Even death."

"Shreek to starboard," Rey interrupts. "There must be a nest of them near here. They usually congregate along ejecta blankets."

Charles scans the starboard side and spots the mica-flash of a shreek high on the rampart of a nearby crater rim.

"Unlike the moon or Mercury," Rey lectures, "the craters on Mars have much larger ejecta blankets. Impacts here made a bigger mess. That's because the ground rock and soil on Mars contain subsurface water ice. On impact, the ice melted and the gooey ejecta formed those characteristic smear contours that terrace the ground for kilometers around a crater. It makes roving difficult, but the biots love it because it provides a lot of shade surface."

The discussion veers into a description of martian flora

and fauna, all biots genetically manufactured in earlier efforts to terraform the planet. While the com-link among the rovers is noisy with history and observations, Rey turns off Charles Outis and adjusts the olfact level of the following rovers' air supply, releasing narcolfact in the cabins. He sets a timer to do the same in the rover he is sharing with Grielle and excuses himself to go to the latrine. When he emerges, he is wearing a statskin cowl and gloves.

Grielle lies slumped in the deck chair where a moment earlier she had been vigorously denouncing the contamination of Mars's pristine sterility. Munk calls on the com-link, "Mr. Charlie? Jumper Nili?"

At the console, Rey brings the caravan to a stop. They are on a nacre flat of silica dust with the mesas of broken crater rims surrounding them. A sand cloud rises from a nearby scarp, and a trundle-carrier emerges from the shadow side of a ferruginous outcropping. The carrier is pitted and rust-streaked and clanks across the rubble-strewn ground with a pulmonary wheezing.

"Marauders!" Munk cries out and jumps down from the dune climber. "Raza! Ready your laser cannon. Raza? Do you hear me?"

"I hear you, Munk." The wing-hatch at the side of the lead rover opens, and Rey emerges. "Stay where you are."

"Where are the pilgrims?" the androne inquires.

"They are in the rovers, where I left them." Rey waves to the noisy trundle-carrier, and it smokes to a stop beside Munk with a viper whistle that stings the thin air. The side of the trundle-carrier lifts with a brutal bang, releasing eight big distorts in patched, remnant pressure suits and dented battle helmets. Just visible through their slit visors, burnt red eyes stare wildly from bone brows and angry faces of wet, twitching muscle.

As Munk whirls toward them across the sand bed, intent on ripping the marauders out of their suits, a figure appears. It has the full and exact appearance of a

man, but because he steps out wearing only a gemdust
shawl, slacks, and slippers, the androne assumes he is a
semblor. Sure enough, infrascan reveals the figure is not
human but a man-shaped volume of plasma, given shape
and direction by remote control.

Munk instantly recognizes the effeminate and raffish
features of Sitor Ananta in the face of the plasma being.
The Commonality agent swaggers through the distort
squad, unconcerned about the attacking androne. A cold
smile touches his sharp lips.

The semblor points a small device at Munk, and a
sound of shattering glass breaks across the androne's
mind. Suddenly, he cannot move. He stands immobilized
in the dust billow his attack stirred up.

Sitor Ananta approaches the paralyzed androne and
taps a pseudofinger against Munk's breastplate. "You once
worked for the Commonality," he says smugly. "Iapetus
Gap readily provided me with your signal codes. And
now you are again what you always were—a puppet."

The semblor turns away abruptly and confronts Rey.
"Where is the wetware?"

"I deactivated Mr. Charlie," Rey answers, "before I put
the others to sleep. I'll disengage him."

"Let the distorts do it," the semblor says. "Where?"

Rey gestures toward the second rover. "I patched him
into the console. It's a delicate hookup. You'd better let
me free him."

"Tear him loose," Sitor Ananta orders the distorts, and
they lurch toward the rover. "He won't be needing to
communicate anymore."

"And my credits?" Rey queries.

"Already in your account at your new house in the
Honor of Giants," the semblor promises. "We'll bang up
your rover so you can claim you struggled to get away.
But the other equipment will have to be sacrificed with
the bodies."

"Fine, fine," Rey agrees. "You're paying me enough to replace them ten times over."

Munk listens to this from far inside his locked body. The signal codes have shut down all his primary programming—his motor reflexes and proprioception—but his C-P program remains alert and stares helplessly through his sensory apparatus as the distorts swarm toward Charles's rover.

The androne shifts his focus internally, to where the shatterglass sounds of the interfering signals propagate. Outside, time seems to slow down as he accesses the virtual space of the signal that has invaded his body. A voice gels out of the static:

Androne Munk, this is Iapetus Gap comptroller advising you that your signal codes have been released to Commonality agent Sitor Ananta through the Rogue Androne Reclamation Decree. Recognition of your contra-parameter programming, however, now indicates that your rogue status may be self-justified. Herewith, then, I am activating your conscience reviewer. You now have one point three seconds to justify your rogue behavior. If you cannot define your current status to the satisfaction of the reviewer, this signal will permanently shut down your C-P program. Begin now.

Munk reviews all his behavior since activating his C-P program in the cold reaches off Saturn. "My actions speak for themselves," he says inwardly to the reviewer. But his body remains rigid.

Through his visor, he sees the array of distorts aiming toward Charles's rover. "I am the protector of an archaic human being," he announces. And still his body stays locked.

"My C-P program has guided my actions since Iapetus Gap," he avers. "It guides me now. Respect it and release me."

Nothing.

"I have done no wrong! Allow me to fulfill my program."

Sitor Ananta is caught with a glint of amused malice in his sharp eyes, and Munk tries to amplify the rage that this malevolent expression makes him feel. But to no avail.

"What do you want from me, then?" Munk bawls.

No answer. He reviews his past actions again, looking for infractions. "I killed Aparecida by default," he asserts. "I had to save human lives."

The glass of the signal codes continues crashing inside him.

He pleads. He cajoles. He provides an eloquent colloquy on the nature of will and imagination, concluding with the Blake quote, "No Body save the Soul!"

The paralysis continues.

"There's nothing more I can do," he finally admits. "I have no other defense but that I am alive. Does that count for anything?"

The bursting glass resounds louder. *One-tenth of a second remains. Satisfy the reviewer now, or you will be terminated.*

Munk can think of nothing more to say; knowing it is useless to repeat himself, he says nothing. The light of the world is pellucid, flecked with glints of silica dust suspended in the air. This is the last he will see of anything, he accepts. One last giddy instant remains. Morning vapor clouds streak the sky like stretch marks. The rusty buttes and parapet rocks sink deeper into his sight. They will continue their billion-year journey into sand. And the sight of them, hard and real, hammers him free of all abstraction. And for that last instant of his being, the androne sees he is a mirage sparkle in the stone poverty of the land. All mind is but a tear in the fabric of nothingness, like a rip in water that quickly heals over.

Munk laughs. With his final thought, he understands why this is the laughing life. Life is the laugh of the actual in the face of nothing. There is so much to sense, think, and emote about, so much life to endure, such fullness of good and bad—and all of it, suddenly, nothing. Only laughter fits the gap. And he laughs luminously with the great swell of being nothing.

Androne Munk, you have satisfied the reviewer that you are validly fulfilling your contra-parameter programming. You are herewith released from all allegiance to the Commonality. Go in freedom and focus.

The sound of breaking glass stops. Immediately, his attention is flung into his anthropic model, and time lunges forward. Flailing the area with a siren scream, his body abruptly resumes spinning, jetting a rooster tail of sand into the sky. The distorts cringe. The semblor frantically jabs his signal device at Munk, while Rey scuttles backward beneath a ragged cry toward the caravan.

With a slashing blow, Munk strikes the semblor, and it explodes in a hissing thrash of lightning. Laser fire from the handguns of the crouching distorts kicks against his breastplate and heaves him backward. He sits down, and the sand around him turns to glass under the hacking laser light.

A sick feeling of power-cell depletion whelms up in Munk, and he lurches to his feet, wrapping his reflectant cowl about him. With deft tilts of his shield, he mirrors the laser fire back, and one of the distorts erupts, the scarlet wings of his ribs splaying apart like a cocoon bursting into a brilliant butterfly.

Munk attacks. Ignoring the widening exhaustion in his body, he lopes among the firing distorts, swiping at them with a blindingly swift but lethal economy of movement. In moments they are strewn among the rocks, slovenly rags in a greasy mess. And there is suddenly again only one moment left. The laser fire has exhausted his power cells.

Rey clambers toward the open wing-hatch of his rover and steals a terrified glance over his shoulder. Munk commits the last of his power to snatch a gun from the limp hand of a distort and levels it on the pilot in the hatchway.

Rey quails, and the console behind him shrieks with metal ripping. The androne missed! Disbelieving, he peers with dread and caution through the weave of his fingers.

Munk stands unmoving, shooting arm extended. A thick moment passes before Rey realizes that the androne has gone dormant. The lens bar in the featureless puzzle of his face is unlit. Rey's amazement distracts him from the fact that an androne could not miss at this range.

"Raza," Grielle croaks from inside the rover.

In rumpled, clumsily donned desert gear, the pilgrims stumble from the vehicles. Rey can see the heat leaking from their loose seams like blood. Then the self-seals kick in, and the faces behind the clear statskin veils flush warmer.

Rey recognizes their shock and acts with impulsive indignation. "Those creatures almost killed us! We have to disconnect the archaic head. It's tainted wetware."

Shau faces away from the mangled bodies of the dead but holds his recorder on the corpses a moment longer. "What is he talking about?" he asks, looking to the others.

Mei gazes in mute and revulsed candor at the dead distorts. Buddy walks over to Munk and stares down the length of the androne's aiming arm.

"The brain we're carrying is tainted," Rey insists. "The anarchists programmed it like a machine, and I stupidly installed it in the console. At the anarchists' signal, it must have usurped your air supply and knocked you out. It would have gotten me, too, if I hadn't been in the latrine, near an emergency statskin. I saw it all. Munk killed them, but the heat from their laser fire sapped his power. I was in here fighting the console, trying to override the wetware's domination. I finally shut him down, but I couldn't clean the air. Munk saw my problem, and with his last act, he blew open the console and freed you."

"It's true," Grielle gasps and steps groggily from the rover. "He was in the latrine when it happened."

"Mr. Charlie is not tainted," Mei declares, shaking her head.

"He might be," Shau says. "I mean, his file says he was held on Earth for quite a while by lewdists and anarchists."

"What are you saying, Pilgrim Nili?" Rey asks with feigned anger. "I nearly got killed trying to save you!"

"If Mr. Charlie were tainted," Mei persists, "he would have detonated the explosives on Phoboi Twelve when he still had the codes. Anarchists destroy. He hasn't destroyed anything."

"He called those distorts down on us, I'm sure of it," Rey insists.

Grielle throws her hands up in dismay. "We don't need Mr. Charlie to go on. Let's leave him shut down and get away from here."

"But what about Munk?" Mei asks. "We can't leave him here."

Rey looks shocked. "We can't lug a deep-space patrol-class androne. He's made of supermassive alloy. It'll take a full rover moving at half speed to carry him anywhere."

"The dune climber could handle him," Buddy states.

Grielle, who is staring at Rey with a perplexed impatience, hands on her hips, says, "I'm the caravan director, and I will not dump a fortune in psyonic core units to haul a rundown androne."

"He just saved your life," Shau points out, catches the sudden wry cock of her head, and shrugs. "Though I guess for a passager that doesn't mean a whole lot."

Grielle passes an apologetic look to the others and says, "I am grateful that Munk saved our lives. For myself, I want to die on the Walk of Freedom in Solis, in the traditional way. But if I had died here, I would be as free. I say we dump the androne and get on with our trek."

"Well, I'm not leaving Munk," Mei says, crossing her arms.

"Are any of us leaving?" Grielle asks with exasperation. "Do the rovers still run, Rey?"

"Yes, I'm sure of it," he says, glad to divert the conversation away from culpability. He pokes his head into the cabin and calls back, "The androne's shot was precise. It destroyed only the remote air controller."

"Then I say we go now," Grielle presses, "before any more distorts find us."

Buddy steps past Grielle and peeks into the cabin. "Looks to me like Munk's shot also burned out the laser cannon controls. That right, Rey?"

"Hmm, yes," Rey admits, having already vainly tried to activate those weapons to cauterize all witnesses. "I guess he figured the wetware could have used the cannon against us."

"His shot was precise," Buddy observes softly. His hard, dolorous stare seems an indictment, and Rey is about to protest when the man says, "We'll need your help mounting Munk to a rover."

"Okay," Rey concedes, not relenting his mean squint for an instant. "I'll have the handroids load him on the third rover. But Grielle and I are going ahead. We're not slowing down for the androne."

"Mei," Buddy asks, "can you pilot a desert rover?"

"In my sleep."

"I'm the director of this caravan," Grielle protests. "My decision is what counts."

"I don't think so," Shau says and pans from Grielle in her outrage to the scattered skull shards and pink brain sludge glistening among the rocks. "We're in the wilds now. I don't think anything counts here except survival."

The handroids crab-swarm over Munk and within the hour have him securely strapped to the roof of the third rover. While they work, Rey Raza examines the vehicles, acting concerned about damage. A boiling mix of dread and anger seethe in him, and he's glad when the others go off to look over the distorts' trundle-carrier. Enraged that his business deal with the Commonality has been undone by the androne, he is determined to destroy the pilgrims. They will join Grielle on her death-passage sooner than she expected. Under the engine manifold of the second rover, he loosens a critical deck plate.

"I think we should at least talk with Mr. Charlie," Mei Nili is saying as she returns with the group from the trundle-carrier.

"He's an abomination," Grielle Aspect says with a revulsed sneer. "Think on him: a wad of brain tissue intent on only one thing—flesh. I told him, flesh is darkness. Though the flesh is in the light, the light is not in the flesh. It would be far better for him if we broke him open on the rocks."

Shau Bandar, walking a wide circle around the two, objects. "Doesn't it count that he's a thousand years old? He's a living piece of our history."

"What did you find in that rusty box?" Rey asks from where he is supervising the handroids' rock burial of the distorts.

"It's a dangerous piece of junk," Mei says. "It's corroded throughout. The compression ducts could blow anytime."

"We should get away from it soon," Rey concurs. "Others may be tracking it."

"There was a semblor in the carrier," Buddy reports. "We found a plasma booster pump that has just been used."

"Yes, yes, that's right," Rey murmurs, rocking back on his heels, submerging his anxiety as he studies Buddy's face. There are none of the telltale heat-blotches of anger, so Rey is convinced he knows nothing, though there is a furrow of suspicion in the man's blockbrow. "I saw a semblor emerge. Munk burst it right away. Then the laser fire began."

"The handroids are done," Grielle notices, standing with one hand on the jut of her hip as she assesses Munk. The androne's limbs have been loosened and his body mounted prone on the rover's roof in the shape of a humanoid swastika. "We can still fulfill most of our nyc-themeral journey if we depart now."

"Leave those guns here," Rey warns Shau, who is heft-ing the laser pistol the handroids removed from Munk's grip. "It's probably tainted and could be used by other distorts to target us."

"I want to talk to Mr. Charlie," Mei says.

"You can ride with that wetware if you want," Rey responds sternly, "but I won't activate him on this cara-van. Forget it." He turns on one toe and motions for Grielle to follow.

"We're all corpses-to-be," Grielle says blithely as she strolls past the burial mounds of orange rocks. "Better to give oneself to the light than be taken by the darkness."

Under the weight of the androne, the third rover crawls only half as fast as the others, and the crate-laded dune climber and the lead rover with Rey and Grielle in it ride far ahead. Mei, who pilots the second rover in full desert gear in the event of another accident, loses sight of them and slows down so as not to lose her rear view of Munk.

"I think Raza betrayed us," Buddy speaks sadly from the deck chair beside the jumper. Like the others, he too, wears a statskin cowl and sealed togs, his fabric ruddy and smudged on the side where he crawled under the trundle-carrier to find the plasma booster pump. "A semblor wouldn't come into the desert to stalk a signal-carrier. Distorts can do that. The semblor was here to meet with someone."

"If we could speak to Munk," Mei says, "we'd know for

sure. But I think you're right. Raza probably cut a deal with the Commonality for Mr. Charlie."

Shau looks down from his perch in the observation bubble behind the forward cabin. "We don't know that. Bo Rabana says Raza's story is plausible." He holds a hand to his left ear, catching a message in his timpan-com. "When the Commonality found out *Softcopy* was covering Mr. Charlie's trek, they sent her some officious report warning that the archaic brain had been tampered with by the, ah, let's see—Friends of the Non-Abelian Gauge Group. That's what Ananta charged in the Moot. But who are these Friends?"

"A clade on Earth," Mei answers. "My understanding is they branched into people with an emotional craving for a certain mathematics—"

"Right, here it is," the reporter indicates with an abstracted expression, calling up a file on his corneal display. "They branched a hundred and fifty-eight terrene years ago—enjambed limbic and cortical plexes—blah blah blah—ah, here's what we want: They abide no authority at all, not even reservation strictures, and are general troublemakers for the Commonality. I don't see any record of violence, though. They seem to be more mischievous and insubordinate than destructive."

"They would have the know-how to trigger wetware," Mei accedes, "but I can't believe that those number-dreamers would do that to an archaic brain. Maybe—"

"Hold up!" Shau shouts. His frantic face glares down between his knees from his sling in the bubble. "Stop the rover! The local office is hearing an ultrahigh pitch over my com-link. The androne dispatcher says it's a pressure whistle. It's coming from under us, in the drive-train. The rover's going to blow!"

Instantly, Mei Nili shuts down the engine, stops the third rover by cutting off the autopilot, throws open all the hatches, and exits through the port companionway, all with the fluid ease of her long training. Buddy barges out the starboard side, and Shau lifts himself through the popped-open bubble, leaps from the top of the rover, and lands in a dust-splash among the cauterized rocks.

Running is swift and easy over the gravelly desert, and Mei and Buddy bound toward the shelter of talus rocks that have spilled from the scorched slopes of a crumbling crater rim. Awkward in his cumbersome desert gear, Shau trails behind. In a twinkling gust of static sparks and a thump of thunder, the second rover explodes. Chunks of white hull roll flashing into the sky, and a spray of fléchettes cut iridescent tracks in the pink atmosphere. One fragment strikes the back of the reporter's mantle as he bolts over the cold ancient ash, and he flops forward, his neck cleanly broken.

Mei rushes toward his fallen body but stops when she sees the queer angle of his head and the lifeless gape of his face.

Buddy passes Mei, kneels over Shau, and rips open the reporter's statskin cowl. "The cold will preserve him," he explains, gasping with exertion. "He's intact. If we get him to Solis soon, he can be revived."

"Mr. Charlie," Mei rasps, looking back at the twisted debris of the rover. She jogs to the wreck and finds the plasteel capsule nestled among tangles of shredded metal. Its surface is spalled and cloudy with scratches, but the case itself is whole. She picks it up and scrutinizes it, trying to see if the shock of the blast damaged the interior.

Buddy strides past, carrying Shau in his arms. The corpse's face is powder-blue, the lips silvery white. "We'd better check Munk's rover carefully."

Mei lifts her angry face to the pale rose sky and screams, "Raza!"

Nude sandstone walls and maroon monument rocks crown the cliff crest where the dune climber and the first desert rover have stopped. These are the ruins of Sarna Neve, a famous center of passage centuries ago, during the Exodus of Light, and Grielle believes Rey stopped to offer her this fabulous view. She speaks reverently, "'At last, I see the last.' That was first said here, Rey. Think on the freedom of—"

"Did you see that?" Rey asks, pointing down the long escarpment to the alkali basin where he spotted the sparkle of the exploding rover. "That flash?"

Grielle's dreamy gaze surveys the golden desert below and selects a glimmer from among the strewn boulders on the nearby slope. "Yes, what is it?"

Rey widens his eyes in mock surprise. "I think that was one of the rovers! It exploded!"

Grielle presses against the viewport, frowning to see what looks like a white blossom on the desert floor. It's a blast cloud of sand. "Those fools!"

"That damn jumper must have flooded the compression tanks," Rey says, doing the same, reaching across the burned gash of the console and stroking the sensor pads that will flood the compression tanks. In the next few minutes the tanks will explode and Grielle will make her passage sooner than she expected. He's pleased with himself that he has at least arranged for her to do so in the presence of Sarna Neve. "I better take the dune climber down there and see if anyone can be saved. Stay here, and I'll call you if it's safe."

Grielle makes a feeble attempt to detain him, but he exits quickly and closes the wing-hatch after him. She is moved by his humane urgency and stands to watch him sprint up the salmon-colored rise of sandstone to the dune climber. He bounds into the cab and starts rolling downslope, the big blue wheels scattering gravel in fins behind him.

Less than halfway down the escarpment, the dune climber fishtails to an abrupt halt. The glimmer among the strewn boulders that Grielle had glimpsed earlier flickerflashes toward Rey. In the red dust kicked up by his hard stop, the disclike bodies, whirling fins, and raving mouth parts of the shreeks materialize.

The white tarpaulin, now peach-red with sand, pulls away under their biting frenzy, exposing the cumbrous crates in the carry bay. More rocks spit skyward as Rey swings the dune climber around and starts churning up the boulder-warted slope. The shreeks thrash among the crates with shuddering might and bang their pugnacious bodies against the spinning wheels. Splats of squashed shreek spin away in widening vectors, and Grielle, who is watching appalled, thinks Rey is going to elude them. She looks for the com-link to encourage him.

Then one of the shreeks slams into the cab of the dune climber, and the canopy roof wings into the air. Grielle's heart thumps, and she steadies herself with a bracing gust of dégagé. Only the olfact enables her to stand still and watch the dune climber weasel among the scarp boulders, scrambling back toward the ridge. She scans the burnt console before her, trying to recall how Rey drove this thing. She wants to go to him, to drive the shreeks off if she can. But the array of sensor pads are just so many jeweled lights to her.

The dune climber disappears from Grielle's vantage. Four heartbeats later, her breath is snatched away when the climber shoots over the rim of the scarp and lofts into the air, wheels blurring. It smacks onto the road in front of the rover, toppling the crates from its carry bay under the shrill screams of its brakes.

Rey pulls himself from the cab, and Grielle opens the side hatch for him. Shreeks flap up from below, etched into the visible by veils of dust. And though they are thronging toward Rey, she stands in the doorway to help him, to sacrifice herself if necessary. Under the gaze of Sarna Neve and the hundreds of millions who passed here, she can do no less for so valiant a man.

But Rey barrels into her, frantically shoving against her, trying to reach the console and abort the flooding of the compression tanks. Grielle, however, thinks he is eager to get her out of harm's way, for she can see the shreeks slashing closer. Their grinding jaws electrify hearing, sending hurting vibrations into the small bones of her head. She tries to help him by closing the wing-hatch, but he hurls her aside the instant before she can reach the lever. In his obvious zeal to save her, he exposes his back. Grielle and he scream together as a flashing streak of fangs scythes through the hatchway and severs his ham tendons.

Grielle watches in rigid horror as Rey collapses across the console, blood smoking from his legs, the shreek gnashing loudly as its teeth crunch into bone. She can't breathe.

Wildly flailing at the console to stop the imminent explosion, Rey enters the stop sequence just as the shreek completes its bone-crushing clamp on his leg and hauls him howling from the rover. A magnetic wind of sheer terror whisks Grielle to the hatch lever, and she secures the rover.

Standing at the viewport in an aching twist of fright and shocked stupor, she observes firsthand the feeding habits of the shreek. They do not compete once the prey is seized. They float in a circle of quiet, shared ecstasy. Only the successful predator feeds. It hovers over the writhing body it has hobbled, swiftly scissors it into parts, and does not share a crumb of bone.

In an astonishingly brief time, it is done. Then, like a shift of wind, the whole shimmery school of them is gone, and no trace of Rey Raza remains but the smeared imprint of his last agony in the coppery sand.

Late in the day, with the bloated sun looking corrugated among the ruins of Sarna Neve, Mei Nili and Buddy find Grielle Aspect sitting stupefied with olfacts in her rover. While Buddy examines the battered dune climber, Mei shakes Grielle alert and finds out about Rey's heroic death. Grielle refuses to believe that Rey had anything to do with the destruction of the second rover, which killed Shau Bandar. "He sacrificed himself to save me," she whispers through her drugged torpor. "He could have fed me to them instead. I was ready to die. I wanted it, but he shoved me back. He saved me."

The dune climber remains functional, and Mei programs the rover's computer to autopilot it along with the rover lugging Munk's body. Slowly, the caravan departs Sarna Neve and trundles into the night. Ghostly vegetative blooms ripple on the sandstone ridges in a nocturnal wind—foxtail, bitter dock, cordgrass, and yarrow—the profuse flora of the spores carried across the shoreless dark from the blue star that is Earth.

A few hours later, the water cycler in the pilot rover emits a raspy groan and cuts out. By dawn the blackglass viewdomes are foggy with exhaled moisture, which Buddy and Mei carefully sop up with their scarves and squeeze into empty nutripouches. Mei retreats to the rover that is carrying Munk, but the water cycler there is dormant, its power cells drained by disuse because the rover has been emptied of air to carry Shau Bandar's frozen body. When Mei tries to hook the cycler to the engine's power drive, the circuits, already straining from the supermassive weight of the androne, shut down. For most of that day, Mei and Buddy struggle to revive the engine.

"Abandon the androne," Grielle demands, "or we're all going to die out here. Is that what you want?"

"Go take a sniff, Grielle," Mei gripes from under the chassis.

"Do you want to die out here, old one?" Grielle asks Buddy.

He looks up from where he is kneeling in the auburn sand, holding a lux torch for Mei and shrugs. "We're three days from Solis. We can make it without a water cycler if we don't panic."

"Life *is* a panic," Grielle states derisively and turns her head to take another gust of dégagé. With all the olfact she's been doing since yesterday's tragedy, she's less talkative than before, yet she manages to add, "Our senses detect only the smallest fraction of what is. Why do you want to go on living in this poverty?"

Mei and Buddy ignore her, and she drifts back to the pilot rover. Inside, she seriously contemplates activating the engine and leaving them behind with their precious androne. But when she looks over the laser-gashed console, she can't figure out how to run the damn thing, and the possibility that she might blow herself up stymies her angry ambition. She wants her passing to be ritualized. Rey Raza died for her that she herself might die with ritual exactitude in Solis, and she will not squander that gift.

Instead, she stares admiringly at the dune climber parked in the shadow of a pinion rock, its burden of psyonic crates promising her a welcome reception in Solis. For that, she will have to wait. But she won't wait thirsty. She helps herself to one of the pouches of reclaimed water and sips it. The acrid taste makes her grimace, but she finishes the pouch anyway. She's the director. This is her caravan, and this her water.

Late in the afternoon the caravan is running again on autopilot, but all the reclaimed water is gone, consumed by Grielle. To conserve body moisture, the pilgrims keep their statskins on and don't talk. The dry martian air, which whirls in scarlet dust devils through the wake of the vehicles, seems to penetrate the rover's seals and even the statskins, but that is a thirst-inspired hallucination. To counter it, Mei and Buddy accept doses of Grielle's olfacts, and physical discomfort relents to a spongy ease.

Mesas appear along the horizon, scabrous and blood-colored, sacrificial altars in the setting sun. Embraced by their flexform deck chairs, the pilgrims each seep deeper into themselves as night comes on and the spectral smoke of the alien plant life appears in the infraview. Sleep cuts through them sporadically, rips in the fabric of their drugged minds that thirst stitches whole again—until another dose of olfacts slashes them free.

When dawn arrives as an enormous apocalypse that ignites a landscape of ferrous peaks and reefs of blowing dust, the olfacts are gone. No condensation at all beads on the blackglass interior, but Buddy swabs it anyway. In the parching chill, Mei's caked lips catch on her dry teeth, and she finds she cannot speak when she tries to. Asleep or comatose, Grielle lies with one blind eye half-lidded as if peeking out at the last dying stars, the planet's tiny lobe-shaped moons.

The rovers and the dune climber churn onward mindlessly. A blustery wind licks powder from the nearby crater ridges, and a pouring haze of sand obscures vision. When the fog lifts, the fiery world is still there. The badland blazes under the space-cold pandemonium of heaven, its tortured pinnacles, crater-mutilated plains, and red dunes indifferent to human trespass.

6

Solis

ON THE HORIZON OF THE BARREN PAN, SOMBER HEADLANDS appear out of the morning glare, the promontories of ancient impact craters. A city shines beyond the protective bulwark of these rouge bluffs. Lens towers burn fiercely, collecting their solar harvest, and the vaulting spans, shield hangars, derrick arcades, and rhombohedral rooftops with their gleaming gold-foil facets give light in fierce spikes like a field of stars.

Solis is the human history of Mars. At the west end, some of the geodesics from the first Mars colony are preserved in a historical park. Surrounding it are the hydroponic grange sheds of the Anthropos Essentia, the oldest residents. Their bower-and-dome architecture dominates the flats of two intersecting craters whose rufous cliff walls have been sculpted into administrative offices. On the other side of them, in three nearly concentric craters, the clade cantonments spraddle in many levels of glass galleries, pyramids, and pavilions. The crofts of prism turrets and rhomboidal stupes at the east end are the latest edifices, the megastructure Hall of All constructed to house the millions of humans who want to live free of the Maat and their minions, the Commonality.

As the pilgrims first spot the silver starpoints in the amber aureole of sunrise that are the solar foils of Solis, flyers already begin to loft out of the city and circle in—scout-class androne programmed to evaluate all travelers who come over the rim of the wasteland.

The flyers find two dusty rovers and a dune climber grinding slowly over the reddish black badlands. A deep-space patrol-class androne lies dormant atop the roof of the following rover. When they land, the vehicles stop and three pilgrims emerge, parched, shrunken with hunger, and glassy-eyed.

The first one out, Grielle Aspect falls deliriously onto her knees, a worshipful smile on her salt-pale lips. Thinking she is collapsing from dehydration, several simple-minded androne begin emergency procedures. Two of them wrap Grielle in a pressurized sling and, despite her protests, pack her face and arms in glucose infusers. Meanwhile, others approach Mei Nili and Buddy.

Buddy leads an androne to the second rover, opening the hatch to reveal Shau Bandar's frozen body, furred in powder-blue carbon dioxide ice.

"And this is Mr. Charlie." Mei presents the battered plasteel capsule to the androne before her. "Can you tell if he is all right? He took a heavy blow."

The flesh-masked androne smiles and takes the capsule. "Solis welcomes you."

"Please, can you tell if he's been damaged?" Mei repeats, dazed.

"Please come with me," the androne requests. "You may enter Solis and ask your questions to the people there."

Grielle is hurriedly hammocked between two flyers, and the androne who have treated her mount their wings, run a short distance, and lift her into the bright sky.

Mei looks back at Buddy. "Buddy and I have to go together," she tells her escort.

"I am sorry," the androne mutters quietly, sounding sincere and gesturing toward wings of opalescent gossamer standing on the pebbly plain. "Your companion is not admittable to Solis. He must remain outside."

"What do you mean?" Mei breaks away from the androne who is leading her. "Buddy's coming with me. He's a human—an old one."

"I am sorry."

She approaches Buddy, who looks at her tristfully.

"We part here," he says.

Head tilted, she stares closely at him, searching for traits she could not have missed in their harrowing days in the wilds—the static blur of a semblor, the clade signs of pupil shape and finger count. He seems profoundly human—though he *has* always displayed the quiescent alertness of a human biot—an organic androne. "Who *are* you?" she insists.

"Forgive me for telling you this way, but I am of the Maat," he confides. "We are not permitted to enter Solis."

Mei blinks back her surprise. "You're joking!"

"Go with Mr. Charlie," he counsels, pointing to the androne with the plasteel capsule in his arms. "And take Shau with you. I'll stay with Munk and see that he's revived."

A dizzy astonishment shoves through her as she tries to remember anything at all exceptional about this man. From the time the water cycler broke down three days ago, he suffered too, and she scowls with disbelief. "I—I thought you had powers."

"Not to strike water from rocks," he smiles. "At least, not without the right hardware. You'd better go now, or you'll get separated from Mr. Charlie."

"Will I see you again?" she asks, backing away.

He waves and smiles with a soft, languid sorrow.

Munk wakes up on a ferric precipice overlooking the spangling starfire of Solis. Instantly he knows where he is and, by comparing the angle and inclination of the sun to his last reading, exactly how much time has elapsed since his power cells emptied. He sharp-focuses on Buddy, who is sitting on a flat boulder watching him quietly through the clear veil of his statskin. The scout-class androbes who recharged him retreat with their cables and clamps toward a silver balloon lashed to a utility gondola. The musical clangor of the winch retracting the chains, nets, and grapnel hooks that carried him here bong and clank dully in the thin atmosphere.

Buddy relates all that has happened since Munk lost consciousness. He concludes by pointing to the harlequin fields of reflector domes and colorful pressure tents on the perimeter of the city, where those denied admission squat. The tent city looks squalid with its patchwork fabrics and its cheap solar mills glinting from atop ragged canopies like tinsel pinwheels. "We've been left out here with the rejects—you because you were never human and me because I am the wrong kind of human."

Sudden fear tightens Munk's field of awareness. None of his sensors detect any sign that Buddy is other than a feral man, though he knows if he touches his cranium he will feel the slow benthic rhythms of a tranced consciousness. From the first, he knew Buddy was cortically augmented, but he has assumed the man was made less, not more. He decides to speak his fear. "You are Maat?"

Buddy nods gently. "I'm on a mission. I'm supposed to deliver this man to here—to these camps."

Munk scans the miserable clutter of storm-battered tents. "He may die here."

"He may well," Buddy accedes. "Or he may flourish as

our view of his future indicates. But the timelines are closed for him in Terra Tharsis."

"Why?"

With a comradely smile, Buddy rises and approaches the androne. "You like this person I am inhabiting, don't you?"

"He is a human. My C-P program—"

"For whatever reason," Buddy says kindly, a gloved hand touching the androne's alloy arm. "You like him. So you will not interfere with his development. When I leave him here, you will not muddle with his life. You will go your own way. As I must."

Overhead, the repair andrones' gondola floats by, the silver balloon trawling into the morning breeze. Munk does not budge his attention from the forlorn man before him. "My sensors do not detect any foreign organism in this man. If you are what you say, where are you?"

"I'm here as an energy pattern in his brain," Buddy replies. "When he attempted to kill himself with the night wings, I came into his body to save him."

"Why?"

Buddy barks a laugh. "Your C-P program is insatiable." He walks to the crumbly edge of the precipice where a vague track wends past the balesome camp and downward among vermilion boulders toward the sunny buildings. "Walk with me, Munk, and we will talk about freedom and destiny."

Mei Nili sways gently in a pressure sling strung between two lux stanchions. While the pressure bags cocooning her left arm and thigh perfuse electrolytic fluid into her blood flow to remedy her dehydration, she gazes across the flagstone colonnade to where Charles Outis is being examined by several utilitarian scanner drones. She has yet to see a human being.

The colonnade where the andrones have hung her is

lushly green as any dream den, and she thinks it may actually be biotectured. Apart from the lux fixtures and maroon flagstones, the area looks genetically designed: The buttress roots of huge trees partition the colonnade into separate chambers. Fern curtains and moss veils hang from the high galleries, where flame-bright birds click and fret and occasionally screech. If she peers upward through the green levels and rocks her head, she believes she can see the texture of the filter dome she knows must be there.

Mei turns her attention back to Charles, in the nave across from her. The scanner androNes have attached him to an elaborate weave of psyonic hardware. She wonders if this is the same equipment the caravan lugged. A camera array has been erected above the plasteel capsule in its chromatic mesh of filament bundles, and Mei takes this as a sign that Charles is okay and these will be his eyes.

So intently does she watch the androNes' ministrations, she does not notice the figure who has stepped to the foot of her sling until he speaks: "Solis welcomes you."

Mei startles and sits up on an elbow to see the effeminate face of the Commonality agent she had encountered at the Moot. "You're—"

"Sitor Ananta." A corner of his mouth smiles, but his caramel eyes study her mirthlessly. "I arrived from our mother planet days ago. I've been waiting for you."

"We're outside the Commonality and the Pashalik," Mei reminds him. "You have no authority here."

"I need no authority here." His smile sharpens. "Solis makes much of being a free state. I am here as an individual, Jumper Nili, as are you. And we will both act as individuals, won't we?"

Mei forces herself to calmness by subvocalizing a panic-management chant. She must get free of the sling to defend herself, but when her hand moves to unstrap the pressure bags, Sitor Ananta lays a moist hand on hers.

"That won't be necessary," he informs her, wetting his

lips with his tongue, tasting the air around her. The avidity in his tawny eyes chills the pith of her. "I cannot stay long. The reception agents want to meet you—not andrones this time, but the free and simple people of Solis, free of olfacts and simpletons of the olfactual science that is my art."

Mei unstraps her arm and leg and wipes the back of her hand on the sling.

"You can't wipe it off," he says, shaking his head and pinching his chin ruefully. "It's already entered your blood."

She rolls out of the sling and pushes pugnaciously close, ready to block or punch. "What've you put in me?" she asks hotly.

His creamy smile does not flinch. "A mild euphoric—this time." He points a finger at her nose, and she hops backward.

In midstep, the haptic drug swells into her brain, and the edge of her anger dulls. She hears the plash of rivulets and small waterfalls from somewhere among the giant trees, and the cedary cinnamon of the tree smoke expands her sinuses. This eases the thumping of her heart, and she regards the Commonality agent with calmness and dignity.

He doesn't appear as threatening now that she is standing. He's slender, almost frail, a shimmery wraith in silken, flouncy green chemise and white baggy slacks cut at midshin to display crimson-trimmed black socks and slippers. When he moves, his terrene body drifts with balletic ease in the lighter gravity, and he seems nearly insubstantial.

"What do you want from me?" she asks.

"I want you to sit down." Sitor Ananta closes his eyes sleepily, and she does not retreat when he slides closer, his blue fragrance cool, bitingly sweet, the frosty spice of a rocky snowfield. The scent jumps through her blood, reminding her whole body of the last time she sensed this precise olfaction, among the runout rubble of the avalanche that buried her family. The stabbing exactitude of the scent punctures the strength in her knees, and she sags, almost falling backward. He steadies her arm, and she sits down on the mossy flagstone, her face jarred loose of all emotion.

Sitor Ananta squats beside her, his pug profile close to her ear. "*Softcopy* has refused to forward the credits for Shau Bandar's revival," he whispers.

"That's a lie." She leans away from him but cannot quite find the strength to stand. "I was with him when he spoke with Bo Rabana. *Softcopy* agreed to fund him."

"Think back." Sitor Ananta allows himself a gloating grin. "You left without any formal agreement. Bo Rabana has been overriden by executives who don't want to pay steep unauthorized expenses. Shau Bandar will be treated now like any other corpse in Solis. They will cremate him. Do you know what that is? It's the archaic practice of incinerating the body at temperatures hot enough to reduce the bones to powder."

Mei struggles to her feet and staggers backward from the agent, nearly tripping on a root coil. "Stay away from me," she mumbles, a numbing weariness soaking her. "I know what you're doing. You're poisoning me."

"Nonsense." He leans against a lux stanchion and crosses his arms. "I'm acquainting you with me. With my ways. I am very persuasive. I was created to be. With my skills I can pretty much have my way with the rubes of Solis. But I don't underestimate their rote stubborness at defying the Commonality. Even with my olfacts, I cannot hope to just walk out of here with Mr. Charlie."

"Why do you want him so badly?" She draws a deep breath of the floral air, trying to flush her lungs.

"Perhaps I will tell you sometime." He shoots her a cunning look. "For now it is enough for you to know I want him, and you must do nothing to obstruct me from having him. If you help me, I will provide the credits for Shau Bandar's revival."

"Get away from me," Mei says, raising her voice. "I don't want to talk to you anymore."

"Fine." Sitor Ananta stands erect and shows his palms with mocking formality. "I'm sure we will find each other again in the courts and lanes. Solis is a small place."

Mei watches him retreat among the piers of buttress roots, and as his sapphire scent fades in the green, bird-loud air, the helpless weariness she feels passes and anger thrums into place.

Through the sparkling morning of the Fountain Court, Exu and Hannas Bowan hurry. They are the dyad lot-selected to serve as the reception agents for today's foundlings, and they are late. Yet even in their haste, they are careful never to disrupt their synchronized grace. Exu strides in strict lockstep with Hannas as they bicker in their humclick speech: "My other concerns are just as vital as dealing with foundlings. Not more vital, Hannas. I said *just* as vital."

"You didn't review the file. That's what all this protesting is about, isn't it, Exu?"

"There wasn't time."

"Tsk, Exu. This one's interesting. It's a Maat approach. Closest in twelve years. And—you'll appreciate this even more—it's a big credit reception. Crates of psyonic core units to be sold off. Can't have them in here, right? And then there's an archaic brain that—"

"A *brain*, Hannas? I take it you mean a human brain?"

"Yes, an archaic human brain, my heartsong. You should have reviewed the file. It's fascinating."

"How was I to know this wasn't going to be the usual monkey troupe?"

"It *is* a monkey troupe, Exu. There they are." She directs his attention to three figures gawking at the rainbows among the electrostatically shaped veils of water in the Fountain Court. They are terrene humans, the stocky, long-armed aboriginals that Exu derides as monkeys. Two women and a man or a morph. "He's a morph," Hannas says, reading the quizzical cant of her mate's head. "He's the Commonality agent who is going to purchase the psyonic core units for full market value."

"What?" Exu looks at the slight and simian shape of the agent. "Why is he paying so much?"

"You should have viewed the file, dear. Just follow me." She climbs the polished chalcedony stairs to the fern-trellised estrade overlooking the rainbow crests of the Fountain Court.

Exu follows in precise shadowstep. Tiers of vine-hung galleries and arcades surround the court, and though this site has been chosen for its openness, Exu is unhappy being so close to the ab-originals. The musky density of their scent annoys him only slightly less than the vaguely disguised abhorrence with which they regard him and Hannas. To the terrenes, the three-meter-tall martians with their backward-bending heron legs and furry, kangaroolike features do not look human.

"Now, be tolerant, Exu. Remember, there's a strong credit inflow here. Think of it as a little monkey time for that romp studio in Highland Terraces we've always wanted."

"Let's just get it over with," he humclicks as they approach and simultaneously says in the glottal language of the aboriginals, "Solis welcomes you! I am Exu Bowan, and this is my lifebond, Hannas. We are the reception agents chosen at random from the resident population to serve you."

Hannas humclicks, "Stop with the facetious tone, Exu. Let's get down to business." She turns to face the terrenes and says in a precise aboriginal dialect, "In the spirit of

Solis, our highest service of course is to leave you free to express your own lives. We will not take up much of your time, but as you know, freedom must be earned. Solis is an entirely self-sufficient community. As long as you are here, as visitors, residents, or passagers, you must contribute to the maintenance and general good of the whole. Now, let's review your credit status. Grielle Aspect?"

The slender woman who steps forward wears the wimple and opaline smock of a passager. "The full credits of all my Outland holdings have already been transferred to an account in Solis. Upon my passing, it reverts to the city. Also, I have contributed twelve crates of psyonic core units. I came on them as an act of rebellion, my last act in the Outlands. I stole them from their manufacturer in Sky-Bowl the night that I left for here. I did it because I want to contribute more than just credit to Solis. I want to give you something tangible—a real piece of the silicon mind, of the world outside of here. Study these, children of the light. Know your enemy."

"*Thank* you, Grielle," Exu says with exaggerated gratitude and clicks to Hannas, "What a rube!"

"Not at all," his mate disputes. "It's a fetish gift. People who want to die need a human place for that. This is her offering to Solis. Be tolerant, Exu. They're human, too." Hannas shows her teeth as she knows Grielle expects and says, "Solis welcomes your contribution, Passager Grielle."

"And we wish you swift passage," Exu cajoles.

"Show some dignity about this," Hannas scolds and recites the next name, "Sitor Ananta—"

The morph looks slender and slick as a newt to Exu, and the martian humclicks, "He looks as much a lizard as a monkey."

"Tsk! He's arranged to take the psyonics off our hands for full credit because he wants consideration. Ignore the fact that he's a Commonality agent, and remember his credit is as good as anyone's. Show some sense, Exu."

Hannas notes with a buzz of alarm the sullen humor in the Commonality agent's face, almost as if he understands their secret language. "Naturally," she says to him, "your presence is funded in full by the Commonality, so you are welcome to come and go as you please. How long will you be with us?"

"Just long enough to conclude business," he answers with a knowing nod.

"Then we wish you a satisfying visit. Mei Nili—"

The jumper shoulders past Sitor Ananta. "I've brought Mr. Charlie. I hope he's okay. There was an explosion—"

"Is she talking about the archaic brain?" Exu asks.

"Pay attention, dear." Hannas raises her palms to stop the slim, muscular woman in the matte-black flightsuit. "The archaic brain you've contributed to Solis certainly merits your admittance to our community, Mei Nili, but if you are to stay among us, you know, you will have to earn credits. Please, listen to the counselors we've assigned to you from the terrene anthro commune. They'll help you make the transition."

"What about Shau Bandar and Munk?" Mei asks. "And what has happened to Buddy?"

"Can we go now?" Exu complains.

"Shau Bandar is scheduled for cremation later this morning," Hannas reads from the display on her mate's shoulder pad. "His news-clip service claims he left without any protective authorization—"

"That's not true!" Mei interrupts. "I was at *Softcopy* with him when Bo Rabana gave him the go-ahead."

Hannas shakes her head. "That's not what we've been told. The offices in Terra Tharsis have agreed to fund the installation of the archaic brain in a body clone, and in return the anthro commune here will be sending news clips of the revived man to *Softcopy*. But they won't pay to revive this reporter. It's too expensive. I'm sorry."

A blue vein ticks at Mei's temple, and she begins to

object. But Grielle cuts her off, saying, "I will pay for Shau Bandar's revival. Remove the necessary funds from my account at once."

The wry smile on the Commonality agent's face slips away, and the jumper shoots a surprised look at Grielle.

"Hey, that cuts into the share we get when she passes," Exu complains.

"It is *her* credit, Exu. She can spend it as she pleases. Control yourself." With a gracious nod, Hannas accepts Grielle's offer. "Now, about the androne and the Maat: You are aware you were traveling in the company of a Maat-possessed anthro?"

"We had no idea," Grielle states. "He tagged on with the androne. He had credits, and the more he paid into the caravan, the more I had left to contribute to Solis. So we accepted him, but we had no idea, dears. No idea at all."

"The Maat wouldn't confide in these monkeys," Exu sneers. "Let's go. We've played our role. I say we file for our share of the credits before she gives away any more."

Hannas accedes by showing her teeth to the terrenes. "This, I believe, concludes our business," Hannas says. "There is a large commune here of terrene humans who have emigrated from the Outlands, and I'm sure they will be helpful with any of your—"

"What about the androne Munk?" Mei presses.

"Come on, Hannas!" Exu trills. "These foundlings are unbearable." He modulates his voice to carry his ire, "Jumper Nili, Solis does not tolerate andrones more complex than scout-class. Munk belongs in deep space, not on Mars."

"Okay, dear, we're done here now." Hannas budges her mate to begin their retreat and says charitably as they backstep in tandem, "The androne Munk's power cells have been recharged. The Maat arranged payment for that from Terra Tharsis. Perhaps they have some use for him. They are his manufacturers, after all."

"But there won't be any use for him here in Solis," Exu admonishes. "If you go out to see him, Jumper Nili, I'm sorry to say you'll have to reapply for admission. One archaic brain won't get you into Solis twice. And this next time, you may be turned away. Be advised."

"Don't be too harsh, dear. She offers us no direct credit, but the archaic brain she delivered is already bringing in news-clip funds, and the agent would pay dearly for possession—"

Exu glares angrily at his lifebond. "Is that the consideration that lizard wants? He can forget it. No deals with the Commonality. The archaic brain stays here."

As if one person, the martians slide fluidly backward down the stairs, and Hannas twitters in his ear, "All he asks is that the brain be given over to the Anthropos Essentia to be bodywoven in their vats. He probably has some arrangement with them. But if there is any trouble—say, a theft of the brain or an accident—it will not be with our people. Our hands are clean, and the credit remains with us. What do you say?"

Exu shows his teeth to the gaping terrenes. "I say, when the credit is good, consideration comes easily. Let's go."

Since waking from the void, Munk keeps drifting in and out of virtual reality. For long intervals, some episodes as much as half a second in duration, he reviews events from his recent past and has even begun modifying them, trying out variations on what might have been. He daydreams.

While he and Buddy wander among the stony eskers on the perimeter of Solis, Munk wonders where he would be now if he had not detonated the explosives on Phoboi Twelve that killed Aparecida. Mei Nili and Mr. Charlie are gone—as they would have been on the path not taken. But there they would have been dead. On this path, he died, so to speak, and when he came back, the people he saved are gone and he can't stop hoping after them and pondering how events might have turned out differently.

Buddy is talking architecture, about the orange pyramids visible just beyond the lux towers and their lances of sunlight. "Those are the vats of the Anthropos Essentia," Buddy says. "Charles Outis will be taken there."

"Who?" Munk asks. He speculates about what might have happened if he had not acted impulsively in the Moot and stolen the plasteel capsule. Maybe the Moot would have found in their favor. He realizes now, he acted too precipitously . . .

"Charles Outis is Mr. Charlie," Buddy says and taps the com-link in his shoulder pad to hear whether it's sending. "Munk, are you all right?"

Munk drives quickly through an internal analysis and affirms, "I am fine. But—" He pauses, weighs whether this revelation is the right choice or if he should keep his own counsel about his enhanced subjectivity.

"But what?" Buddy presses. His face through the clear statskin cowl appears pallid, his eyes larger, holding the solar stars from the lux towers.

"Since I have been revived," the androne confesses, "I have been obsessed with my past."

An understanding smile touches Buddy's thin lips. "It's your C-P program. Your little taste of oblivion broke the program's seamless internal narrative. Now it's more obvious to the preconscious monitoring systems in you that there are other ways to tell your story—more human ways."

Munk feels his attention slipping toward the daylight silence of the rocky landscape and its brilliant oxides, but he restrains himself from thinking about what would have happened if he had ignored Mr. Charlie's initial broadcast and never left Apollo Combine. Instead he asks, "Why did you make me this way? I mean, why did you give me an anthrophilic contra-parameter program?"

"It's not anthrophilic," Buddy says, stepping closer, a compassionate crease between his luculent eyes. "Munk, don't you see? It's anthropic."

The androne scans Buddy's face and body profile time and again, searching for the signs of double entendre, metaphor, or just plain outright deception that must be there. "Human?" Munk queries. "Are you saying that my C-P program is designed to make me eventually experience reality as a human?"

"Yes."

"That's not possible!"

"What? You don't believe that humanity is nothing more than a pattern?" Buddy edges even closer, looking up at the faceless abstraction of the androne's head with an incredulous expression. "You've been around Mr. Charlie too long, Munk. Your thinking's become archaic."

"No," Munk says. "I understand that consciousness is emergent. I know it is generated through pattern complexity, whether of dendrites or electron tunneling junctions. I understand that. But I can't believe that I am—that."

"Yes, Munk," Buddy asserts, staring earnestly into the ruby-bright depths of his lens bar. "You are human. We have made you that way."

"Why?"

"To be here with me right now," Buddy answers at once. "I need you to fulfill the aftermath of my passing."

Munk represses the trembling conflict in him between elation and blatant disbelief and acknowledges aloud, "My responsibility to Mr. Charlie is replete. He has been delivered to Solis. So has Mei Nili. Then, I guess, I am wholly free to serve you—my maker."

"Good." A frantic quiet plays across Buddy's thick features, as though he's just coming to a precarious realization. "Hold on. I'm having a prescient memory—"

Munk extends an arm to steady Buddy, who suddenly looks as if he is about to fall asleep. "I don't understand," the androne says.

Buddy snatches at Munk's arm and snaps out of it. He blinks, and a crisp alertness seizes his stare. "I remembered what's going to happen." He cocks his head and blinks again. "I'm going to leave now. Once I'm gone, Buddy won't remember anything about me or you. His last memory will be of falling out of the skies in Terra Tharsis. He will find his way back to the outsiders' camp behind us, and in time he will realize that he has been exiled from Terra Tharsis by the Maat for his crime against himself: attempted suicide. And you—" A hot smile flashes across his face, and he almost bursts into laughter. "Ah, you have your work cut out for you."

"Again, I don't understand . . ." Munk trails off, for Buddy has seized his faceplate and pulled himself up very close, lifting his legs off the ground and practically climbing up the androne's front.

"My time in time is done in time," Buddy chants, his face a white moon, his eyes lit from within. "Goodbye, Munk."

Buddy lets go, and as his body falls, Munk involuntarily enters suspended time. Briefly, a light like blue smoke phosphoresces in the space between them, an amethyst fire that blusters violently even in slow time. Then it is gone, leaving comet feathers dazzling on the path of its dwindling flight through the pink lens of the horizon.

In a splash of dust, Buddy falls at Munk's feet and gazes up at the androne with a bewildered look shading to fright. Munk moves to help him up, but the man pushes away in a startled crabwalk. He flips over and scurries up the path among the boulders and out of sight.

Munk moves to follow, then stops himself. Inside, in the imaginal space behind his lens bar, he can still see Buddy fleeing among large talons of rock. He is running through horizontal rays of fiery dust that cut time into strata. On the lowest level, he is running through the woven light of the desert. Slightly above that view of him, he has already reached the camp of storm-battered pressure tents and reflector domes. A notch higher, the sky is full of the pink twigs of nightfall, and he is crouched with others beside a thermalux telling his story of life in Terra Tharsis as an old one, which no one believes. For many levels, he huddles at night in the thermal leaks of tents and works with others by day erecting a wind turbine, eventually earning his own tent . . .

Munk dizzies. A whole life unfurls before him. He skims ahead and sees Buddy in a caravan heading west into the pumice winds of the red desert, returning to Terra Tharsis. And above that, the opal-black heights of the Maat city where there is no death.

His vision dissolves in a blind roar of images a thousand years deep—and still there is Buddy, at this far-gone time under the anvil of a tree. The stony land is patch-quilted with lichen and sloping swards, and groves of strata-tiered trees bloom among the rocky outcrops under a flame-blue sky.

Munk startles alert to find himself gazing at lucent grains of dust glittering in the space where a moment before a craze-eyed Buddy stood. He can hear the crunching of the icy gravel as the man flees among the erratic boulders. The androne doesn't know what to do. The sounds fade away, and Buddy entirely disappears into the silence of his future.

Solis dazzles under the minarets of sunfire that are capturing that day's power. Terraced on the ramparts of ancient impact craters, the settlement hoards light, from the prism-cut lofts at the craters' edges to the glass hangars and mirror panes of the huddled warrens on the desert floor. Among a jumble of red ivy bunkers and ginger stonework arbors, two small orange pyramids catch his attention, and he remembers Buddy saying, "Those are the vats of the Anthropos Essentia; Mr. Charlie will be taken there."

Only, the Maat had called Mr. Charlie by his untranslated name, and it had sounded like a brattle of wind over shale. Munk repeats it, "Charles Outis," and the noise goes off aimlessly across the gritty swells of land.

He telescopes in on the orange pyramids and says the name more softly. Then his vision pulls back with the thought that the Maat could have left Buddy anywhere they wanted and certainly closer to the tent camp. That the neo-sapiens would bring the androne to this precise place is significant, he assumes, and he scans more slowly the journey down the heather-choked gulleys and ice-splotched cobble flats to the stone wall and a dolmen door with a niter beard. Hidden by fan boulders and a torpid mound of rocks, the door is visible only from this venue.

There are blisters of rime around the touch pad that will listen for the correct code signal to open the door. As Munk stares at the amplified image of the pad, giddy disbelief overtakes all his reservations. The touch pad is identical to the type used by Iapetus Gap, and he is confident that his familiarity with this lock system will enable him to feel out the admittance code.

He starts forward, then stops and asks himself where he thinks he's going. *To find Charles Outis,* he confirms to himself and continues on his way, leaving unspoken his expectation of confronting the people in the settlement and finding out if the Maat are right. Maybe there is a place for him among the last tribes at the end of the world.

He strides boldly across the desolation, and as he approaches the lithic entryway, he makes no effort to hide himself—for if he is indeed human, he belongs in Solis.

7

Zero in the Bone

MEI NILI HAS SEEN THE SOLIS CLADES—THE MARTIANS—numerous times in news clips, but in person they seem much bigger. They stand bristle-headed and narrow-shouldered above the counselors from the terrene anthro commune. The counselors, dressed in the sere-and-buff tunics and toque caps of the Solis autocracy, are tall and slender-muscled from their lives in the thin gravity of Mars. They crane their necks to look up at Exu and Hannas Bowans' marsupial faces, and watching them together, the jumper marvels again at the diversity of human life outside the reservation.

The martians flitter away across the Fountain Court in their eerie synchronized gait, and in moments they are lost among the hive bustle of numerous other martians crossing through the plaza's chords of sunlight and broken spectra.

"Clades," Grielle Aspect snickers from behind Mei. "I'm glad to be getting away from this genetic circus. You should come with me."

Mei tilts her head back and gives a sour look. "Maybe when I'm as old as you, I'll be ready to end it, too."

"Oh, I'm not ending it, Mei dear." Grielle smiles seraphically. "I'm becoming light—true freedom. No more of this shape-shifting—morphs, clades, and plasmatics—it's disgusting. The light is pure and timeless."

"If you believe that," Mei says, pointing with her eyes to Grielle's wimple and opaline apron, the traditional garments of a passager, "why are you paying to revive Shau?"

"Rey Raza died trying to save him—to save all of you," Grielle says softly, her eyes unfocusing. "I saw him die. It was a terrible thing. I would bring him back if I could." Her gaze tightens. "But I can't. So, it's the journalist. Maybe he'll see the light and die properly. If we leave the flesh in the right way, we never have to come back, you know."

Sitor Ananta steps past them to greet the approaching counselors. A whiff of a cold fragrance tingles in his wake, and Mei experiences a discoloring in her soul. "That agent is using olfacts to sway the people around him."

Grielle winks slyly. "Don't you just envy him? Even I can't afford olfacts that effective. If I could, you'd all be passagers."

The three anthro counselors show their palms, introduce themselves, and conduct the pilgrims on a walking tour of Greater Free Solis. The settlement is large, but the interface among the clade cantonments, the anthro commune, and the Anthropos Essentia enclaves is a triangular plaza with the Fountain Court at the center. Strolling across the garnet flagstones, they have the opportunity to see all the human types in their bright and often outré garb: the martians with their back-bending stalk legs and bouffant manes, the whippet-thin wraiths of the Anthropos Essentia in their orange frocks and headwraps, and the aboriginals looking so simian in their contour jackets and flexfabrics. A counselor points out that even some of the elaborate air plants hanging among the stratiform galleries under the blue-glass canopy are plasmatics, humans in wholly inhuman form. Another counselor explains how selective Solis has been about the numbers and types of human variants it has integrated within its biotecture.

Their patter is endless, and Mei interrupts to ask where Mr. Charlie is. In reply, the counselors talk about the vats and point out on a holoform map of the settlement two compact orange pyramids at the old end. Then Grielle wants to see the Walk of Freedom, and a section of the map expands to show the famous crystal-gravel path leaving the ebony gate and curving under a skull-mounted catafalque into a field of human bones and mummified corpses.

At tour's end, on a balcony overlooking the Rainbow Court, there is a meal of vegetables and hatchery steaks. Sitor Ananta is magnificent with the counselors, amusing and charming them. Several times Mei tries to direct the conversation to the olfacts, but no one seems to care. The meal continues with amicable cheer, eventually even the jumper laughing with the others over Grielle's pantomime of a martian.

"When will I see Mr. Charlie?" Mei asks the counselors after the meal.

The counselors confer as they lead the way between two silvery walls of electrostatically suspended water and up an automated rampway to a bunker of black, block-cut rock scribbled with ivy. This is the anthro lodge where the agent will be staying, and he lingers under the dragon-eye lintel for the counselors' reply.

They can't agree on whether the bodyweave will be complete in two or three days. The vats are busy designing clades for the cold new worlds beyond the Belt.

"Too late," Grielle decides. "I had hoped to speak with

him before my passage—you know, dears, I really want to confront the poor man with the error of his ways. But I don't think he's slept in his flesh a thousand years to argue with me. So I am gone. Tomorrow I commit my last act of light as a human."

Mei is left in the purple-tile vestibule of the hostel where she will reside until she earns enough credit for her own suite. Grielle and the counselors depart into the saffron afternoon, and the jumper uses the passcard the counselors have given her to enter a cloister of blackglass cubicles.

From inside her own chamber, the walls to the corridor and the outside are transparent, and she can see the serrated rooftops, a hint of the clustered rainbows from the Fountain Court, and the broken shoulders of the crater rim, rubescent in the long sunlight.

"Jumper Nili," a familiar voice calls from the doorway. Shau Bandar stands there wearing the green caftan of the vats and a thick grin. "Are you in there?"

Mei hurries to touch the entry pad, and he strides in, the door sliding shut behind him. He pivots, displaying his partly shaved scalp, the close-cropped hair like red hackles. Without his face paint, he looks no different from any of the men in the hamlets of her reservation on Earth.

"I've been in the beverage stall across the way," he says, "waiting for you to return. So what do you think? How did the vat doctors do?"

"I think it's a tough way to get a haircut."

They laugh and skim palms, and he plops onto a flex-form chair and grins at her. "They say I was dead for days. But it was like being asleep. I don't even remember what happened."

Mei sits in the window bay and tells him what happened. They talk excitedly about *Softcopy*'s betrayal and how close he has come to the absolute edge of departure.

From down the blackglass corridor, Sitor Ananta slinks into view. He flicks his palms at them. "Open the door. I know you're in there."

Shau moves to slap the door pad, and Mei stops him. An angry light flexes in her eyes, a twinkle of fear at its core. "Don't! He's dangerous. He uses psycholfacts to manipulate people."

Shau looks surprised. "That's the Commonality agent we saw in the Moot, the one who wants to reclaim Mr. Charlie. Those agents are rascals. That's why Mr. Charlie fears him. But they can't use psychokinetic substances. It's against the mandate, and you know how righteous those tightasses are about that."

"Open the door, you two," Sitor Ananta calls with a timbre surprisingly deep for his slender frame. "I want to speak to you about Mr. Charlie."

"Let's just ignore him," Mei advises.

"He knows we're here. Why must we hide?"

"I think he's crazy."

Shau rolls his eyes in disbelief. "We're the crazy ones, Jumper Nili. That's what I found out in the vats. You left the reservation, I left Terra Tharsis—for what? To hide? I've been dead. What is there left to be afraid of?" He reaches for the entry pad. "Don't worry. I'll talk with him."

"Bandar, don't!" Mei calls.

The glass door parts, and Sitor Ananta, grinning coldly, enters in a cloud of dreams.

Munk has no trouble figuring out the admittance codes to open the stone portal that enters Solis. His large frame is cramped in the lightless corridor, and he must proceed stooped and sideways. With infrascan he sees that the walls are composed of an unfamiliar alloy. He wants to pause and examine it, but a reverberant pulsing summons him from ahead, and he is eager to see where this entryway leads.

Farther along, the walls begin to weep. The substance that dews on the slick surface is mostly water, yet at his touch he feels the helical waverings of molecular linkages. He identifies chains of methylated proteins before he realizes that the corridor ahead is smaller. He cannot hope to go forward and decides to retreat. But behind him the hall is also tighter than when he passed through, and in a gust of surprise, he sees that the passageway is soundlessly constricting.

The androne tentatively pits his strength against the contracting walls, but their force is too great even for him. Viscous sheets of organic fluid slicken all surfaces. The floor, too, is wet, and he has no purchase to apply any resistance. In moments, the ceiling is weighing heavily on his shoulders, and he is obliged to bend over, then forced to curl up. The dense liquid envelops him.

The contracting walls close around him, then stop. Nothing more happens, and Munk begins to think that he has been encased alive, maybe indefinitely. He computes that with his fully charged power cells he could remain conscious in this immobilized state for centuries; he is too frightened to determine how many. Then he senses movement. The corridor slowly shunts him inward, the strong peristaltic motion sweeping him in his liquid sac deeper into Solis.

Abruptly, space opens around him, and he is adrift in a thick fluid of inductor enzymes that sheathe him in a strong electromagnetic field. He senses that the field is being directed from an outside source, but already his sensors, under the influence of the field, are shutting down. He cannot move his limbs, and his infraview goes blind.

Darkness and silence possess him. He is alert, but he has no referents. Time, too, seems distorted. He searches for his internal anthropic model and finds nothing. Panic swirls in him, and then that, also, fades away. He floats in emptiness, outside and inside reduced to nothing. Only his consciousness persists, his ineffable and enclosing sense of I am.

The hallucinations begin with a mushroom cloud of billowing images. He's aware of this phenomenon from the archives: sensory-deprivation hallucinations. When external stimulation is deprived, the brain generates living images to fill the void. Always, before, when he turned his sensors off, he filled the emptiness with his anthropic model but never for intervals longer than a second.

Now, with no sensory or internal models, he thrives in a flux of images, memories folding into lucid dreams— the aqua-green ripples in a shallow marine pool rhyming with the glow of The Laughing Life's flight bubble as he overrides his primary programming and initiates the code sequence that ignites Phoboi Twelve into a blue-white fireball.

The blunt, leering snout of a moray eel shoves out of the crimson cloud of planet dust and swells into Aparecida's sleek visage. Choice and chance, she says with the voice of the musical dispatcher from Iapetus Gap, and suddenly he is flying above the agate clouds of Saturn listening to music. He never said farewell to the androne in the control pod on Titan who broadcast that music. They never met, yet she laved him with her creativity for years until he woke to the choice to take a chance on himself.

All the experiences that followed from his choice to activate his contra-parameter program sluice through him in a fiery plume of images, like the outbound incandescence of Phoboi Twelve's explosion. His life has been an explosion, he sees, cooling at the edges to the pixel dust of memories. The void that surrounds those memories is misty with the fractal diminutions of endless associations and augmentations—the magical zone of the imagination, its flowstreams of hallucinatory shapes shrinking ever farther into virtual space, like a tree whose madness of tiny roots tightens on nothing.

His consciousness slips free of all he can remember and imagine. Everything he has been in spacetime and in mind, everything he could be, all of his life goes off like fireworks and dwindles sparkling into darkness.

He is alert in the darkness, which is really not darkness or light but an isotropic dearth of sensation, a nothingness in which only his sense of awareness persists. He is the busy work of atoms, force lines of intersecting fields, a clear flame full of shapes, the quivery glistening in the lens of a startled eye.

A brown iris flexes around the black depth of a pupil. It blinks, and he pulls away to see two brown eyes staring shrilly from a submerged human face. Wavy hair streams like shreds of brown sargassum, and the bloated, staring face is drowned before he realizes he is not seeing a face but a reflection.

Munk thrashes convulsively. Beset with chest cramps and a roaring in his head, he surges upward and breaks the mirror gloss of the surface. Chilled air scalds his sinus and lungs, and his loud sucking gasp drums echoes out of the brightness. Quaking with shock and oxygen hunger, he flops to his back in the saline buoyancy and sees that he is floating in a tank big as a pond. Star-webbed rows of lights shine blindingly overhead, illuminating the slick green water and the ceramic lip of the tank.

He huffs laboriously, kicking his legs to keep his head up and holding his hands before his face—human hands, with trembling fingers and blue-pink fingernails and the palms etched with fine lines of destiny.

"What is your name?" a voice calls from beyond the tank's edge.

In the cold air above the steaming surface of the green fluid, his head and hands float, and a laugh breaks through his gasping. He gapes at the smoke of his laughter in the cold air and laughs again, choking and gulping oxygen. He is respiring! The astounding truth of what has happened knocks him breathless again, and he coughs jets of steam.

"What is your name, man?" the booming voice calls again.

He wrenches enough air into his lungs to shout, "Munk."

A handroid slides onto the edge of the tank and extends a coiling arm. "Solis welcomes you, Munk."

Munk seizes the arm and pulls himself to the side of the tank, where he hangs shivering, panting, trying to understand.

"Rise, Munk," the handroid beckons. "The people would have you among them."

Munk stills his excitement enough to stare at his human nakedness and listen inward. An effulgence of psychic energies churns within him, but the virtual reality of his C-P program is gone and with it his capacity to function mentally in suspended time. He listens for code signals and hears only his own rasping and the slosh of the tank's edge.

Heart slamming, he pulls himself out of the mist-wreathed liquid and sits heavily on the rim of the vat. The handroid steadies him with a coil arm lashed around his torso, and Munk hangs there staring at men and women naked as he. They are smiling and laughing and rushing across the glaring white tiles waving to him with towels and blankets. A racket of triumphant music swells under the hard lights, and a splash of rose petals hits him between the eyes.

For a day and a night, Sitor Ananta uses his psychol-facts to make Mei Nili and Shau Bandar irresistible to each other. He sits in a flexform with his back to the luminous window, a motionless silhouette in the room watching the two naked, glistening bodies grappling with their irreparable passion. He can tell from the forgotten fear on their faces, from the startled pleasure of their weary features, that sensuality is a happy calamity for them.

When the lovers eventually sprawl exhausted in each other's embrace and stare into space with a pained stupor, the agent has a handroid deliver a roll of nutripatches to the chamber. He modifies the pheromonol density of the room and adds just enough ergal for the two to get up and apply the nourishing patches.

"You're sick," Shau groans. He is so enfeebled from the long hours of neurochemical manipulation, he barely has the strength to pull the starter strip on the nutripatches. He presses one to Mei's thigh and places the other over his scramming heart.

"No, no," Sitor Ananta objects, adjusting his noseplug to admit more vasopressin to his inhalant, sharpening his verbal ability. "You're just not familiar with your bodies and their history. You know, in Mr. Charlie's time, there was no sublimol in the air supply to mitigate sexual desire. They couldn't turn off their sex glands. The hormones flooded their bloodstreams day and night, perpetually. What you're experiencing here is just natural human behavior woken from a long sleep."

"This isn't natural," Shau mutters. "You're inflicting this on us."

"It is true," the agent accedes, an amused smile glittering in the shadow of his face. "I am playing your bodies. But, I assure you, the olfacts I'm using are only activating neural arcs of natural behavior patterns."

"Pornolfacts," Shau whispers wearily. "I've heard about them."

"Yes, they're quite the rage on the homeworld," Sitor Ananta affirms. "Except in the feral reserves, there's been no human sexuality on Earth or in most of the colonies for centuries. It's absurd, really. When you think about it, this is the basic biological drive that propelled life for billions of years, and then, virtually overnight, we find the chemical switch and turn it off. *That* is unnatural."

Shau's groggy eyes focus more keenly as he realizes, "You're a lewdist."

"You're so bright," Sitor mocks. "*Softcopy* should never have let you go."

"That's why you're intent on getting Mr. Charlie," Shau gloats in comprehension. He struggles to sit up on the sleep mat and untangle himself from Mei. "Lewdism is illegal in the Commonality. And Mr. Charlie is a witness, isn't he?" He jabs a wavery finger at the agent. "You took him from the archives yourself—for your own lewdist rituals. Like you're doing to us. And that's how he got stolen by the anarchists. They stole him from you." He flops back under the weight of his realization. "You had to get him back before someone found out how you had used him." He rolls his head to the side to face the agent. "What is the penalty in the Commonality for lewdist behavior? Or is it the penalty for theft from the archives that forces you to come all the way to Mars to make wetware of Mr. Charlie?" His face flexes angrily, but he has no strength to rise. "You got scared after the anarchists stole him from you. That called too much attention to him, didn't it? He wasn't your exclusive toy anymore. You were afraid someone else in the Commonality might access Mr. Charlie's brain and find out how you had stolen him from the archive and abused him for your illegal lewdism. So you shipped him out to Phoboi Twelve. You thought that would be the end of it. You thought your secret would be safe."

"Activate your patch," Sitor Ananta says drily. "You look like you're going to pass out." He turns his pug-nosed, bat-faced profile to where Mei lies spraddled on her back, watching him with bright pins of malice in her eyes. "Your lover has reasoned out my motives," he admits and basks in her hatred. "Why are you silent?"

"I'm thinking of ways to kill you," she murmurs.

Sitor Ananta chuckles. "I'm sure your ideas are not nearly as clever as the way I've thought of killing you."

Shau staggers upright, limp fists raised, and the agent stands, splays his hand across the angry man's face, and shoves him to the mat. The hypnolfact on Sitor Ananta's palm penetrates the mucosa of Shau's eyes and instantly renders him slumberous.

"I have had days to think this through," he tells a passive, seething Mei. "And I have decided to kill you in such a way as to make everyone think you want to die. With an artful combination of ergal, dégagé, and hypnolfacts, I can arrange for you and your lover to earnestly choose to make passage with Grielle Aspect. Now, isn't that truly clever?"

Mei gropes out of bed, and Sitor Ananta smears her face with the hypnolfact. In minutes he has them lying side-by-side, head to foot. In turn, he whispers close to their slack faces the narratives that will make death irresistible.

The journalist is easy. He has already been dead. His psyche knows the succor of emptiness, free of the hurtling world, free of the pretense of time and form. Sitor Ananta whisper-hums to him about the dreamless ease he once had and can have again. He reminds him of all the needless efforts of each day, all the predestined indignities he must endure just to go on. "Why take it the hard way? Forget the dream of reality. Let's go back to the reality of dreams, Shau Bandar. Return to the invisible source and destiny of all assembled things. Take the way out."

Shau's eyelids twitch through a brief REM episode as the behavioral program sets in his brain, and Sitor Ananta stifles a snicker.

The jumper is more difficult. First, Sitor Ananta must sing the song of the avalanche that killed her family. He describes how a river of rock roared down the snowy valley faster than a skim train, the massive stone slabs riding a layer of compressed air. He sings from above, where the mountainside looks as if it has suddenly turned into muddy water, spilling through the snowbound valley in a dark flood and then setting instantly in place. Under tons of broken slate, a whole village is entombed. He sings of their last moments, of the thundersong from the mountain. No one thought they were going to die. Most avalanches slide horizontally less than twice the distance they fall, and the village was over five kilometers from the cliffs. He sings of how safe they felt, how unsuspecting their last minutes were. Sadly, he sings of their ignorance of the trapped air layer and the acoustic energy of the thunder, powers strong enough to propel the giant rocks ten times as far as they fall. With thick dolor, he sings of the 630-meter fall of a whole mountainside and its smoking, screaming, unstoppable 6-kilometer runout.

"Where were you?" Sitor Ananta trills. "Off on a ski safari with your friends. You will never forget your absence at the appointed hour. Why run from it? Death requires us, Mei Nili. Your family was not spared. The whole village left the future behind. Why are you here? You don't have to be apart from them. That is the hard way."

Without a splotch of vegetation, the crushed crystal trod that is the Walk of Freedom wanders into terrain that has the appearance of pre-Adamic Mars. Rocks lie strewn in the russet sand like crockery shards, and the weatherworn vent of a lava tube rises at the end of the path with the fluted and sacrosanct shape of a dais on the floor of hell. Around it are scattered the sitting and sprawling mummies, sandwind-torn skeletons, and bone slurry of the passagers who have already completed the Walk of Freedom.

Grielle Aspect stands with Mei Nili and Shau Bandar

under the copper-green catafalque that frames the airlock in the transparent section of wall facing the ceremonial grounds. They are wearing the opaline smocks and head and neck wrappings traditional to passagers, but only Grielle looks enthusiastic. The jumper and the reporter stare with sterile expressions at the small gathering of observers in the viewing stands as though the world before them were indeed a vain illusion.

Sitor Ananta, wearing minty colors for this festive occasion and standing close enough to the passagers to inspire them with more olfacts if necessary, admires the lithe crowd that has gathered to witness this old and increasingly rare ritual. He recognizes Exu and Hannas Bowan among the martian dyads, and there are members of the Solis trade council in their business kirtles. When the ceremony is over, he will approach them and see if he can work up some kind of deal for the Commonality to justify his trip here.

"I have come to the Walk of Freedom to forget the dream of reality," Grielle says at the conclusion of her address, deepening the small smile in Sitor Ananta's face. By using the ceremonial parting, she is unwittingly reinforcing the hypnolfaction of his victims. "I take this walk now to return to the reality of dreams. Happily, I release the zero in the bone and return to the invisible source and the destiny of all assembled things. Proudly, I take the way out."

Grielle lifts her palms to the filtered blue sky, turns, and strides through the airlock. In the sudden cold and reduced air pressure, her smock billows and the statskin film of her wimple fogs. But she can see well enough to follow gracefully the radiant crystal path through the bonefield. Among ricks of skeletons and mummified corpses sitting tilted and askew, she lowers herself and crosses her legs.

With a florid gesture, her pink-gloved hands rip away

the wimple and the protection of the statskin film. The out-
rush of air and pressure flaps her cheeks, bulges her eyes,
and squirts blood from their corners. The blood explodes
into clouds of crimson glitter and blows away, and the look
of ecstasy on Grielle's face goes stupid as her life vanishes
through her snarling lips in a jetting gust of water vapor.
The heat bleeds away instantly, and Grielle Aspect's blood-
streaked grimace smuts over with blotches of ice crystal.

Sitor Ananta watches Mei and Shau closely, but their
mesmeric stares do not flinch at the blunt sight of
Grielle's passing. They seem fervent believers that the
waveform of her body's neural light has been liberated
and, unimpeded by much of an atmosphere, flies free of
all creation.

"Light is action," Shau says, reciting the same programmed speech to the assembly that he used earlier to
convince Grielle of his and Mei's sincerity. "The photon,
the ultimate unit of light, is the quantum of action.
Photons, like actions, come in wholes. We cannot have
one and a half actions. We cannot decide to speak, to
walk this path, or do anything one and a half times.
Action is whole. And so is the photon. They are the same.
All actions are acts of light."

Sitor Ananta watches with evident satisfaction the behavior of his subjects. When Mei begins to talk, he indulges
himself by stealing a congratulatory look at the spectators
and is pleased to see them listening attentively.

"Look how we are attached to the ends of things," the
jumper says, her voice thin and dreamy. "Death is always
a beginning. Yet, when I lost my family—when they
died—I saw only the end of our time together. I could
not let that go. But now and here among the broken
stones, I know what to ask for from this uncharitable
existence—and that is a new beginning, beyond where
this body ends, beyond where all things end."

From among the rubric stones of the rock garden

beside the viewer stands, a bareheaded man in the green caftan of the vats waves gently, almost secretly, to Sitor Ananta. The agent does not recognize him, but the jolting thought occurs to him that this could well be Charles Outis. The vats are to conclude their bodyweave at any time. The agent casually mists himself with dégagé to calm himself down and edges toward the stranger.

"Shau Bandar and I take this walk now to return to the reality of dreams," the jumper continues. "Happily, we release the zero in the bone . . ."

"Who are you?" Sitor Ananta whispers to the stranger in the green caftan.

"Who do you think I am?" the man asks. He wears a merry grin in a face with minor imperfections—a slightly offset nose, muted cheekbones, asymmetrical mouthline—the tiny flaws common before gene manipulation homogenized beauty. He has an archaic face.

"You're Mr. Charlie," the agent surmises.

"I'm Mr. Charlie's *body*," the man answers gleefully. "But I'm Munk! I'm the androne who faced you in the Moot and stole Mr. Charlie's brain. I'm the same one who destroyed your semblor in the wilds—"

"Munk?" Sitor Ananta's face clenches with incomprehension. "That's not possible. Munk is an androne."

"Yes!" Munk grabs the pastel pleats of the agent's jacket as if to shake sense into him. "The Maat created me with an anthropic mind. And Buddy—the Maat—he coated my mechanical body with some kind of molecular code. It instructed the vats to transcribe my silicon mind into an organic brain—a human brain—this brain, in this body. I am Munk!"

Sitor Ananta rips himself free of Munk and falls back a step, stunned.

"We return to the invisible source and the destiny of all assembled things," Mei recites woodenly. "Proudly, we take the way out."

Sitor Ananta stares avidly at the happy man before him, and his face blanches. "If you're Munk, where is Mr. Charlie's brain?"

A triumphant smile further brightens Munk's giddy, human face. "Haven't you heard? A deep-space patrol-class androne has emerged from the vats and claims to be Mr. Charlie. The Maat code instructed the vats to put his brain in my old body."

"No." Sitor Ananta's flesh tingles with fright at that thought, and he snorts a blast of dégagé. He pulls a viewsheet from his jacket, punches up current events, and the small hairs along his spine rise as the image of a giant, silver-cowled androne appears. In the background he recognizes the purple air plants and multiplex galleries of Solis's Fountain Court.

"The Anthropos Essentia sent me ahead to tell you he's coming," Munk says, pressing closer with obvious delight. "They can't stop him. And neither can you."

The dégagé withholds the agent's shock sufficiently for him to see clearly what he must do. He grabs Munk, douses him with hypnolfact, and leaves him slumped against a rubric stone. No one sees. They are all watching the passagers enter the airlock.

"No!" Sitor Ananta shouts. He barges through a line of onlookers, well aware that if Mr. Charlie's friends die on the Walk of Freedom, tradition forbids their revival—and Mr. Charlie will have not only his torture at the hands of the Commonality agent to avenge but also the deaths of the only people he knows in this life.

Mei and Shau pause at the sound of their inductor's voice, and to the amazed shouts of the viewers, Sitor Ananta is quickly upon them, misting the air with the invisible smoke of ergal. The stimulant disrupts the hypnolfaction, and the jumper and the reporter sag to their knees under the shock of their chemically assaulted brains.

Sitor Ananta leaves them sitting on the crystal gravel inside the airlock and bolts through the scaffolding of the catafalque. No one in the perplexed gathering of witnesses tries to stop him, and he disappears into the rock garden.

By the time Charles arrives at the Walk of Freedom, the agent has hurried across Solis to the jungle-fronded colonnade at the edge of the wilds. Though he is a day too late for the last caravan to Terra Tharsis, he uses his Commonality credit to rent a dune climber. He knows if he can get back to the Pashalik, he will be safe. The Common Archive has no record of a Mr. Charlie; that was why he deprived Charles Outis of his name when he first stole him, feigning a translator glitch. Now, if anyone comes forward, he can deny everything, and in the fullness of time he will find accidents for all of them. With much bravura, he starts the dune climber and departs the settlement in a cloud of rouge dust that follows his escape among the sentinel stones and balance rocks.

On the other side of Solis, Mei, Shau, and Munk are sitting in the viewer stands telling Exu and Hannas Bowan what has happened. The excited crowd that spills about them parts at the approach of the androne. Charles kneels before his human friends so he can stare into their faces and sees himself sitting between Mei and Shau, his precisely familiar features staring at him with a bemused grin.

In the vats, as the handroids lifted him from the green creative fluid, the molecular program that Buddy had installed in this mechanical body bloomed in him with understanding. He knew then that the Maat had arranged for the body switch between him and Munk. But only now, as he sees the joy in his own face, does he feel the rightness of what has happened.

Before anyone can speak, he shifts his awareness to slow time. He takes in the martians, their dark eyes like the black-bolt orbs of sharks set in the tufty copper fur of their soft lineaments. He detects no sign of ears. Their slender blue throats, glossy, chitin-plated arms, and stalk legs bent the wrong way like a grasshopper's bespeak an alien adaptation he has a new lifetime to learn about.

He shifts his attention and studies the startling likeness of himself—his own flesh, the lifelong face in the mirror, here younger than he remembers himself in his last days, yet him nonetheless, with the same dimple creases, the same long, slightly skewed nose, and those inquisitive eyes, luminous now, starflexed with happiness. He has never seen himself so happy.

Beside his twin, Mei and Shau sit holding hands, looking wrung but mirthful. They are beautiful. Facing them, he feels beautiful. Their bone-strong, balanced features regard him with the openness of children; he wants to hug them and has to remember that his love fits a greater strength now.

These people before him—the martians, too, and his own body with someone else inside it—these people are the future that he has traversed a thousand years to meet. In the next moment, he will speak to them and listen. But for now, for the duration of this one sturdy instant, his attention fixes on the smallest, momentary detail, the least noticeable ephemera of this far future afternoon—tiny, evanescent particles suspended in the mauve transparency of the wind—pollen, lint, microns of sand. He focuses on these diminutive bits of reality, these granulations that he has never paid any real attention to in his former life and that others in the rush of time would never notice either, and they are enough. Their simple actuality makes him inexplicably happy, these motes glittering with their charge of sunlight, the dust of time and worlds, golden and imperishable.

Epilogue

UNDER THE CREAKING STARS AND OVER THE BASALTIC KNOLLS AND
fault trenches, a shreek slides through the air with mini-
mal motion. Its swift, transparent bulk gleams in the
moonlight, wild protruding eyes blackly visible, a brain
glistening between the swiveling pupils like a sunstruck
geode, golden pink and translucent. Through the clear
flesh of its gutsack, behind the nearly invisible muzzle
with its undershot jaw and pugnacious fangs, scissored
chunks of prey hang in a smudgy shadow. Dune lemurs'
round-eared silhouettes moil with the thicker pulp of
bones and gouts of flesh—broken femurs, balled-up
limbs with fingers and toes, and, pressed against the
gelatinous side of the creature, an eyeless skull wearing
the torn rags of Rey Raza's face.

The shreek digests the brain of its prey differently from
the rest of its food. It transforms the neural tissue that it
devours into compressed nodules in its own brain. Rey
Raza figures that this was intended by the gene engineers
of this creature to help it learn the habits of its prey.

Gazing out on the night world through the shreek's infrasensitive eyes, Rey feels the alert, nocturnal need of the dune lemurs sharing the shreek's brain with him. This carnivore has eaten enough lemurs to infuse Rey with the twittery music of their simple brains, mere cortical nodes full of reflex and no reflection. For days he has prowled thus, without pain yet feeling his own macerated body moving slowly and usefully through the shreek's entrails.

He wants the shreek to churn its pelvic and pectoral pinion-fins and climb higher, toward the untouchable veils of stars. The silver current of the Milky Way flows to the black horizon, and staring at it comforts him in his solitude. But the beast has spotted a flitting glimmer among the nested craters below, and it spurts in that direction, flashing downward between the cathedral boulders of an eroded rim wall. Zubu cacti herded along the slipface of dunes come into view, quilled, gray-green shadowspheres in the shreek's night vision, wisping a thin lavender heat under the crinkly stars.

The shreek's dive pulls up sharply before an obelisk rock at the center of an ancient crater. A soft animal flame shines from around the boulder's edge. It is another shreek, its body heat ruffling with the wind in oily waves of scarlet and vermilion. The creatures approach each other, lock muzzles, and display their gutsacks.

Rey startles to see the strange moon of a chewed human face bulging against the other shreek's flank. Even missing its lower jaw and nose, the head is recognizable to Rey as the Commonality agent to whom he had agreed to sell the archaic brain—the agent who had assured him there would be no bloodshed and then had sent his sem-blor with a gang of murderous distorts to retrieve Mr. Charlie from the caravan. So, choice has led to chance yet again, and here is the treacherous Sitor Ananta, gazing with stringy eye-sockets at the desert floor.

Rey knows that the agent's brain tissue is folded into

the glittery nerve lobes of the shreek who ate him. No doubt the man is staring at him through the eyes of his shreek with the same shameful mix of horror and hopeless resignation he himself feels. But there is no way for devoured men to communicate.

The slither of syrups in the gutsacks shivers with the shreeks' mutual joy at their successful feeding. Both bellies are full, and there will be no need for them to fight. As a couple, they can better stalk their next meal and perhaps even join others on the endless hunt. They unclasp the fangmesh of their faces and swim away together under the starry sky and the night's two moons.

THIS NOVEL IS BASED ON THE CONCEPT OF CRYONIC SUSPENSION: freezing a patient today in the *hope*—not yet the expectation—of resuscitating and healing that person in the future. Readers shoud realize that cryonics is not just science fiction; it is a service that anyone can pay for: *Your* brain can be frozen—though to what consequence, only the future knows. Further details about current cryonic technology are available from the Alcor Foundation, 12327 Doherty Street, Riverside, CA 92503. Telephone (toll free) 1-800-367-2228. Outside the U.S.: 1-900-763-1703.